PRAISE F̶ R̶

Woman Commits Suicide in Dishwasher

Debra Daniel's novel, a why done it, is a funny, tragic, poignant story of family, friendship, love, revenge and madness. Fasten your seatbelt for a wild and thoroughly delightful ride.

-Phillip Gardner, author of SOMEONE TO CRAWL BACK TO

WOMAN COMMITS SUICIDE IN DISHWASHER is as poignant as it is humorous. Myrtle, as she should, has the last word in a story that moves steadily from dark comedy into unexpected depths of feeling. This novel confirms that Debra Daniel is a superb fiction writer as well as a superb poet.

-Ron Rash, author of SERENA

Go ahead: let Daniel's title catch you laughing. Assume that the bizarre manner of Myrtle Graham's death and the ensuing inquest-by-committee is a signal that you're in for an *As I Lay Drying* parody of southern gothic. That will quicken your appreciation of the real accomplishment here, which is the methodical excavation of a personality in crisis and the culture that created it. This book is in part an evocation of a bygone era, told in the language of loss, but primarily the cubist portrait of a woman who fights for her dignity by striving mightily against it. Remarkably, Daniel shows us that the better we come to know someone, the less we understand them.

-*Jon Tuttle, author of DRIFT*

WOMAN COMMITS

SUICIDE

IN DISHWASHER

MUDDY FORD

This Copy Courtesy ⟨

MUDDY FORD

PRESS

WOMAN COMMITS SUICIDE IN DISHWASHER

By

Debra A. Daniel

WOMAN COMMITS SUICIDE IN DISHWASHER

FIRST EDITION

LIBRARY OF CONGRESS NUMBER: 2013952603

ISBN 978-0-9838544-7-0

Acknowledgements

Thanks to my literary family at Wildacres Writers' Workshop where this novel came into being, and especially to Judi Hill, director, and to Ann Hood who led my first workshop there and whose guidance and inspiration helped me fill the dishwasher. I'd also like to thank my friends and fellow writers: Carolyn Elkins, Bill Spencer, Jerry Eidenier, Janice Fuller, and Donna Vitucci for always believing that this would happen. Thanks to Cynthia Boiter and Robert Jolley at Muddy Ford Press for making my book real. I'd like to thank my family for their lifelong support. Finally and most especially, unending gratitude goes to my exceptional husband, Jack McGregor, for filling my life with music and laughter and love.

Dedication

This book is dedicated to the most special characters I have known and loved whose names are not printed here on this page but inked indelibly in the chapters of my life.

CONTENTS

DISHWASHER MAY TAG WRITER FOR LIFE

Prologue

She threw Myrtle Graham's death at me like
a water balloon, hoping it would douse my morning
and put me on the defensive for the rest of the day.
"Hey, Mr. Anchored Man," she said, "Here's a big
wet one for you. 'WOMAN COMMITS SUICIDE IN
DISHWASHER. The body of Myrtle Graham was
discovered yesterday by long time neighbor, Ruth
Overton.' Blah, blah, blah. 'Distraught husband
Hamilton Graham said he had no idea his wife was
suffering from depression or that her mental capacity
had diminished in recent years.' Blah, blah, blah. 'A
note was found but shed little light on Mrs. Graham's
motivations.' Pretty pathetic stuff, eh? And close to
home, too. Hot story right in your own backyard."

With that, Delia tore the article from the paper
and tacked it on the message board. Delia dislikes
me on principle. My job should have been hers and
every time the opportunity arises, she slams that
fact down on the table like a pastrami on rye. You
can't not notice it. She scorns my lack of experience
as a real reporter, calls me "Mr. Hair-do with a
Microphone," laughs whenever someone brings up
my cancelled television career. She enjoys baiting me
with comments about members of the media preying
on other people's pain. Tossing the latest scandal in
my lap, she'll say, "Well, Mr. Hotshot Newsman, how
would you handle this one?" or "Too bad you're only
a communications specialist now, because this one
could be your Pulitzer." Usually I let her goading slide
off, but slowly, for some reason, Myrtle Graham's
death seeped into my mind. I'd find myself in the

kitchen staring at the dishwasher wondering how the woman had fit into the tiny cubicle. It became impossible to rinse, wash, dry a dish, place cups on the top rack, even to open or close the dishwasher door without picturing a dead woman crammed inside.

Somehow Delia knew she had hit a nerve. Circulars announcing appliance sales began appearing on my desk, Delia's trademark purple highlighter emphasizing the dishwasher prices. Inside my stationery drawer, I found an envelope already typed with Myrtle's home address. Ruth Overton's name was placed in my Rolodex.

At least twice a day, Delia would stop by my desk to ask, "Hey, Mr. Word Processor, how many chapters have you written?" or "Washed any good dishes lately?"

I don't know if it was because of Delia or just because my curiosity became insatiable, but when I couldn't stand it anymore, I contacted Ruth Overton, and once I did, the flood could not be sandbagged.

I found myself listening to the stories and secrets of the people in Myrtle Graham's life, first in person and later over and over again as I replayed tapes of my interviews, searching for the best way to tell the tale. Finally I realized the most effective way was not my way at all, but theirs. I couldn't create people more pitiful or tenacious, more hopeful or cynical, more maddening or lovable than the ones that already existed. I wasn't clever enough to make up quirks of fate any stranger or slap-in-the-face realities any crueler than the truth of what they told me. That is a writer's deathblow.

So I am loath to admit that what you are about to read has little or nothing to do with me. These are not my words. None of this is mine. Not the cut-to-the-quick comments of an old soldier. Not the poetic lost love memories of a broken-hearted girl. Not the frantic erratic flight of the hummingbird neighbor in a non-stop buzzes from image to image. And certainly not the letters, recipes, or final instructions of a woman who chose to die in a dishwasher.

A suicide note doesn't disclose every reason why a person decides to take that path. For every decision a person makes, no matter how large, no matter how small, there are reasons that are hidden and those that are revealed. Secrets are kept for secret purposes. We are charmed and held captive by them.

Everyone, from the teenage boy in a digital-imaged world to the listener-deprived nursing home resident, has at least one bear-trapped secret that could destroy something or someone they love and cast themselves in an unflattering glare. Sometimes a person guards that poisoned truth a lifetime and dies, like Romeo, with it on their lips. Sometimes they confess.

The people of Myrtle Graham's death rinsed themselves clean. They craved relief, so they passed on their lies and deceptions to me. Slowly they're recovering, though Hamilton still washes dishes by hand in the bathroom sink. I am passing those secrets on to you.

NEIGHBOR'S MEMORY SCALDED BY DEATH

Chapter 1 - Ruth Overton's Story

I'm the one who found her. It's about time somebody talked to me. Oh, the police asked questions when it first happened, of course, and the newspaper quoted me once or twice. Then everything quieted down. You're the first reporter who's been here since. Took you long enough. I thought you reporters always wanted to interview the witnesses. Well, I am a witness, I can tell you that. Yes, indeed, the witness with a capital THE. I found her crammed in that dishwasher. Terrible, terrible sight. But at least she was clean, except for the spots on her eyeglasses. I used to get spots, too. On my drinking glasses, that is, until I switched detergents.

But you're not sitting in my kitchen, a handsome young man like you, to hear about that. That is not the interesting part of the story. I must be getting pretty old when the only thing I talk to a handsome young man about is detergent. No, indeed, a smart woman doesn't entertain a man by doing all the talking, now does she?

Well, it doesn't take a smart woman to know why you're here. You came about Myrtle. I'll tell you all I know. Probably enough to leave you with your mouth hanging open. I guess you could say I found her because of the cow manure. Calvin, he's the young boy who comes around to help me with the yard, well, he had stored six or seven of those forty-pound bags of manure and compost in my shed. They were on sale at Wal-Mart, you see, so I sent him to stock up. When he came back with them, I wasn't home to show him what beds to put them in, so he just stacked them in the shed. Stacked them right on top of the wheelbarrow. How on earth he expected me to use the wheelbarrow with two hundred and fifty pounds or so on top, I will never know. But that's what he did, so I had to go out there and shift things around. And me, with my back the way it is.

I was on my way to the shed where I have all my garden things – my gloves, trowel, and the like – because it was time to plant the impatiens. I'd almost decided on marigolds to help keep insects and rabbits away. Marigolds have a weedy stink to them, you know. I like them, but I just wasn't in a yellow mood. I'm partial to pink and fuchsia. And the flats of impatiens had just come in at the market. They looked healthy and so sweet this year. Such lovely pinks. If you plant them in the right spot, they'll last a long time. Speaking of impatiens, you'll be getting pretty impatient with me if I don't stop talking my fool head off and get to the point.

You want some coffee? It's real coffee. Henry, he's my husband, he won't drink decaf. I say, "Henry Overton, caffeine is going to kill you. Caffeine and cigarettes." And he says, "Ruth, the only thing on my tombstone will be, 'Henry Overton – Nagged to Death.' "

That used to be funny. But these days, death is no laughing matter. Not with Myrtle and the dishwasher and the impatiens. Oh, yes, the impatiens. Let's see where was I? I remember now. I was on my way to the shed. I got my wide-brimmed straw hat that ties around the chin so the wind won't take it and out I went. It was Wednesday. Early. Around ten. By then, Myrtle Graham had been missing almost twenty-four hours, as close as anybody

could figure. They couldn't be sure for certain because
Tuesday is seniors' day at the bowling alley and
Hamilton, that's Myrtle's husband, he always spends
the entire morning there. He'd gotten home around
two o'clock, and Myrtle was nowhere to be found.
Still that wasn't unusual. She had a habit of going to
the movies right by herself, so he wasn't alarmed. But
it was strange that she didn't leave a note. She always
fussed something terrible if he took off somewhere
and didn't leave her a note. The stupid thing is, her
car was right there in the garage. I don't know how
he thought she would've gone to the movies with her
car at home. Myrtle would never walk. Not with her
knees.

When she hadn't come in by five, he called
me to ask if I had seen her. Well, I was worried
right off. Henry always says I am a worrier, but,
for heaven's sake, that was something to worry
about. A woman Myrtle's age out all alone. It's not
safe. Henry was outside with his roses, as usual. I
marched myself out to him and the two of us went
straight over to be with Hamilton.

Well, Hamilton was upset. Of course, he
was. Don't let anyone tell you he wasn't. I could
tell. He's gruff as an old warthog sometimes, but he
never fools me. He kept taking his glasses off and
rubbing his eyes. Then he'd look out the window,
walk to the front door, stare at the phone, pop his
knuckles, walk some more. Over and over again.
Like to drove me crazy. Hamilton was a nervous
wreck.

I told him, "Hamilton, call the police. Myrtle
would not have gone off without telling somebody."
It was like something from a TV movie.

I could tell he hated to call. It was admitting
something was bad wrong. He said, "I'll give her
thirty minutes." Then he paced and stared and
popped those knuckles till I thought I would scream.
Henry went home and started calling our friends,
anybody who might know something. We didn't want
to tie up Hamilton's phone in case Myrtle tried to call.

By six-thirty, we had a policeman sitting on
Myrtle's sofa in Myrtle's den looking at Myrtle's
photograph without a clue in the world as to where
Myrtle was. No one thought she was a runaway.
There was no sign of a struggle and nothing was
missing. Her purse was there. And her car. They
asked about Alzheimer's. She didn't have that. Not
that anyone knew of, at least.

Everyone was baffled. Hamilton, most of all.
When he left to go bowling, Myrtle was in the den
folding clothes and watching *I Love Lucy*. You know,
if you have cable, you can see Lucy four times before
noon. That meant an awful lot to Myrtle. She was a
redhead, too. Hair looked terrible when I found her.
All wet and matted down.

Hamilton said when he left her, she was fine.
But I ask you, how fine can you be to crawl into a
dishwasher and kill yourself? Hamilton's not telling
everything he knows. Plays his hand close to the
chest. I believe if you'd question him long enough,
he'd break down.

Or offer him money for one of those TV movies.
Then we'd find out what really happened to poor
Myrtle. Oh, now don't go getting that look. I don't
mean Hamilton killed her or anything like that. I
certainly don't want you getting the wrong idea. I just
think that Hamilton must have had some clue as to
why she'd do that to herself.

It breaks my heart to think of her. Wet and matted hair. Arms and legs all folded up like a card table. And Myrtle was no small woman – big-boned, bad arthritis. Lord, she had to have struggled just climbing in.

Makes me want to cry. I would, too, but my tear ducts are all dried out. I'm having that laser surgery to open them up. It's a real problem when you need to cry. Getting old is no picnic, believe me. You're handsome and young right now, but you'll find out one day, sooner than you think. One of these days when you look in the mirror and you see some shriveled up old raisin staring back, it will scare you so bad you might start trying on kitchen appliances for size, too.

It was a long night tending to Hamilton until his brother, Joe, came up from Garden City Beach to stay with him. Joe's a retired army recruiter. Barreled in like he owned the place, barked some orders at Hamilton, complained about the police not doing anything. Hamilton explained it was too early for an official missing person report. Then Joe started in on Myrtle, about her being nuts and causing a commotion. Henry and I went on home. There was no need for us to hear Joe fussing at Hamilton. He had enough to worry about without being embarrassed by his brother in front of his friends so we left. Henry slept some, but I stood at the window most all night, staring at Myrtle's house.

She drove me crazy sometimes, rattling on for hours, repeating the same story over and over like a faucet that drips and drips all night long. Then the faucet stops. No warning. It just stops. And this unbearable silence takes over. Silence is the worst thing about death. You can keep a picture of somebody, keep it with you all the time, but you can't keep their voices.

Next morning, the morning I found her, I just had to do something. To tell you the truth, it wasn't a good day to plant. Calvin wasn't there to help, but I had to keep busy. The flowerbed runs between our driveways. We'd been next-door neighbors for – goodness, how long has it been – more than forty years. We always took turns doing the driveway bed. I'm partial to impatiens. Pink. Did I tell you that?

Myrtle always wanted something leafy like a caladium or a coleus, but I like flowers. Impatiens spread out and give a full bed. I hate gaps. One year, my impatiens didn't make and I had gaps like you wouldn't believe. It looked like starving rabbits had visited an all-you-can-eat salad bar. Myrtle never let me live that down. Lord knows I'm going to miss her. And Hamilton, I don't know what will become of him. She did everything for him.

She wanted to, of course. Myrtle loved taking care of him. She was always cooking and cleaning. Why, that house was spotless. Those dishes we found in the sink – that should have been a clue something was wrong. We should've checked the dishwasher as soon as we saw dirty dishes. Myrtle would have never left dirty dishes in the sink. No, sirree bob, that Myrtle was a cleaning fanatic. She didn't just swipe the surface either. She went after baseboards and windows. Why, she'd take the blinds down and soak them in the bathtub once a month. I've known her to vacuum the mattress. Hamilton used to say that if he went to the bathroom in the middle of the night, Myrtle would have changed the linens and made the bed before he got back.

She never left a dirty dish in the sink, especially
not Hamilton's breakfast dishes. He ate two eggs,
over easy, every morning of his life. Cholesterol never
scared him. Myrtle said his name should've been
Hamilton "Over-easy" Graham. So there they were,
those dishes in the sink. You know how hard it is to
get dried egg off. What am I saying? Of course, you
don't. Not a handsome, young man like you. You
probably don't ever eat eggs. Well, let me tell you, it's
near impossible to get dried egg off.

We should've known when we saw those
dishes. Should have known there was a reason she
didn't put them in the dishwasher. I don't know what
Hamilton's eating for breakfast now. It's too sad to
think about. Poor Hamilton, all alone.

They had one son, but he died a long time
ago. If you had asked me to pick out the time in
Myrtle's life when she would have killed herself, I
would've said when Gerald died. Hamilton, too,
for that matter. That boy was their universe. Tall.
Good-looking. His eyes were like a blue spruce. He
had red hair, too, but not like Myrtle's. His hair was
rich-people red like an Irish setter. Thick and shiny.
Hair like that was wasted on a boy. Once on a trip
to Tennessee, he knocked out his front tooth, but
after they got that fixed, Gerald was uncommonly
handsome. And smart. He could've had a scholarship
to any college he wanted, but he wanted to sing and
dance.

Now that suited Myrtle just fine, but as you
might expect, Hamilton was against it. He went
along with the plans though. Couldn't stop Myrtle
anyway. The truth was Gerald had enough talent
to be a star. Lordy, he should have been good what
with all those lessons. Madame Fouché got rich on

the money they paid her to teach him to dance. If Myrtle could've figured how to fasten tap shoes onto that poor boy's knees, she would've enrolled him in dance classes while he was still crawling. She used to brag, "Broadway's gonna snatch him up in a minute. He'll be bigger than Fred Astaire and Gene Kelly combined." Oh, Lordy, how she went on about him. She had it all mapped out, but Gerald decided on a different road. Only time I ever knew him to defy her.

Gerald thought country music was the best, said he thought Nashville was the place to be. He liked everything about it long before it was popular. That just goes to show you how smart he was. Way before his time. When all his friends were going through folk music and the Beatles and that heavy rock, he was listening to the hillbilly stations and practicing his twang.

It was terrible, the way Gerald died. Such a freak accident, it was. Why, it makes killing yourself in a dishwasher sound as peaceful as dying in your sleep. Gerald was spending the summer singing at one of those outdoor dramas. He auditioned through the college theater department. Actually he wasn't even in college yet. He'd just graduated from high school, but Madame Fouché worked it out so they let him try out anyway. Shows you how good he was, doesn't it? Almost all the summer stock companies offered him a job. He could take his pick. Well, he chose a theater in the mountains so he could hike the Blue Ridge Trail on his days off, he said.

One weekend we drove up with Myrtle and Hamilton to watch him perform. What a lovely time we had. Nice and cool in the mountains, and the scenery could just steal your breath away. I see that look, young man. I know you're thinking staring at a

bunch of colored leaves is a bore. I declare, scenery
is wasted on men. But we girls just oohed and aahed
and made the men stop at every overlook.

Gerald's little girlfriend, Rebecca, had driven
up with us. We were all so proud. Oh, that boy could
take the stage. I clapped until my hands hurt. Well,
after Sunday's matinee, Gerald and his theater friends
took off for Slick-as-Glass Falls with us following
along in Hamilton's car. The young people loved that
place, and Gerald was anxious to show it to Rebecca.
You ever seen it? It's a sight, that's for sure. It was
like a giant sliding board, the water skimming over the
surface of the rocks. It was worn smooth and slippery,
and everybody thought it was safe.

We saw it happen. That's what was so bad.
We watched Gerald die. He slid down fine. When he
got to the bottom, he swam over to the side but not
the side that everybody else went to. I don't know
why he did that, but that was his mistake. He put his
arms up to lift himself up, and pulled his body onto
the bank – right onto a copperhead or rattlesnake
– whatever kind it was, it was poisonous. It struck
him in the throat. Right where his vocal cords were.
He screamed once and grabbed at his neck. He
probably fell onto the snake. It kept biting him. Or
maybe there was more than one. The doctors said he
probably could have survived a single bite, but there
were just too many.

He lived a little while, but by the time they
got him up the ridge, he was unconscious. Gerald's
beautiful voice, gone.

Myrtle and Hamilton caved in. They grieved
hard for months. Gradually they built themselves
up again, but their walls were never as strong as they
once were. I always felt Myrtle could give way any

time. At any given moment she could crumble and
fall in on herself. Hamilton? Well, Hamilton got
through the way most men would. Stiff. Stiff upper
lip, stiff shoulders, stiff heart. After the first wave of
shock passed, he refused to let on how he was hurting,
but I knew. Hamilton loved salvaging junk, had a
little backyard repair business on the side. I'd hear
him in the garage fixing somebody's lawn mower.
He'd be listening to the country station on the radio.
Hamilton Graham, listening to break-your-heart
songs. Now, if that doesn't tell you something, I don't
know what will.

But that was a long time ago. That shouldn't
have any bearing on Myrtle and the dishwasher. No,
it had to be something recent that set her off.

On the way to get the manure, I was thinking
Myrtle's house had the same empty look it did when
Gerald died. Looked like the house itself was grieving.
Of course, at that point we didn't know Myrtle was
dead right there in the kitchen, but the house knew. It
surely did.

The sky was gray, a get-you-down kind of gray.
Henry had driven Hamilton and Joe to the police
station to talk to them again. I could've gone along,
but somehow I couldn't bring myself to leave the
house. I have feelings sometimes, and I felt I needed
to stay home. Henry makes light of me and my
feelings, but I put a great deal of stock in them. I trust
them. I do.

I'd been feeling funny all morning. The alarm
had gone off at six, as usual. Henry and I listened
to the news. It felt so odd when the reporter talked
about Myrtle's disappearance. Henry was saying how
the police must have thought it was serious after all
because somebody had notified the radio stations. He

was talking on and on, but I blocked him out because
the strangest sensation came over me. Not sorrow or
fear, not dread even. An eerie feeling.

I pictured Myrtle standing in her kitchen
heating grease for Hamilton's eggs. I pictured her
turning around and around in the kitchen, slow and
wobbly like a top at the end of its spin. Then I could
see her falling onto her side, her hands over her eyes,
crying. I didn't tell anybody about that, but that's how
I saw her. I never related it to where Myrtle might be.

Henry and I drank coffee, real coffee. Strong.
Coffee that means what it says. Before seven, our
phone was ringing. Young people think when you
retire, you sleep late. That's not so. Retired people
are up at first light. We're so happy not to have to
go to work that we get up early just so we can enjoy
not going anywhere. So anyway, all our friends were
awake and on the phone as soon as they heard Myrtle
was still missing. Henry answered most of the calls.
I like to talk. You've probably noticed that by now.
But I do not like to talk about something I don't have
any control over. I like to have a say-so. I like gossip,
I'm ashamed to admit, but I don't like spiteful rumors
or mournful news. And this was mournful news
of the worst kind. All those questions and all that
speculation just made me tired.

I was glad when Henry left. I went outside so I
couldn't hear the phone. I thought I'd just put those
flowers into the bed. Calvin had already tilled the soil.
I could plant without his help. I needed to and that's
the truth. Therapy, I guess. Something to make me
feel hopeful. I figured pink flowers ought to do the
trick. Pink flowers have an innocence that yellow ones
don't. They're so naïve, like little girls in bonnets.
You ever notice that? Of course not, handsome, young

men like you don't notice things like bonnets and flowers. But I'll tell you, gardens bring old people a lot of joy. Planting should give peace. How was I to know that getting ready to plant would lead me to discover Myrtle's body?

When I opened the shed door, I saw them. Myrtle's dishwasher shelves on top of the peat moss and cow manure bags. I didn't know they were Myrtle's until I got closer. First I thought maybe Calvin put them there, but what would a teenage boy be doing with dishwasher shelves? Then I noticed the little silverware holder with the split side. And, bam, I knew they were Myrtle's. I always asked her, "Myrtle, why in the world don't you get a new one?" And she'd say, "Ruth, it works just fine. It's not like it's got to hold water." Lordy, that woman hated to throw anything away. You know, when you think about it, that sure doesn't fit with what she did to her very own self, now does it?

She must have put the shelves there after Hamilton went bowling. I'm surprised Henry didn't see her. He'd been in the backyard with his roses for most of the morning. The roses are his pride. He stays with them quite a bit. Says they don't like to be alone. He furnishes roses for all the ladies on the street. He always set a jar of his best on Myrtle's back steps. She made sachets from the petals.

Myrtle knew I'd already bought the impatiens for the beds. I guess she meant to be found pretty quick. She knew I'd be going into that shed. I'm sure she meant for me to find the shelves. I get irritated just thinking about it. I certainly didn't enjoy finding Myrtle's body in that dishwasher. It's not a picture I want to remember. On the other hand, I guess Myrtle must have trusted me, depended on me to know

where she was. I'm glad I was the one to see her in
that position. I'm glad it wasn't Hamilton who had
to see her that way. I touched the body, you know. I
didn't tell the police that because I didn't want them
to know I tampered with what might have been a
crime scene. You're not supposed to do that. Anyone
who watched *Matlock* or that old Angela Lansbury
detective program or any of those crime scene shows
as much as I have knows that. Anyhow, I put on some
Playtex gloves first, so I didn't leave any fingerprints.

Now I don't want to go getting ahead of myself.
I hadn't even found her yet, but seeing those shelves,
I knew. I don't remember crossing the yard, but I
remember thinking maybe I shouldn't go in Myrtle's
house with nobody home. Of course, Myrtle, the poor
thing, was at home. She'd never left. I got the key
from the hiding place. I knew where it was because I
always checked their house when they were away.

She had this little planter shaped like a burro
wearing a sombrero. The plants grew out of the
saddlebags. She got it at South of the Border. You
know that tourist place on the North Carolina -
South Carolina line? There are dozens of billboards
advertising it on I-95. Anyway, the little sombrero
lifted off so you could put a key under it. Myrtle said
she'd never forget where she put it because she'd
think, don-key. Get it? Don-key.

It rattled me to go inside. Those dishes
screamed at me like signal flares or big neon arrows
pointing to Myrtle. I went to the dishwasher and
just stood there for I don't know how long. How in
the world had she locked herself inside and turned it
on? Why would she kill herself like that? Why not
use pills and go to sleep? Why would she put herself
through the pain of wash and rinse?

If I were going to kill myself, I'd use pills and
I'd do it on Tuesday afternoon, because that's when I
have my hair shampooed and set on Tuesday morning
so I'd look my nicest. I'd fill my bedroom with lots
of fresh flowers and candles. Then I'd put on my
prettiest gown, the white eyelet with the lacy bed
jacket. I'd turn on the soaps. Of course, I'd probably
get interested in the story and forget to take the pills.
Then Henry would come in and think I'd gotten into
an amorous mood. Lordy, would you listen to me.
I'm embarrassing myself and you, too. Just look at
the way you're blushing.

I shouldn't tell you this. I hope you won't go
and print this part, but Myrtle told me a while back
that she didn't care if she ever had sex again. I asked
her why in the world not. She said, "Ruth, I just
feel all used up." I told her, "Now Myrtle, honey, a
new car is fun to drive. It smells all clean and fresh.
Everyone admires it, says you're lucky to have it.
Pretty soon though, you spill hot dog chili or ice cream
on the seat or the door gets a little ding in it. Starts to
smell musty, but it still gets you where you're going.
You can put it up on blocks and leave it to rust or you
can crank it up every now and again to keep the old
battery charged."

I thought I was pretty cute using all that car
talk, but it was all wasted. You know what she said?
She said, "I think it's time to tow the old heap away
and sell it for scrap."

Lord knows, I thought she was talking about
Hamilton, but thinking about it later, I realized she
was thinking about getting rid of herself. I wish to
heaven I had been able to say something to encourage
her to keep living.

It was premeditated. There's no doubt. The police said she used a timer to start the cycle. She'd looped a cord through the latch so she could pull the door closed. She was determined. That is one thing you can safely say about Myrtle Graham. I'll have to give her that. For a makeshift operation, it worked fine. Henry can explain better how she did it. He's mechanically inclined. He says he could come up with a more efficient system, but he better not. That's what I tell him. He better never do to me what Myrtle did to Hamilton.

I don't believe she thought it through. Not what it would do to Hamilton. You should see him now. He can't even go into the kitchen. He's got a cooler in the den. Lives out of that thing. Mostly, he eats out or comes over here. We set up a TV tray for him. Pretty soon he leaves. Hardly says a word. I'm hoping time will heal him. I expect he'll sell the house. He's got no reason to stay.

You ever feel like you're watching yourself do something while you're doing it? An out-of-your-mind experience. Is that what you call it? Well, that's the way I felt standing in front of that dishwasher. When I tried to open the door, it seemed to be stuck. I pulled again. It opened. At first I was just going to open it a crack. I only wanted to make sure she was really in there before I called the police. But once that door was open, I was like Pandora with that awful box of evils. I had to look. I had to. Not just for curiosity. For Myrtle. What if her skirt was up around her waist and she was in an indelicate situation? Death is embarrassing enough as it is, without strangers seeing your personal parts. That's why I think Myrtle wanted me to find her, to look after her dignity. I just put those Playtex gloves on and fixed her a little.

Sometimes in life a woman needs another woman. In death, too.

I don't like to think about what I saw. She seemed bruised and scalded. Her glasses were shoved halfway around her head. I already told you about her pitiful hair. Her clothes were rumpled and she was barefoot. Her shoes were inside though. Somehow she must have taken them off after the door closed. She didn't have long to wait before the automatic timer started the cycle. That's what they think anyway. She wedged herself in tight, with no room for second thoughts.

The police found a note. Problem was, she left it in her pocket so the ink ran and the words smeared. You could make out a little. A couple of "good-byes." Something about "a sorry excuse." Leave it to Myrtle to write a suicide note in disappearing ink. Not real disappearing ink, but you know what I mean.

Did you notice those impatiens when you came in? Cheerful, aren't they? When I see them I remember Myrtle. I'd like to take the lawn mower and demolish them. Just mow and mow until they are a pile of mulch. They've got no right to be so pink.

What are you going to write about a woman who kills herself with a dishwasher? I'm not sure why she did it. Maybe she was tired. Maybe she just decided to clean out her system and got carried away.

I wish I knew because the truth is, Myrtle's life was a lot like mine. I wish I could figure out what she couldn't stand anymore. Then maybe I could avoid it. I'm scared I'll end up the same way. I'm scared one day I'll wake up and look out at the impatiens and think, what's the use. Those damn pink things are going to die anyway.

You'll have to excuse me. I hope you won't quote that. I don't normally curse, especially in front of a handsome, young man like you. Ladies don't behave that way. They don't go around committing suicide either.

I wish she could talk to me. Talk and talk and talk. But Myrtle's voice washed right down that drain.

Lordy, I've been sitting here too long. Why don't you walk around back? Henry's out cutting roses. You have a girlfriend? Of course, you do. You're too handsome not to. Well, you just find Henry and he will make a nice bouquet for you to give her. He's got plenty now that he doesn't have Myrtle's jar to fill.

Roses are perennials, you know. You plant them once and they stay around. You can count on roses. Impatiens bloom like crazy – but just for one season. Then you have it to do again. Waste of time, when you think about it.

WOMAN'S DEATH NOT FULLY AUTOMATIC

Chapter 2 - Henry Overton's Story

Ruth finally let you go? Still got your ears? You're luckier than most. She's pickled hundreds of ears. Talked them right off those pitiful people she trapped in that kitchen of hers. Stores them in jars. Serves them with barbecue sauce. Tastes like chicken. I'm pulling your leg, son. Don't look so serious.

She sent you for roses, I reckon. Roses, I can give you. Roses are meant to be cut. Pick out anything you like. This one over here, it's a new one. I'm testing it. The Bunyon Rose Company has folks all over the country trying out new roses, recording data about leaves and blooms and thorns, if the bud is a fast opener, if the perfume lingers. Whole process takes a couple of years. Then if the rose passes muster, we submit ideas for names and Bunyon markets it. This one is number 413. White, tinged with peach. This little lady is a gem. Look how delicate she is. Fragile but resilient. Take a whiff. Inhale the bouquet. Like you'd do with wine. You'd like to sip it, wouldn't you?

Yes, sir, number 413's a keeper. I submitted a name for her. Don't think it's got much chance though because the name I chose isn't romantic enough, not poetic. Still, I think it's an a-number-one name. Haven't told a soul my suggestion, not even Ruth. It'll be awhile before I know if I win. By then, everyone will have had some healing time.

About Myrtle, I mean. Wounds are still pretty tender. Ruth's having a time dealing with all this. She doesn't let on, but she is. No need getting her upset about a name for a rose. By the time it's been decided she'll be ready for a memorial.

Yep, you guessed it. Myrtle's the name I sent.
That's why they won't pick it. Myrtle isn't a feminine,
lacy word. Of course, Myrtle herself wasn't either,
but she was just what a woman should be. New
women are too strong, too self-reliant for men of my
generation. But take Myrtle. Take Ruth. They're the
kind a man like me can trust. They let us men be men.
They depend on us. Maybe new men are different, but
the men I grew old with enjoyed being needed.

Myrtle. Ruth. They liked needing us. It
worked out fine and dandy.

Myrtle fancied my roses. Used to stroll through
my roses two, three times a week. "Henry," she'd say,
"it pleasures me to be around something so cared for,
so tended." She liked the arrangement of my rose
garden, like a chorus line, she said. Old number 413
was one of her favorites. She said it reminded her
of homemade peach ice cream. Hand churned, old
fashioned.

It'd be fitting if Bunyon picked Myrtle's
name for this rose. A nice little eulogy. She was old
fashioned. Hand churned, if you will. Unassuming.
You could take Myrtle at face value. That's what I
thought, anyway.

I guess Myrtle was dealing with more thorns
than I realized. It's been tough on everybody. The
four of us – Myrtle, Hamilton, Ruth, and me – we
spent lots of time together. It's hard losing somebody
so close. When you get older, death's a regular
visitor. You get accustomed to funerals, to reading
the obituaries. Pretty soon, you know more dead
friends than living ones. It's like they've been invited
somewhere and you haven't. Not yet, that is. You
expect death to do what's right. But this time, death

deceived us all, dared Myrtle to do something she
shouldn't have done. Myrtle should've known better
than to kill herself. She made us distrust death.
Ruth's lost. Hamilton sinks lower every day. Me?
Lots of nights I lie awake feeling too bad to sleep.

Ruth had no call to tell you I could explain
how Myrtle did it. I don't let my mind wander
that direction. Timers and cords, drowning and
smothering all at once. Tell you the truth, I didn't
think she was that original. Why did she do it? We
might never know. Hidden meanings? I don't
even think about the meanings right there in broad
daylight.

To tell you what I know I'd have to start at the
beginning. That's part of the problem with getting
old. Nothing's simple. Everything's connected to
something connected to something else. You couldn't
tell a simple story if your life depended on it, but if
you've got the time, I'll tell you my estimation of what
happened.

I've known Hamilton since World War II. We
were in the same unit. He was a pilot and I was a
ground mechanic. We were stationed at Fort Jackson,
waiting to be shipped out. That's where we met
Myrtle. Local girls rode buses out to Twin Lakes on
the weekends to dance with us soldiers. Big morale
booster. Lots of scared young men, some away from
home for the first time, getting ready to partner up
with death. Those sweet homegrown girls were just
what we needed. Some fellas wanted a last fling, but
mostly, we were satisfied to hold a pretty girl in our
arms and sway.

Myrtle was one hell of a dancer. She never
hurt for partners. Everybody wanted to spin and
dip Myrtle. With her even the clumsiest left-footed

recruit would glide like Astaire. She wasn't beautiful, not pin-up material, but she was lively and fired up to do her part for the war effort. She was so patriotic she even looked like the flag. Blue eyes, hair so red it seemed ready to explode, and skin whiter than powdered sugar. She didn't look pale though; she looked pure. No, sir, she wasn't beautiful, but she did startle you into looking twice. All the GIs liked her, but no one was painting her name on their planes. Not until Hamilton came along. He named his bomber "Marryin' Myrtle."

When she wasn't dancing, she poured punch or passed applesauce cake she'd baked herself. In those days it was hard to bake anything what with rationing, but Myrtle had ways of substituting. She always said Hamilton married her because of that cake. It was a secret family recipe. The only way he could get it was become a member of the family.

Hamilton just plain liked Myrtle. She was a large woman, not in the sense that she weighed a lot, but she was big boned. Tall. Most women, when they're taller than men, will slouch or hang their heads trying to look shorter. Not Myrtle. She held herself straight, seemed proud to look a man eye to eye. Hamilton used to say short girls gave him a crick in the neck because of always having to bend over to kiss them. But Myrtle's lips, he said, were easy to find. They lined up perfect with his.

The first night we went to Twin Lakes, we were just in from basic training and pure-t overwhelmed with the fact that war was our next stop. Hamilton and I were both innocent Tennessee country boys so we buddied up. Yes, sir, it was June 1943, so muggy you could practically swim in the air, but an afternoon thunderstorm had cooled down that particular night.

I remember because the wind was blowing the girls' skirts. Plenty of leg to see.

Finally, you smile. You must be a leg man. Well, you should've been there, son. Nothing more tantalizing than dozens of angel-faced girls trying unsuccessfully to keep the breezes from raising a fella's eyebrows, not to mention his hopes.

Enough girls for the army and the navy. Moonlight and sugar-voiced, long-haired, rosy-lipped girls as far as you could see. GIs smoking outside propped along the docks. Girls giggling and leaning into them. Everybody packing fun into a few hours, especially the boys shipping out the next week. Hamilton met up with his brother, Joe, who was on his last weekend pass himself. Three sheets to the wind, he was. Grabbed Hamilton around the neck and said, "It's up to you to carry on the Graham legend. Women'll be grief stricken. Comfort them, Ham. Make a name for yourself."

Hamilton and I both were holding him up when Myrtle came sashaying over. I remember it like it was yesterday. She said, "Joe, you only have three hours to break your dance partner record. You're wasting time latched onto these soldiers. Handsome as they are, and they are handsome, you gotta move on to someone in a skirt."

Joe pulled himself together and shrugged Myrtle off. He said, "Keep your distance, girlie girl," then staggered away. Hamilton was embarrassed that Joe'd been rude. He tried to apologize, but Myrtle laughed and said, "Can't please them all." Then she left, went about five steps, turned, winked, and made some clicking sounds with her tongue. She said, "Stand back, boys. I was born to dance." Hamilton liked her immediately. I have to admit, so did I.

We stood in the crowd, watching Myrtle dance
with one GI after another. Fellows were breaking in
on her all the time. She never finished a dance with
the guy she started with. Was she good? Son, she
was Cyd Charisse. And she could do them all: tango,
jitterbug, rumba. Most girls wilted after a while,
but the more Myrtle danced, the more she glowed.
I was getting my courage to ask her to dance when
Hamilton started across the floor. "I'll Be Seeing
You" was playing when he tapped the fellow on the
shoulder. When he took Myrtle in his arms, they just
fit. He didn't waste time dancing a polite distance
from her either. No, sir, he pulled her close. She
looked up at him once; then she put her head next to
his cheek and she was his. The whole world knew it,
too. While they danced, not a soul broke in on them.

Myrtle and Hamilton tried dancing with other
people, but it was no use. They kept coming back
to each other like they were on springs. I wouldn't
say it was love at first sight. Hamilton was too
sensible for that; so was Myrtle for that matter, but
it was the strongest attraction I've ever witnessed. I
think, looking back, it was more serious than love
at first sight. Maybe it was realization at first sight.
Realization that they were going to fall in love and be
together forever.

That sounds mushy coming from an old man
like me. But son, I was there. Saw it with my own
eyes. I think, nowadays, young people don't have
that same kind of initial knowledge of commitment,
so there's no care taken to respect the stages of a
relationship. They just lunge in and figure if it doesn't
work out, they'll get a divorce and start over, like they
can recycle their lives.

You young men should step back and examine
things the way we did. When we made a decision,
we stuck to it. Living was serious. We faced the
Depression, Pearl Harbor, the war. Comfort came
from things we counted on, consistency. We craved
habits, patterns, customs. Put our faith in traditions.
Pardon my preaching, son. I get carried away
sometimes.

Anyway, that was Friday. Saturday was the
same, the two of them dancing about every third
song, gazing lovesick at each other over the shoulders
of their other partners. At one point Joe cornered
Hamilton, got right in his face. I was standing
across the room with Myrtle and one of her friends,
but I could tell Joe was furious. Looked like he was
snarling. Myrtle noticed me watching. She said, "Pay
no mind to Joe. He hates me. Probably thinks it's
his brotherly duty to warn Hamilton to stay away." I
asked her why she and Joe didn't get along. She said,
"That's Joe. He's hard to like." The other girl piped
up that Joe was a sweet guy, funny and charming.
Myrtle rolled her eyes and said, "You must be talking
about some other Joe." When Hamilton came back,
he was hotter than Hades. Myrtle nestled up to him.
Soon he was smiling again and dancing her out to the
docks.

She invited us to Sunday dinner at her
home, even drove a friend's car out to the fort to
pick us up. She'd piled her hair on top of her head.
Sunlight fired it so bright you almost had to shield
your eyes. Marigolds. Orange ones. Myrtle's hair
looked like a bunch of marigolds. I commented on
it. Hamilton grinned, said it was the exact color of his
Grandmother Eva's. Cheerful, he said.

Hamilton wore himself out trying to please Myrtle's parents. He set the table, raved about the chicken, helped dry the dishes. Her mother was fidgety with a high-pitched laugh that called attention to itself. She entertained us in the parlor playing the piano while Myrtle and her father sang duets and acted out comedy routines like George and Gracie. They were so polished, it was clear they'd rehearsed. Myrtle's father was the biggest surprise. Before dinner, he sat in an armchair reading his paper. No smiling. No conversation, but when he began singing, he lit up. Myrtle was definitely the second banana, and he was the star. When they finished, he folded into his chair again and clammed up.

Later we had applesauce cake on the front porch. Hamilton and Myrtle sat close together on the swing, and finally when her mother went inside, he put his arm around her. I've never seen two people more content. I walked around the block a few times so they could be alone. We were stationed at the fort for about two months before we shipped out. During that time Hamilton and Myrtle got to know each other better, as if they needed to. They spent all their free time together, were settled in and snug like they were already an old married couple. At Twin Lakes, she still danced with other fellas, but word got around pretty quick it was paws off. Of course, like I said, most men weren't dying to kiss Myrtle, but for Hamilton's benefit, his buddies pretended she was the cat's meow. She wasn't a beauty, but we all liked her. Yes, sir, Myrtle was a party.

Hard to believe she ended up dead in a dishwasher. I still see her dancing under those colored lanterns at Twin Lakes. Still see her tilting her head, looking over her shoulder, hands on her hips in that famous Betty Grable pose she liked to imitate. She always used to say, "Hamilton, those eyes of yours are dangerous weapons. One look and I surrender." Of course, it was Hamilton that surrendered to her.

He loved Myrtle so much it was pure-t embarrassing. After we went overseas, he was consumed with getting back to Myrtle. Nothing else mattered. Wrote her two, three letters a day. That was probably what got him through the crash. "Marryin' Myrtle" went down. He took a hit, but somehow got back to the landing strip before he crashed. It would've been okay if it hadn't caught fire. All but one man got out. Hamilton broke his arm, had some serious burns. His wounds healed, but he was bad off. Felt responsible for the man he lost. Without Myrtle's letters and loving her, he might've given up.

War is hell, son, no doubt about it. But Myrtle was life, and Hamilton held onto that. Now Myrtle's death. It's been a blow. I'm not sure he'll come through. Always before, he had her. Even when his son died, he had Myrtle. Who's he got now?

We've tried to help. Ruth cooks for him, checks after his clothes but she doesn't know what else to do. Sometimes around Hamilton, she doesn't say a word. You've met her. That's highly unusual for Ruth. They both look emptied. Myrtle deserted them. Stranded. That's what they are.

Me? Well, Myrtle and I had a brother-sister relationship. To me, her death is like a prank a mean-hearted kid would pull. No consideration for the consequences. A game gone wrong, like when you read about children who play hide-and-seek in an old refrigerator and smother themselves. Myrtle bullied me into a cruel joke. How could she do that to me? To all of us? It's like the years we were together meant nothing.

June of '47, that's when the four of us got
started. After the war was over, Hamilton high-
tailed it here to marry Myrtle. He got a job, went
to school so they'd have security. Took a while, but
he got established. I went back to Tennessee. One
day Myrtle called me to come for the wedding, be
Hamilton's best man. I was surprised, figured Joe'd
stand up for him, but I felt honored. Bought myself a
new suit. The wedding itself was formal, but Myrtle
insisted on dancing at the reception. Lots of dancing
and laughing people. That was where I met Ruth.
Prettiest girl there. Ugliest hat I'd ever seen, but the
girl underneath was a pure-t wonder. I truly believe
she wore that hat so she wouldn't outshine the bride.
She'd never admit that, but it's something she'd do.
She's considerate that way.

I went back to Tennessee, packed my things,
moved here, and started selling cars. That was when
men made a career of automobile sales. We took
it seriously, handled folks with dignity. Regular
customers came back car after car after car. They
trusted us. We weren't like these high-pressure
twenty-year-old hotshots pushing cars nowadays, in it
for big bucks, trying to swindle folks with rebates and
add-ons. We were different. We were honorable and
willing to wait.

You young fellas don't understand what my
generation went through. You've had everything
handed to you. We wrestled with life. For you,
everything has to be instant. No such thing as
patience anymore. Young men don't grow roses.
Roses take time and care. Year-round care. Men
of your generation won't know the satisfaction of
growing roses, of sitting on the porch of the house
where you've spent your whole adult life, of being

married to the same woman for fifty years. Growing
old will be harder on your generation than it was on
ours because nothing is a constant with you people.
Remote control life. Switch. Switch. Switch. You
don't know how to ease into anything. Sure as hell
don't know how to stick with something.

We were constants, the four of us, neighbors
from the beginning. For all accounts and purposes,
I saw Hamilton and Myrtle every day. They were
as much a part of my life as Ruth. When I close my
eyes, picture my past, those two are in every stage of
it. Starting out and ending up, the best friends I ever
had. I can't get Myrtle out of my mind, can't let go of
it. Death shouldn't be a slammed door. It wasn't like
Myrtle to be that way.

We had good times, especially early on. We
bought these houses, side by side. Cooked out. Went
on vacation together. Once a week we played hearts
or bridge or rummy. They got their television first and
together we'd watch the shows about married couples.
Always two couples in zany situations together. *The
Honeymooners* and *I Love Lucy*. Myrtle would say,
"That's us." She even wore her hair and dressed like
Lucille Ball.

After the war life relaxed. No worries. We
used to say if I could sell enough Pontiacs to fill up
Hamilton's parking lots, we'd be rich. He was in the
paving and grading business, you see, and shopping
centers and housing developments were going up all
over. That meant streets, driveways, parking lots,
curbs. Hamilton got us where we were going.

We always had a pet project. I didn't have
a garage so the two of us built that little shed over
there. Gave me a place to putter around with dirt and
flowers while he fixed lawn mowers. Hamilton glued

together model airplanes. I was happiest under the
hood of a car. Anybody looking for us, all they had
to do was holler to his garage or my shed. The girls
would bring sandwiches out to us, but they wouldn't
stay. They said there wasn't a place clean enough for a
lady to sit down.

Ruth and Myrtle always complained that
our fingernails never got completely clean. Myrtle,
especially, liked clean. She didn't like anything out
of place. Hamilton was neat, too, but he wasn't
overboard with it. He used to worry about Gerald
because when he was a little boy, Myrtle would
change his clothes five times a day trying to keep the
child clean. Hamilton said, "Let him be a kid." See,
Hamilton and I had grown up in the mountains, the
woods. We played at building forts, swam in ponds,
ran outside after breakfast and didn't come back until
suppertime. I don't think Gerald ever got dirty.

In fact, it was rare to see that boy in the yard.
Hamilton would buy train sets, baseballs, BB guns,
but the two of us played with them more than Gerald
did. All that boy did was dance. For years, before
Hamilton and I fixed up Gerald's practice room,
Myrtle'd put sheets of plywood on the back porch
so he could practice tap dancing. Hamilton and I'd
be in the garage, and we'd hear Myrtle and Gerald
rehearsing song after song. Reminded me of Myrtle
and her father dancing in their parlor.

Hamilton loved Gerald, but they didn't
have much common ground. The older he got,
the more time he spent at dance school with that
Madame Fouché woman. Hamilton hardly ever
saw Gerald. He worried. I think he was scared
Gerald wasn't manly, if you know what I mean. He
never said anything, but he sure seemed relieved

whenever Gerald had a date, especially with Rebecca Montgomery.

Gerald liked music and acting. Myrtle pictured him on Broadway. She talked about it constantly, and Gerald definitely had the face. He looked a lot like Hamilton except for his hair. He had hair like Myrtle's, not a wild red though. Myrtle's was like a jack-o'-lantern. Gerald's, more like pumpkin pie.

When Gerald died, Hamilton closed off. He mourned, but in a lot of ways Hamilton was mourning a stranger, like he was mourning the son he never had.

During that time, Hamilton stopped growing roses. Up until then, we had a friendly rivalry over our gardens. But he let his go. That's how Myrtle knew something was wrong. Hamilton made some big mistakes. There's a name for that now. A mid-life crisis. Maybe it was age. Maybe it was Gerald's death or the depression Myrtle went into afterwards, but for whatever reason, Hamilton had an affair. I never suspected, not until Myrtle came over one day when I was cutting roses and questioned me. She thought Hamilton would've confided in me. He hadn't though. Hamilton was discreet. I don't think he meant for anyone to ever find out.

Myrtle was thin, too thin. Grief had taken all her appetite for living. Suffering takes a toll on a woman. Even her voice was weak when she spoke. She said she hadn't been a proper wife since Gerald died, that she didn't have the heart for day-to-day living. She asked me to talk with Hamilton. Suspicion was killing her. She needed to know for sure.

She pointed to his roses, pointed out the neglect. They showed Hamilton's state of mind, all right. His betrayal. Roses are like women. They need to be noticed daily. Those roses had been abandoned.

I knew then Hamilton had put his attention somewhere else. I wasn't sure if it was an affair, but Myrtle said she had other clear signs indicating another woman. Butting in wasn't natural for me, but she looked so hollow I couldn't stand it. Myrtle had always been my image of everything that was right with the world. She didn't need me very often, but when she did, when Hamilton couldn't or wouldn't come through, I helped her. She knew if there was anything I could do, I would.

She made me swear I wouldn't tell Ruth right away, not until we knew for sure. She wanted to protect Hamilton's reputation. That tells you something about Myrtle. She didn't want Ruth to think less of him. There are things a man will keep from his wife if there's a good reason, so I agreed. I can count on one hand the things I didn't tell Ruth over the years. I had good reasons, but I'm not proud of myself.

Anyway, a couple of days later Hamilton and I rode up to the lake. On the way, he was quiet, kept staring out the window. I said, "Hamilton, I know things have been hard lately. It might be best if you talk about it."

He turned to me with that haunted expression I hadn't seen since the war. He said, "I've bought myself a ticket to hell, Henry. One way. And if it means eternal damnation, I'll accept it. I just can't live the rest of my life on earth like this."

He let go of the whole story. Hard as it was to hear, I could understand the temptation he felt. You see, in those days most people went into marriage without much experience and took it as a lifetime agreement. Divorce wasn't accepted. You didn't want to admit you couldn't take care of problems, that there was something you couldn't handle. But every once in a while, when a beautiful woman walked through your life, you couldn't help but wonder, what if. Most times, it was harmless fantasy. But Hamilton was so miserable and this woman so available that he was involved before he knew it.

Her name was Lydia. She worked in the county office where Hamilton got permits for his paving business. He'd known her for years. She'd always been pleasant and helpful and very proper. If she'd been flirty, then Hamilton probably wouldn't have taken her seriously, but she was nice. Hamilton said she had dark hair and warm soothing eyes that gave the kind of pleasure you get from coffee, not from drinking, just from stirring. She had delicate features and tiny hands and dimples. He liked her soft-lipped smile.

After Gerald died, Hamilton took some time off. When he went back to Lydia's office, it'd been a while since she'd seen him. She said, "Where in the world have you been, off on vacation?" She had no idea what had happened and Hamilton said he couldn't find his voice. He realized he was going to cry, to lose control. She took one look at the tears coming to his eyes, pushed herself back from her desk, and ushered him into a little file room so he could compose himself. He broke down in her arms. She comforted him in a way that Myrtle, with her own grieving, hadn't. They went for lunch, and over the next few weeks Lydia became Hamilton's reason to keep living.

Hamilton's a gentleman, he never told me details. I never asked. But he did tell me Lydia was generous and giving and he felt a freedom with her that, because of heartbreak and pain, he'd lost with

Myrtle. He knew that he would cause trouble for
them all, but he didn't have the will to stop. He said
he needed Lydia, and as long as Myrtle didn't know,
he thought he could fill his needs.

Myrtle knew, I told him. He put his face in his
hands and sat for a long time without saying a word.
Then he sighed, said he'd deal with the truth of his
lies. We drove back to town. I never heard Lydia's
name again. Myrtle seemed to pull herself out of
her mourning and they went on. Hamilton didn't go
back to his roses. Unless Myrtle told her, Ruth never
realized the crisis.

Things settled down. They seemed fine.
Hamilton had some improvements done to the house,
modernized the kitchen and bathrooms. That's when
they put in that dishwasher. Changes don't always
make your life easier. You know what they say about
idle hands.

Ruth thinks Hamilton will move to a condo.
It'd probably be best. I couldn't live in that house
now. It hurts me to look at it.

I can't speculate how she did it. That's not for
me to say. I know she used a timer. She used me, too.
She knew I'd do anything for her. Any little favor she
wanted, all she had to do was ask Henry. If Hamilton
was too busy, ask Henry. Pick up something at the
hardware store; show her how to use something, ask
Henry. Good old Henry. Myrtle played me for a fool.

About a year ago, Ruth and I went to the
Grand Canyon. Myrtle looked after things while we
were gone. All she had to do was get the mail. She
didn't have to go into the house because I'd bought
automatic timers to turn the lights on and off so it
would look like we were home. Myrtle was intrigued
with those timers. Asked me to pick up some for her

the next time I went to the hardware store. She said
she wanted to play a little trick on Hamilton. I hate
to think she was planning this that far back. Worse, I
hate to think I gave her the idea.

Don't print that part about timers. That's one
of the things I never told Ruth.

Take your roses and be on your way. Women
love a man who brings roses. Not in a box from a
florist. They like to be handed roses personally. She'll
like these better than store-bought ones. Point out
number 413, the one that's taller than the rest.

Yes, Hamilton's home. His car's there. He
won't talk to you though. He barely speaks to me and
I'm his best friend.

HUSBAND DRAINED BY
DISHWASHER DEATH

Chapter 3 - Hamilton Graham's Story

I thought you were from Goodwill. They're coming today to pick up Myrtle's clothes. Somebody ought to get some wear out of them. Shouldn't be wasted. Good money spent. I boxed everything up according to season. There's also a box of purses and belts and the like. Shoes, too. Boxes and boxes of them. My wife was very particular about her accessories. Hell, she was particular about everything. She wanted to look nice when she went out. She liked to think she was stylish.

That's why I wouldn't let them open the casket. People tried to talk me into it, but I knew Myrtle would have been furious if anyone had seen her like that. Let them speculate all they want, dammit. Nobody was going to have a last view of Myrtle that wasn't complimentary.

You might as well come in and sit down. At least you're not another widow with a casserole. It's only been a few weeks and already those damn church women, some I don't even know, have started dropping by with chicken-and-something in cream sauce and inviting themselves to share it with me. So I won't have to eat alone, they say. Hard as hell to get rid of them. They set about making themselves at home in that god-awful kitchen, rummaging through Myrtle's cabinets and drawers. Then after we eat, they make not-so-subtle comments about staying to help me get through the lonely nights. I don't want the old biddies here, but I don't have the strength to fight them off. Mostly, I sit and stare at the television and finally they leave. Desperation isn't attractive in an old woman.

Desperation. I keep telling myself that Myrtle must have been desperate to do what she did. Desperate enough to punish herself and all of us she left here to deal with all our hurting. Dammit, what the hell was she thinking? How could she hurt me like this? We had problems like everybody else, but nothing that should have caused her to do this. I'm so damn mad I can't talk about it without wanting to smash something.

"Perfectly natural reaction." That's what Dr. Know-it-all said. Told me I'd go through stages. Stood right here with that blasted dishwasher in the next room and said, "At first, you'll be in a state of disbelief, Mr. Graham." Hell, the only thing I couldn't believe was that he was old enough to be a doctor. He had the nerve to say I'd feel guilty. Wanted me to take tranquilizers and meet with some blubbering support group to help me, let's see, how did he put it, to help me "articulate my anger."

Damn poor excuse for a doctor. He doesn't know me and he sure as hell didn't know Myrtle. He just waltzed in and took over Bud Riley's practice when he retired last year. I'd never even seen him except when I got my flu shot. Myrtle had a couple of appointments with him when she thought she might have diabetes, but he told her to stop diagnosing herself and let him worry about her health. Riley would have seen what was going on. These modern doctors don't have a clue about respecting their elders. I don't need his lectures or his put-on sympathy. He can't begin to know what I feel. He doesn't have any idea about life, much less death. He's what? Thirty years old? Big-time doctor with his sports car and his

three-hundred-thousand-dollar house. Hell, I'd like
to see him go through one day of this kind of reality.

Do you want a beer? Soda? I've got some in
the cooler right here. Nobody has to go in the kitchen.
I've got chips and bananas, peanut butter, bread,
raisins right here. All the comforts of home. See. I
moved the microwave and the toaster out here. A
man doesn't need a whole house. A man can live just
fine out of a couple of rooms.

So you interviewed Ruth and Henry already.
They're good people. Good friends. I can't stand to
be around them very long, but they're good friends.
I'm painful to them, too. They look at me as if I must
know something they don't, some blackheart secret.
Hell, I'm as much in the dark as they are. Damn
mystery. Not even Angela Lansbury or *Law and
Order* could figure this out.

I haven't talked about it much. Truth is,
nobody's asked. The police did, of course, but
everybody else tiptoes around me, afraid to mention
Myrtle's name. Even my brother Joe, who never kept
it a secret that he didn't like her, even he doesn't say
anything. Hell, what do they think I'm going to do? I
guess it's time for some things to be said. Out loud.

It's your job to listen. That's what you get
paid for. Right? Myrtle would have liked you. She
had to have somebody listening to her. She wasn't
always so stuck on that, not until she started watching
those damn talk shows. They're always harping
on communicating. Get it all out, they say. Then
everybody starts blubbering and hugging. Hogwash.
There's nothing wrong with keeping stuff inside. No
need to go smearing yourself around. Some things are
meant to be kept private.

You have to know the balance, when to speak and when to keep your mouth shut. I'll talk, but I won't lose my dignity to you or anybody else. People try to steal dignity, especially from an older person. I'll keep mine or die trying.

Funny I should put it that way because that damn doctor told me that suicide is a big thing with senior citizens. Happens all the time. They get to a point where there's nothing left, not even dignity. I didn't think Myrtle was that far gone.

The day it happened, I went bowling. Myrtle was in here when I left. She didn't seem odd. Not any more so than usual. She was folding clothes. I asked her if she wanted me to bring back some lunch. She liked certain things on certain days. Most Tuesdays, after bowling I would stop and pick up Whoppers from Burger King or the baked fish dinner at Captain D's. She liked the hush puppies. It depended on whether or not she had coupons from Sunday's paper. The joke was, she always clipped them, sorted them, and handed them over, but I never used them. I hated those damn coupons.

The only strange thing was she said she didn't have much appetite, that maybe she would fix a tuna salad later. I can truthfully say that Myrtle always had a healthy appetite except for two times in her life – when she was pregnant and when our son Gerald died. Hell, she hated tuna salad.

I don't remember saying good-bye. After you've been married so long you take things for granted. I know why I didn't say good-bye. I was coming back in just a little while. But Myrtle, she could have said good-bye. That was the least she could have done. Dammit, she knew it was the last time she was going to see me. There's no way I'm

going to believe that she folded the last towel, and
on the spur of the moment said, "Hey, I've got an
idea. I'll go jump in the dishwasher and kill myself.
Hamilton won't mind."

She planned it. She knew when I left what she
was going to do. She had all the laundry caught up.
When the police were here, they found the pantry
full of food and the freezer stocked with microwave
dinners. That was enough to convince me she had
planned it. She never bought those things. Cooking
meals was a source of pride for Myrtle. She swore
she'd never rely on the microwave oven. What she
was doing was making sure I'd have supper. Another
way I knew she planned it was she had written down
all her secret recipes and left them in a box for Ruth.
It was in the back of her underwear drawer. I haven't
even given them to her yet. I don't want to start her
crying again.

I found some other things too. The police think
all she left was a washed-out note. But there was
more. Some notebooks and lists. A sealed letter to
Henry. She was crazy if she thought I was going to be
her little helper, if she thought I'd pass out her little
death messages. If she wanted to say something to
somebody, she should have done it before she killed
herself. I'm not going to be manipulated into reading
that stuff. If she had something to say to me, she
should have said it to my face. She was a coward.

As far as I'm concerned, the police will never
know about those things I found. They see a lot of
bad things, but I don't think they had ever run into
something like this before. They kept talking about
the way she did it. Said most people use pills or
shoot themselves. We didn't have a gun in the house,
haven't since Gerald was a baby. As far as pills are

46 Debra A. Daniel

concerned, Myrtle hated to swallow pills. Had a hell
of a time getting one down, much less a bottle full.

The dishwasher was probably Myrtle's way
of getting back at me. Her way of saying all the
things she loved had changed so much she wasn't
comfortable with them anymore. When we were first
married, we used to eat supper and then we would do
the dishes together. Take turns washing and drying.
Gerald never did a dish in his life. I never realized
how much she liked doing dishes with me until I had
the kitchen remodeled. Hell, I thought she'd be happy
not to have to work so hard.

The first night after everything was finished
and the kitchen was back to working order, I was
looking forward to watching the news after supper.
Took my dessert in the den with me and left Myrtle
to load the dishwasher. During the commercial, I
went back to take my plate, and there was Myrtle
filling the silverware holder and crying her eyes
out. I asked her what the hell was wrong. She said,
"I miss you washing the dishes with me." You can't
figure women out. She would throw that dishwasher
up in my face every time we had an argument. It
always came back to the fact that I didn't talk to her
enough. "Remember washing dishes," she would say.
"That's when you really talked to me, when you really
listened."

Men don't need all that talk. You can
understand that. You're a man. Women don't think
you love them unless you talk to them. They want to
hang your feelings out to dry. I'll keep mine to myself,
thank you. I'm sick and tired of all this sensitive
garbage. If she didn't know after fifty years that I
loved her, then to hell with her.

Wait. I don't mean that. Myrtle was my wife. I'm just
not good at expressing myself. Sometimes my words
start punching out like I'm a prizefighter. I used to do
that with Gerald. I wasn't good with him either.

He was more Myrtle's child than mine. When
he was little, it wasn't so bad. I got to play with him
some, and on a trip to Tennessee once, he seemed to
take a shine to being in the woods with me. But the
older he got, the less we had in common. He didn't
like a single thing I did. Didn't play ball, except
tennis. Hated hunting and fishing. Myrtle had him
taking damn tap and ballet lessons by the time he
was five. She loved dancing better than anything,
and she didn't rest until she had transferred that to
him. She had dreams of Gerald following the path
she would liked to have taken. The nights I spent
watching Gerald in those damn dance recitals were
torture. That Fouché woman bustling around him
and dressing him in tiny tin soldier or sailor costumes
like he was a little Gene Kelly doll made me nervous.
And the worst thing was he was good at it. He was a
natural. For years, I kept hoping he'd get tired of it
or suddenly look at himself in those ruffly-shirt Latin
costumes or those god-awful tights and say, "Hey, this
is sissy stuff." Then he'd jerk the tights off right there
on stage and show everybody, in no uncertain terms,
what a man he was.

Gerald made me feel unsure. Having a
conversation with him was next to impossible for
me. What the hell could I talk to him about? How to
pick out a toe shoe? I couldn't get a handle on him.
He wasn't exactly girlish, but he didn't seem strong
and masculine either. Didn't even have a driver's
license. Watching a football game on television wasn't
for him. He liked to read and go to movies. He was

smart in school and had friends. Kids seemed to like
him. In fact, he was a cheerleader. When we went to
the games to watch him cheer, I felt foolish. I wanted
a football player for my son. During those years, I'm
sorry to say, I was embarrassed by him. Even when
he danced with a partner or sang the love songs in the
school plays, it didn't seem right to me. There was
one pretty little girl that he went out with on a regular
basis. Guess you could call her his girlfriend. Rebecca
Montgomery. Sweet girl. Myrtle didn't like her,
pestered Gerald about getting too serious. I thought,
hell, he needs to get involved with a girl. I prayed he'd
come home with passion marks on his neck, that he'd
break curfew, that Myrtle would find a girlie magazine
under his mattress.

He didn't act like a normal, hot-blooded
American teenaged boy. He didn't go prissing around
the house either. I couldn't figure him out, and I
couldn't make Myrtle understand my concerns. When
it came to Gerald, she wore blinders. She would sew
his little costumes and sell tickets to his performances.
If Fouché needed volunteers or the playhouse wanted
donations, Myrtle was the first one they called. She
spent as much time at rehearsals as he did.

Gerald was talented. The dancing part came
from Myrtle, but no one could figure where he got
the singing voice. When I sing, I sound like I need
to be oiled. But Gerald's voice, it was exceptional.
That caused problems. He wanted to go to Nashville
and try to get on The Grand Ole Opry stage. Myrtle's
opinion was that a voice like his would be wasted on
country music. New York was the place he should go.
You know, Broadway. That was what she thought.
That was about the only time I ever remember
them clashing. Myrtle wasn't accustomed to being

challenged. If she didn't get her way right off, she'd
pout or mope around until she did. That worked on
me when we first got married. Worked on Gerald, too,
until that country music argument came up. They
were having some serious set-tos right towards the
end of his life. It pleased me to see he had some damn
spunk. Plenty of times I thought he was a pantywaist.

During Gerald's senior year in high school, they
put on *OKLAHOMA!* and he was chosen to play Curly.
That's the lead role. On opening night he left for the
theater early, then realized he'd forgotten his dance
shoes. He called home and asked if we'd bring them
backstage when we got there. When I walked into
the boys' dressing room, there was Gerald, his hair
in rollers and his face all done up with eye shadow,
rosy cheeks, even lipstick. He looked exactly like
Myrtle did whenever she was getting ready for a fancy
party. Scared the hell out of me. All I could think of
was that Gerald had turned into Geraldine. Nobody
else seemed to notice, and, in fact, all the kids had on
make-up. But that image is still burned in my mind.

He belonged on stage, pretending he was
somebody else. The other kids, they did a good job,
but Gerald was at home there. Rebecca was probably
next best. She was in the show, too, but didn't play
opposite Gerald. She was the girl that can't say no.
Gerald had to kiss another girl on stage in front of
about three hundred people every performance. I
think her name was Lindy. Hell, you'd think if he
could kiss in front of an audience he'd do all right
alone. At least that's what I counted on. I'll have to
admit that he looked like he knew what he was doing.
Watching your son kissing in public is awkward,
but hoping he's necking in the backseat after the
performance is worse. Most parents are scared to

death their son is going to get a girl pregnant, but that would have been a relief to me.

I wonder what I would have done if Gerald had told me he was homosexual. I mean, I don't know that he was, but the thought crossed my mind. There's a hell of a lot of talk about that these days. Gay men. Everywhere you look. So open about it. Getting married even. I know they've been around forever. Even in the war, we suspected that some of the men were. But people kept it quiet then. I hear on talk shows that it's difficult for them to tell people, but it's also hard for them not to tell. Coming out of the closet, not coming out of the closet. I'll tell you the truth, and I know I'm not being modern, but it's easier for me not to know, not to have to deal with it.

Myrtle would probably have accepted Gerald no matter what. Me, I loved my son, but I never felt comfortable with him. I can't say how I would have reacted. It's hard for me to think about it now, even after all this time. I wonder where he would be if he had lived. If Myrtle had gotten her way, he would be in New York. I picture him there, living in a brownstone with a male lover named Geoffrey who raises Pomeranians and runs a coffeehouse in Greenwich Village, marching in Gay Rights parades, and volunteering Myrtle to pass out fliers promoting AIDS research. I imagine us going to see him opening in a Broadway show, hearing the audience applaud louder for his curtain call than anyone else's. Dinner afterwards with him and Geoffrey. Me being completely at ease with Geoffrey's affectionate pats and private jokes. Happy little foursome.

Hell, I'm too old for that kind of scene. Life has turned upside down on me. My patience is gone. I've never been a very tolerant man. If Gerald had lived

and if he had been gay, I don't think he would have
told me.

It would have suited me fine if Gerald had
settled down with Rebecca. She still lives a couple
of blocks from here. She went off to college and
got married. Lived somewhere in the Midwest for
years. Then she got divorced and moved back with
her parents, supposedly until she got her feet on the
ground. Both her parents have since died and she's
still in the house where she grew up. Her son, Cal,
helps Ruth in the yard since Henry's gotten so he can't
do the heavy jobs. That Cal, he's all boy. Athletic and
full of energy. Hard worker, too.

I can't help but think that if Gerald had lived
and married Rebecca, I might have had a grandson
like Cal. They came over when Myrtle died, brought
a ham. Rebecca was still as sweet as she always was.
She took Cal into Gerald's old room and showed him
the cast picture from *OKLAHOMA!* She told me that
was the happiest time of her life, that she treasured
Gerald. That made me feel good, that a woman
besides Myrtle treasured him.

I can remember Gerald coming out to the
garden, asking if he could have some roses for
Rebecca. Hell, I would have given him every damn
rose I grew if he wanted them for a girl. We'd cut a
dozen or so, and then he would snap the thorns off of
each stem. He didn't want her to prick her fingers.

Besides the time in Tennessee, the only time I
ever felt close to Gerald was when he would help me
with the roses. He loved them. As a boy, he'd come
out almost every evening and we would weed or spray
or fertilize the plants. He would go around and chant
the names of each one. Checking for insects was his
most important job, he thought. I taught him how to

prune and why it's healthy to cut them back. He had
a million questions. Rose-talk was easy for the two of
us. Sometimes when Henry was out at the same time,
Gerald would holler over to him. Ask him how many
new buds he had. No matter what number Henry
would say, Gerald would say, "My dad's got more."
Henry was a damn good sport about it.

I let my roses go after Gerald died. Henry's
garden is still a showplace. He's won prizes for his
roses. Do you know what he did for Myrtle? He
cut almost all the roses he had and took them to the
florist who made the casket spray. Myrtle's casket was
covered with roses Henry had grown himself.

Sometimes I miss my roses. But I can't go
back. Even if I wanted to, everything's too grown
over. Damn weeds snake into your life and choke the
good out of it. You ever notice the kudzu, how it can
surround a tree or even an old farmhouse until you
don't even see what was original anymore? I lost sight
of what I had.

Myrtle's gone, so this can't hurt her anymore.
It won't matter if you know everything, print
everything. I've tried to figure out where life went
wrong, why Myrtle killed herself. I have to go back to
letting the roses go.

When Gerald died, Myrtle almost did too. For
weeks she wouldn't eat and she stayed awake most of
the night. She refused to go out of the house, didn't
fix herself up. Barely combed her hair. It was like she
hated me. Snapped at me all the damn time. Hell,
I was grieving, too, but she kept saying I couldn't
possibly know the pain she felt.

For a while I tried to be patient, but instead of
getting better, she got worse. When I touched her,
she would actually cringe. If I mentioned going back

to work, she would glare at me. It would have suited
her for us to lock the doors, shut the blinds, and starve
ourselves to death. The temptation to close down
and join her depression was strong. Guilt over the
doubts I had felt about Gerald was burying me. It
was a struggle to pull myself out of the tomb she was
building.

But I made myself go back to work. At that
point I was hating Myrtle for not helping me cope.
I resented her. She had always been in control.
Actually she was still trying to control me. But,
dammit, I couldn't let her make me die inside. I had
to fight it.

I'll give you some advice. Don't let yourself
believe in forever. As sure as you do, something or
someone will come along and prove what a fool you
are. You get married and you take those vows and
you have every intention of standing by your word.
Even if it gets hard, you try to follow them because
you promised. But then you realize that person you
made those promises to is only a figment of your
imagination. You turned her into what you thought
you wanted. In your mind. She was only in your
mind. The real person next to you at the dinner table
isn't what she used to be. Maybe she never was who
you thought her to be. Life changes people. They
grow apart. And all you want is a little happiness and
some genuine affection before you die. You just want
to breathe.

So you know how that feels? You meet
someone you're not supposed to be attracted to, but
you find yourself aching to sit next to her and hold her
hand. To have her look at you and say your name like
she believes you could change her world. You need
to feel that one more time before you die. I needed to

be discovered. Myrtle was lost to me and I was lost to her.

That was when I started seeing Lydia. Damn, she was a beautiful woman. She was gentle with my grief. But she could be. See, she was removed from it. If I needed to be sad, she would give me sympathy. But if I needed to laugh or forget about Gerald for a while, then she didn't make me feel guilty about it. You think "affair" and you think passion, sex. We had that, sure. But a lot of the time, we just acted like a normal couple. Watched television, went for rides in the country, played Scrabble.

Myrtle was painful to me then. It was like she had betrayed me by not going on with life. With Lydia, I was starting over. I liked the danger of doing something forbidden. I felt alive again. Two or three nights a week, I would stop by her house on the way home from work and have a drink with her. Sometimes only iced tea or lemonade. Sometimes we'd have fast sex, sometimes not. But it didn't matter. I never left feeling unsatisfied. Lydia restored my confidence.

I hurt her. She didn't deserve what she got from me, not after she had made me so happy. It was a pleasure just to look at her. Her hair was very dark and shiny, and it curved around her face going all different directions. I could take my hands, muss it up, and it would spring right back. She always wore tiny pearl earrings, like a damn trademark. Her beauty was calm. Nothing with her was forced. I never met anybody like her before or since. I remember the last time I left her house. She was never so beautiful as she was when I knew she'd never touch me again.

Myrtle found out about Lydia. She didn't know her name, but she knew there was another woman. She sent Henry to me. You could tell he felt awkward as hell to be put in the middle, but he had a soft spot for Myrtle. He listened to the whole story without giving advice. He didn't act like I had sinned, but I felt his disappointment. And his understanding. He didn't have much to say. Henry was just Henry. Quiet and honorable. Letting him down felt worse than betraying Myrtle.

I hate to say it, but I never imagined leaving Myrtle. Not the whole time. I used Lydia and I'm not proud of it. Now I wonder if Lydia could have made my life happier. But at the time, I went back to my marriage and tried to put things right. Myrtle's fear of losing me shocked her into living again.

We went on, pretending we satisfied each other, but it was a make-believe life. Truth was, we had a lot of hollow years. We went through the motions, but it seemed like we were in a play about marriage and we were just waiting for the final curtain to fall so we could take off the costumes and be somebody else. After I retired, it got a lot harder to fill up the hours. Myrtle kept signing us up for classes and trips. I always went along with her ideas. Guilt makes you very cooperative.

If you asked people what they thought of Myrtle, they would say she was jolly. She was always bustling around at the shopping center or the church. But they didn't see her at home. Damn, some days she would sit and watch television for hours, one talk show after another, lately that shopping channel. Or she'd go off on a damn tangent about something she had read in the newspaper. For example, there was a story about a man shooting a neighbor's dog for no reason. Right in front of the kids. And Myrtle fussed at me like I should do something about it.

Around other people, even Ruth and Henry, she acted lively, laughed a lot. But it was too loud. Artificial. Still I didn't realize she had gotten to the point of killing herself. I guess the craziness came on so gradually I got accustomed to it. I should have listened to Joe. He told me not to marry Myrtle. He's the only other person I told about Lydia. He told me I was a fool. He told me to grab my sanity, slam the door on Myrtle, and not stop running until I was safe in Lydia's arms. I can't count the number of times I've heard him say, "I told you so."

There are days when I hate Myrtle. Who the hell did she think she was to go and wreck everybody's peace of mind. She's fixed it so I don't even feel comfortable in my own home. I want all traces of Myrtle out of here as soon as possible. Get her clothes out. That damn flowery bedspread. Out. And all that yarn and those lacy towels nobody was supposed to use. Those boxes of rose petals and the notebooks and letters she left behind. Out. Take them. Myrtle wanted out so bad. Okay, she's out.

But she won't force me out. Joe says sell the house. Hell, no, I'm not selling. I'll strip the kitchen so nothing of Myrtle remains in there. It'll be easy as snapping the thorns off a rose.

OTHER WOMAN RINSED OF BLAME

Chapter 4 - Lydia Carlozzi's Story

Are you the man who's doing the story about Myrtle Graham? Thank heavens I found you before it's too late. My name is Lydia Carlozzi. You've been trying to find me. Look, I don't know how you tracked me down, but please don't call my home anymore. I have a husband who doesn't know anything about Hamilton Graham. I'd like it to stay that way. He'd never understand.

That's why I've come to see you. I'll agree to talk with you if you can disguise my real identity. There is no sense in causing trouble over a short affair that happened more than twenty years ago. I really don't see how you can blame Myrtle's suicide on that. She killed herself in a dishwasher. That should tell you she was not normal. Myrtle Graham was crazy, long before the affair and long after. Way off balance. I'm not the cause. I was only a side effect.

You're not planning on blaming me, are you? Because if you are, it wouldn't be accurate. I mean, Hamilton went back to her. If anyone should have been distraught, it should have been me. I was the loser.

I was the fool. But I can't blame my foolishness on youth. I was plenty old enough to know what I was doing. I guess that's why I thought Hamilton really loved me. I wasn't some little twenty year old with a centerfold's body and a fun-for-the-minute attitude. I was established in a good job. I had a home and decent friends. I wasn't looking for a dead-end relationship with a married man. I lived the tired plot of a very bad TV movie.

But you have to understand. Falling for
Hamilton was easy, painless. He had an air about
him, a certain rightness. You noticed it the minute
you met him. He was the good guy. Add to that his
handsomely sad face, and you've got an irresistible
package.

I imagine you could turn a woman's head the
same way. You're good-looking and there's a clean-
cut openness about you, but you don't radiate the
aching that makes a woman want to soothe away the
troubles. That was what I did for Hamilton. I helped
him. For all the heartbreak it gave me, I can truly say
I helped him. I did. So I can't be all bad. Can I?

The whole time I was seeing Hamilton I never
told anyone about us. I can't believe that when I
finally do, it's to a reporter who can ruin me. You have
to understand the power you have. Don't take this
lightly, please. I can't lose what I have. My husband
is a good man. He loves me.

Nowadays, people are so open about their love
life. It seems you can do anything you want with
anybody, the more outrageous the better. In fact,
if you're wild enough, you'll probably end up on a
talk show. But when I grew up, we were expected to
walk the straight and narrow. You got a reputation
if you had sex before you married, or with a lot of
boys, or even if you acted like you wanted to. A bad
reputation. The same rules applied when I started
working. In fact, they were stricter. You couldn't be
a flirt or a tease. Men wouldn't take you seriously.
Any woman in the workplace was fair game. That
was hard enough, but I was also divorced. I had to be
careful. Men thought of divorced women as easy.

I was working in an office where a lot of men
came and went. My conduct was very formal. Nice

and friendly, but formal. Even so, I heard every
come-on in the book from men you would never
have expected to be on the make. Some comments
or compliments from harmless jokers. Some grimy
propositions from real wolves. I sloughed them all off
and kept my business lips buttoned. I couldn't afford
to be perceived as a hussy.

I was all I had. I had to support myself. That's
the irony of the whole story. You see, the man I
married left me for another woman. My first husband
was a big mistake. Of course, it took a while for me to
figure that out. At first, he was charming and sweet.
Young girls are easily impressed, especially by an older
boy. Jerry was a friend of my big brother Pete's, and
I'd had a crush on him for years. When I was a little
girl, I would climb the tree next to our backyard fence
and watch him cut the neighbor's grass. When he
came over to see Pete, I would make a pest of myself,
anything to get his attention. The most he ever said
to me then was, "Get lost, Wormbrain." That was his
nickname for me. Wormbrain. Because I had done a
science experiment to prove worms were smart enough
to crawl through a maze.

Until I was a sophomore in high school, Jerry
thought of me as a wart on the nose on my brother.
Then suddenly in January of that year, he finally
noticed me. I remember the day it happened. It was
Pete's birthday and I was in the kitchen putting candles
on his cake. Jerry came in, leaned against the counter,
and said, "If it were my birthday, I know what I'd wish
for." Of course, I asked him what it was. He got this
really serious expression on his face, and he said, "I'd
wish I had never called you Wormbrain." I burned my
fingers on the match. A couple of days later, he called
me for a date and pretty soon we were going steady.

That spring, after his graduation, he left to fight in the Korean War. We must have written a thousand letters full of silly romantic ideas. While he was away, I planned the wedding. Church ceremony. White dress. Candles and flowers. Storybook, all the way. We were happy and innocent and stupid. Jerry was the only man in the world as far as I was concerned. We had absolutely nothing. No jobs, no money. But we were so much in love we survived on fumes. I was fresh out of high school and he had just gotten back from overseas. He didn't get any medals for bravery, but he managed to survive. He always said that was courage enough for him.

The only thing I could do was type and put things in alphabetical order. He couldn't even do that. I managed to get a job with an insurance company filing and addressing envelopes for fliers. Jerry worked on construction jobs.

As hard as it was, we were okay for a while. Then I got pregnant. From the beginning it was doomed. I was sick all the time, so much I couldn't go to work. I got fired. That wouldn't happen nowadays, but things were different then. And to top it off, I miscarried. It was for the best, but at the time I didn't think so. We had doctor bills to pay and never enough money. Jerry had no idea about how to deal with my depression over losing the baby.

That was about the time he came up with the idea of night school. Another man on his job was going. He convinced Jerry that college was the place to be, even if you had to be there at night. And the best thing was that he could use the GI Bill. It was the beginning of Jerry's getaway.

He never got a degree, but he got enough education to get a job with IBM working on office machines. He worked his way up to a decent salary and a three-piece suit. It was quite a ways from the skinny young man I married who had taken his sandwich to work every day in a metal lunchbox.

I got pregnant two more times. Lost my babies both times. With the last one, I almost died, so we gave up.

We were married for fifteen years. The last three of those he was seeing a young college-educated junior executive, a very classy woman who knew what she wanted and didn't have any problem stepping on a few toes to get it. She wanted Jerry. Everybody knew about them, except me. I found out when she got pregnant. So she gave Jerry what I couldn't, a baby.

She suddenly transformed herself from the IBM climber to an ad for Hallmark Mother's Day cards. He left me and married her. She won. The whole situation was a cliché. They didn't mean for it to happen. It was bigger than both of them. He didn't want to hurt me. But the bottom line was, he walked. The public embarrassment alone was enough to make me want to quit living, not to mention the feeling of betrayal and rejection. I could have killed myself. But, thank goodness, I had pride. That kept me going to work. I had started a job at the highway department. It took a while, but basically I survived.

In the office where I worked, Hamilton Graham was a regular. He was the nicest man. Honest and decent. He never made a pass at me or treated me rudely. He came in maybe four, five times a month. Talking with him was a pleasure. He was older than I was. Maybe ten or twelve years older. Distinguished. Handsome. He always smelled like Old Spice. That seemed very solid to me, especially after Jerry's expensive colognes.

I pushed his paperwork through channels for him, cut as much red tape as I could, and at Christmas he'd bring me candy or a poinsettia. He almost always had a little nick somewhere on his cheek or neck from shaving. That was so endearing. His hair was too short, and I imagined he must go to the barbershop every week whether he needed to or not. Precise. He was very precise about his work. His handwriting looked like a teaching model. I wasn't surprised when I found out he had been a pilot. I would have felt very safe with him steering me through the skies.

I got used to seeing him and then he didn't come in for a while. I didn't know what had happened, that his son had died. When he came back, he looked almost invisible. It scared me and I asked him where he had been. When he tried to answer, his voice broke and he teared up. I was so afraid he was going to cry right there in front of everybody that I took him into another room. And he did cry. The need to comfort, make everything better rushed out of me and I was hooked.

It was around lunchtime, so we left the office and went to a little café where Hamilton could relax and gather himself. His hands fidgeted, folding the napkin, rearranging the salt and pepper shakers, stacking the sugar packs. I finally reached out and covered his hands with mine. I said, "Be still, Hamilton." I could feel him settle and he turned his hands over and held mine back.

He didn't open up completely that day, but he didn't have to. I think he was grateful just to have the calmness. My first impression of Myrtle was that she must be incredibly self-centered not to have noticed that Hamilton was consumed with grief. I guess that's unfair. She had lost her son. But Hamilton's suffering was sitting at the table with us. It was that real.

The next day Hamilton sent an African violet from the florist. It was the perfect gesture. Roses would have been too romantic, overdone. A dish garden would have been too impersonal. The violet was simple but it said he was thinking of me. I kept it for the longest time, watering it from the bottom, making sure it got indirect light. Not everybody can grow African violets. They take a lot of care and the right circumstances. Your windows have to face the right direction.

The next week he called and asked if I'd have lunch with him again. I knew I shouldn't go, but I couldn't stop myself. We met at the same café. He was awkward, nervous. He spilled his drink and got mustard on his shirt. He was a mess, a charming mess. At the end of the meal, he reached into his pocket and pulled out a lavender satin sachet, edged with lace, heart-shaped. The fragrance was like musty roses. Hamilton said it reminded him of me.

Over the next months, he brought me dozens of those sachets, enough to fill my dresser drawers and closet shelves, my hatboxes and pillowcases. Thoughtful. Romantic. It was those little things that drew me closer to Hamilton.

No one plans to have an affair with a married man, certainly not me. But the more we talked the more we liked each other. Hamilton told me so much about himself, what he was like as a boy, the peace he left in the Tennessee mountains, how much he wanted to go back there. I felt flattered that he wanted me to know things he had never said out loud.

Although we both felt an attraction, there was nothing physical for weeks. We didn't even speak of it. I think we knew what would happen if we gave it a name. We pretended we were having an innocent friendship. Then one evening, I was at home. It was about seven o'clock and the doorbell rang. I looked out of the window and there was Hamilton's car in my driveway. My stomach flipped over like a teenager's when her first date comes to pick her up and he's standing on the porch. When I opened the door, we stood staring at each other. Finally he said, "Lydia, I had to see you. If I don't touch you, I won't be able to sleep again tonight. I haven't slept a whole night through in such a long time."

Then he didn't say anything else. He came into my living room. I closed the door and he put his hand on my cheek. That was all it took. For a long time, we stood holding each other. That night I stepped over the line I had drawn for myself. I was falling in love with Hamilton and I stopped fighting it.

It was hard keeping my feelings secret, not going out in public with him, but I kept telling myself he would come to me free and clear one day. He couldn't leave his wife so soon after the death of his son. He needed time.

At the office, we pretended there was nothing between us. Business as usual. No one suspected a thing. But it was so difficult not to reach out to him when he walked beside my desk. Gradually he seemed to reform himself. He lost that haunted expression you see on someone who is grieving.

You always hear the old line that married men use about how their wives don't understand them. It was the opposite with Hamilton. He told me he didn't understand his wife. Myrtle had been a mystery to him for a long time. He said she had been deeply involved with Gerald's life and made a good home for them both but that she seemed to have something missing. Something made her sad and wistful. She was always sighing. While Gerald was growing up, he said, he wouldn't have been surprised to come home one day and find that Myrtle had taken him and run away to be in the movies.

Hamilton thought her problems were because of movies. She was consumed with show business. Even Myrtle's bedtime stories had been movie plots or the amazing ways stars had been discovered. She would act out the old musicals in Gerald's bedroom, singing and dancing like she was in a big production number. At first Hamilton thought it was charming, teased her about wearing her tap shoes to tuck in their son. But then it got stranger and stranger. Hamilton would hear her teaching his little boy the lyrics and the steps to Shirley Temple's famous routines.

The older Gerald got, the more left out Hamilton felt. He said it was like Myrtle and Gerald had a secret code. At any moment, Myrtle might blurt out the name of a dance step and she and Gerald would start tapping. When they went on trips, instead of playing count cows, Gerald would sing the songs from Broadway musicals. Hamilton said it drove him crazy. Sometimes he would pick Gerald up at the dance school, Madame Something-or-other's. The doors would open and dozens of little girls in pink tights, giggling and pointing their toes, would come prissing out to the parking lot. Right in the middle would be Gerald. His dark red, wavy hair standing out among all the blonds and brunettes, completely comfortable, surrounded by tutus.

Hamilton confessed to me that he was afraid Myrtle had turned Gerald into a mama's boy. Guilt was eating him alive. He had been ashamed of his son and resentful of Myrtle for encouraging Gerald to be different.

Hamilton was questioning himself. He was afraid
he was incapable of loving someone unconditionally,
even his own child. I did my best to give him support.
I desperately wanted to be the one he could love with
all his heart.

That didn't happen. Hamilton called me one
night and said that Myrtle knew about us, that he
needed to come over and talk to me right away. When
I hung up the phone, I was overjoyed. I just knew the
confrontation had taken place and Hamilton had told
Myrtle he was leaving. But he came to tell me it was
over between us. I couldn't believe my ears.

For almost a year, I had been living with the
dream of making a public life with Hamilton. The
dream of being his wife. I know people don't feel
sorry for the other woman in these cases. They figure
she gets what she deserves.

But let me tell you, I didn't need anybody else's
sympathy. I felt sorry enough for myself. I loved
Hamilton. I let him go gracefully though. To him, I
was kind and unselfish. I told him we could remain
friends and that I'd always be there if he needed
me. But I put in for a transfer as soon as I could and
moved to another department where I would have no
contact with him. Seeing him was too painful.

Once in the grocery store, I saw him and
Myrtle. They were in the checkout line. She was
very tall and solid looking. But she struck me as
needy. I think it was because the back of her hair
wasn't brushed, and evidently she was searching for
something because she had emptied her purse onto
the conveyor belt and everything was sliding away
from her. The cashier just stood there watching
Myrtle's stuff roll away while Hamilton grabbed
lipsticks and candy wrappers and compacts. I

couldn't tell for sure from a distance, but I think he
was gritting his teeth. People waiting behind them
were making faces. She was holding up the line and
talking on and on. I felt sorry for him because he gave
me up for someone he had no patience with.

That makes me sound cold and conceited, I
know, but the fact was, I was better for him than she
was. He made the wrong choice.

I never wished her any harm, or him either. I
am truly sorry he's had to go through this dishwasher
tragedy. He doesn't deserve what he's gotten in life.
But he made his choices. I've gone on. I can't help
him now. When I heard about it, about Myrtle, the
thought crossed my mind that I should call him. But
why? What good would it possibly do? Him or me?

One strange thing happened after Hamilton left
me and went back to Myrtle. His brother Joe called
and asked if he could speak with me. As far as I knew,
Hamilton had never told anyone about us. I couldn't
imagine what he wanted, but I said okay. It turned
out that Joe couldn't stand Myrtle. She had gone to
him and asked him to talk to Hamilton, to find out
if he was involved with another woman. He wanted
me to know that he had not been the one to confront
Hamilton. He was actually glad Hamilton had found
someone else. He said he had never seen Hamilton as
contented and relaxed as he had been in the months
we'd been seeing each other. He didn't know what
the difference was at the time, but once he found out
about me, he put two and two together. When Gerald
died, as terrible as that was, Joe felt it gave Hamilton
the chance to break free from Myrtle and find some
happiness.

From Joe's point of view, Myrtle was like
poison ivy. Irritating. Impossible to get rid of. He

said she was pushy and demanding. He said he remembered going over to their house when Gerald was a little boy and hearing Myrtle fussing at him because he wanted to skip dance practice for a friend's birthday party. She was preaching to this little seven-year-old kid about dedication to the arts.

Joe wanted me to contact Hamilton. He begged me not to give up so easily. Fight for him, that's what he wanted me to do. I was torn. I loved Hamilton deeply and it gave me tremendous pleasure to hear Joe say I was the best thing that had ever happened to Hamilton. But when it came down to the decision, my pride won out. I was too stubborn to crawl after him. I should have. I love my husband, but there will never be another love in my life like Hamilton Graham.

Joe called me several times trying to make me change my mind. He finally gave up. He should have kept trying. I was very close to the breaking point.

After Hamilton left me and went back to Myrtle, I swore I'd never get involved with another man. Men meant pain and I had had enough. For a long time, I stuck to that. Then I met Gene Carlozzi. He's actually younger than I am. Not so much that people gossiped about it, but young enough to make me feel beautiful again.

Gene doesn't know anything about Hamilton and I want to keep it that way. What's in the past should stay there. Myrtle Graham caused me a great hurt once before; I won't let that happen again. I won't lose another man because of her.

I've told Gene I had some casual relationships. But he doesn't know I was in love with a married man.

I can understand why a woman would feel the desire to end her life. I've been at that point plenty of times myself. You get so tired of dealing with trouble. And trouble keeps cropping up. You can't get away from it. It's like playing solitaire. You almost never win. You go through the same rules and patterns and sometimes you get down to only a few cards left, but you never win. The card you need to make you happy is buried somewhere under a stack directly behind another card you have no use for at all. You could cheat, but then where's the satisfaction? The really sad part is you keep playing. You keep hoping. You shuffle the same damn cards that brought you trouble before and you deal yourself another game.

Myrtle dealt herself out, and if her life was a losing hand, then I don't blame her. She made a wise decision. Hamilton may not have been the sole cause of her trouble, but it seems to me that she knew he didn't love her, that he wanted more than she could give. I wouldn't be surprised if Hamilton had more than one affair. I don't think going back to Myrtle changed one thing about their relationship. He just wasn't brave enough to end it.

Women never forget. What a man would consider to be a throwaway remark, a woman will hold forever and bank her entire future on it. Women are hopeful romantics. They believe. I fell for Hamilton, sure that he was going to be my rescuer. I want to show you something. The only thing from Hamilton I kept. The sachets I threw away. One per week until they were all gone. It was a kind of therapy for me. I told myself I would get Hamilton out of my life a little bit at a time. I would let go of a part of him with every sachet I threw away. They smelled dead anyway. But this I kept. It's a necklace. Heart-shaped, as you might expect. The back is engraved. Can you read it? It says, "You hold my heart."

How can a man say that and then leave?
Hamilton hurt me and it's my belief that he hurt
Myrtle too. The hurt he brought to her was something
she could never forget. No matter that he came back
to her. She knew he had given part of himself to
another woman. There were parts of him she would
never be able to lay claim to. They had a history,
sure, but Myrtle's future was tarnished. She never
forgot and Hamilton was a constant reminder of her
failure. If he had left, she could have shed the image
of betrayal.

It was easier for me to go on. I didn't have to
see a traitor lying in the bed next to me each morning.
I didn't have to worry every time he came home late
or got too quiet at dinner. There was no reason for me
to confront myself in the mirror before bed wondering
how I compared to another woman. Not this time. I
blocked the betrayal from my mind so I was able to
go on. Gene Carlozzi is a better man than Hamilton
Graham. Myrtle would have been better off without
him. Hamilton would have been better off with me
instead of her. But then, where would I be now?

Sometimes I can't help but imagine Myrtle
closed up in a dark box, hearing the motor start,
feeling the wet heat. She must have been scared. And
relieved to have the whole thing over with.

Thinking of Hamilton going through another
cycle of grief, another pain, makes me ache. For all
the hurt he caused me, I can't forget the gentleness in
him. He always held my hand after we made love. He
was a simple man. Give him a peanut butter sandwich
and he was happy. When he left me at night, the
pillowcase smelled like Old Spice. To me, it's the
fragrance of regret.
I never see an African violet that I don't think about

Hamilton. But I don't grow them myself. My
windows don't face the right direction.

OLD GIRLFRIEND CAN'T MAKE SUDS LAST

Chapter 5 - Rebecca Setters' Story

I'm Rebecca Setters. Montgomery was my maiden name. You've found the right house. Cal's my son, but he isn't here right now. He's playing basketball with some friends. He'll be home by six. What do you want with him?

You're a writer? I see, research on Myrtle Graham? Wait a minute. I remember you. You used to be on the news. No, not the news. It was that magazine show, the one that isn't on anymore.

Well, I guess it would be all right for you to interview Cal, but I really don't think it will help you. He doesn't know anything about Myrtle. The only connection he would have is that he does yard work once a week or so for the Overtons. They were her next-door neighbors. You can wait if you like, but I think you'll be wasting your time.

Cal hardly knew the Grahams. We went over when Myrtle died, but that was my idea. The Grahams and I go back a long way. You're actually better off talking to me. You don't mind if I keep working, do you? I've got a special order to finish. Silk bridesmaids' bouquets. A lot of girls are using them these days. Saves money. Some people say you can't tell the difference. But actually, even though I make money on them, I don't think artificial flowers are right for a wedding. No fragrance. No life.

On the other hand, there's something sad about real flowers. Especially cut flowers. They're so temporary. Reminds me of the Grahams. Not Myrtle. Oh no, definitely not Myrtle. They remind me of Mr. Graham and Gerald. I was once very close to Gerald.

Actually, he was my first serious boyfriend, so I knew
the family well. I liked Mr. Graham. Hamilton. He
was nice to me. But Myrtle. Well, a boy's mother
never thinks her son's girlfriend is good enough.
Right? You probably went through that with your
mother. You'd expect that Myrtle wouldn't exactly be
my biggest fan. That would be normal. That would
also be an understatement.

It upset me then, but that was a long time ago
and it doesn't do any good to speak unkindly of the
dead. Yes, I agree. Killing herself in a dishwasher
does lend itself to speculation. It's bizarre. I imagine
in your business you see a lot of shocking things.
But what's really shocking about that is that it didn't
surprise me. Myrtle Graham was a very odd person.
Even as a teenager I could see that. Even before
Gerald died.

And things had only gotten worse. When Cal
and I moved back here after my divorce, I got a job at
the craft shop doing these silk flower arrangements
and Myrtle would come in at least once a week to buy
ribbons and trims for her sachets. If I saw her first,
I'd try to dodge her because she'd corner me, grab me
so tightly it hurt. She had huge fingers that would
clench my arms. I got the feeling she wanted to shake
me.

People stared. It was uncomfortable. On and
on she would talk about Gerald and how much she
missed him. Like it was yesterday that he died. It
was more than twenty years ago. And you know how
sometimes a person will stand too close to you, invade
your space? That's what she would do. I kept feeling
the urge to back up, to get away from her.

I had this horrible vision of what it would
have been like if Gerald had lived and we had gotten

married. This horrible image. Of Myrtle Graham. As
my mother-in-law. How she would have hated me!
She preferred for him to devote his time to studying
and performing. That was made very clear. In her
opinion, Gerald had bigger things in store for him
than a hometown girl and a nine-to-five job.

Before I really got to know Gerald, I knew a lot
about him. You can probably identify with that, being
a television personality. People don't see you as a
stranger, so there's immediate acceptance. I felt that
as soon as I realized who you were. Your reputation
precedes you. Gerald's did, too.

My parents bought this house the summer I
turned twelve. That was when I met Lindy Hayes.
She lived next door. For the entire month of August, I
listened to Lindy mooning about Gerald Graham. She
and I would dial his phone number and then hang up
when he answered. We were starting junior high, and
she was dying to be in his homeroom. I thought Lindy
was the only one fascinated by him, but the weekend
before school opened, she had a slumber party. It
was like a meeting of the Gerald Graham fan club.
To those girls, Gerald was bigger than the Beatles. A
couple of them argued that he was a sissy, but they all
agreed he was the cutest boy in school. I couldn't wait
to see what he looked like. And when I finally did, I
found out they were absolutely right. As we used to
say, he was "tuff enough."

We weren't in any classes together. But I also
started taking dance at Madame Fouché's Dance
Studio. My mother had asked around and everyone
said Madame Fouché was the best. I had already
been taking for four years, so I was enrolled in a real
pointe class in ballet and intermediate tap. It turned
out I was more advanced in tap, so they moved me

to another class which, lucky for me, met the same
time Gerald had a private lesson across the hall with
Madame Fouché herself. That honor was reserved for
the students who, as Madame said, had destiny. So it
was there that I finally came face to face with the great
Gerald Graham.

Let me ask you something. How old were
you when you felt at ease mingling with a room full
of people? I'd bet that even with your television
background you'd have to say at least twenty. Twenty-
five? Gerald had command of a crowd at twelve. He'd
arrive for his lesson and circulate through the waiting
room speaking to each little pocket of people like a
politician, charming and good looking.

Don't get me wrong. Gerald was not phony. He
sincerely liked people and they flocked around him.
He was mannerly with mothers and silly with little
kids. The girls loved the way he flirted, just enough to
make each one feel special. What a sense of humor.
A quick wit. He was always making jokes. Even if
they were corny, his delivery was so good that people
laughed in spite of themselves.

Lindy had already told me that Gerald was
the best dancer at the studio, and she wanted more
than anything to be picked to perform a duet with
him at the annual Christmas program. Lindy had
taken dance for six years already. She would have
been a shoe-in for the part, but between August and
December, she hit a growth spurt. By Christmas, she
was a head taller than he was. It killed her chances of
shuffling off to Buffalo with Gerald.

No, I didn't get the part either. That would
have happened on your television show maybe, but
not in a dance school where I was still considered
the new kid. Dancing with Gerald was special, not

because a boy that takes tap is rare, but because he was so talented. Watching him was like holding sparklers. You know the way they sizzle and flash, the energy you can feel in your fingertips. The first time I saw him on stage was that Christmas. It seemed every time the curtain opened, there he was.

Do you know what a triple threat is? In theater, not in sports. It's a dancer-singer-actor. That was Gerald, a triple threat with a voice that could break your heart and tapping that was crisp and clean. And fast. He got solos because nobody else could keep up with him. Effortless. His life on stage was effortless.

Gerald Graham was magic. No braces. No pimples. His voice changed practically overnight, without a trace of the crackly, screechy sound that other boys had. All the girls said he had the dreamiest eyes and eyelashes. Bedroom eyes, like Paul McCartney's. And his hair was a rich dark auburn that caught the stage lights. He seemed to glow.

You look like you're about my age, maybe a little younger. What grade were you in when the Beatles were first on Ed Sullivan? Remember how girls reacted? I could imagine throngs of screaming teenage girls fainting in the aisles like that when Gerald sang. I would have done that myself except that Gerald was so down-to-earth and good-hearted I didn't want to embarrass him by creating a scene.

My second year at the studio, I got to dance with him. The teacher decided I had potential as a comic lead, so I got to audition for Madame Fouché. Other girls who had entered Madame's private studio had been reduced to tears, had run white-faced from the building, had vowed never to tap again. I was petrified, but I was determined to impress her.

She was probably in her mid-forties but
seemed much older and much younger all at the same
time. Impossible to define. There was a smooth
gracefulness about her that reminded me of a rare
orchid, exotic and dramatic. Everything about
her was elegant from the tilt of her head to the silk
kimonos she wore over her leotards. Ballerinas have a
signature stance and walk, a bit sway-backed with toes
pointed outward. Even standing still they look like
they're about to leap, and I always had the feeling that
Madame could leave the earth any time she wished.
But she was equally at home in tap shoes, so there was
also the vitality and peppy step of a female Astaire.
She reminded me of whipped cream and chopped
nuts. I idolized her.

You were in television. You know how
important auditions are. I decided that if I were
auditioning for a funny part, then it would be crucial
to make Madame laugh, at least smile; so when I
entered the room I faked a tumbling trip, à la Donald
O'Connor, and ended up back on my feet with a
"ta da." I actually caught her by surprise. And she
smiled. With teeth. The audition went off without a
hitch and she called Gerald in to try out a few steps
with me. That was unheard of. My head was so
swollen I could barely make it out of the door when
we were finished.

Madame conferred with my teacher, then
called me back into the studio. It was like judgment
day. Madame did everything with a flourish, so she
floated around the room for a while. Then she struck
a pose like she was ready to have her portrait painted.
When she started speaking, it was almost a whisper,
and her French accent intrigued me so intensely
that I remember every word. She said, "Rebecca

Montgomery is a lovely name for a dancer. It has
enough syllables so that it flows. It has extension.
You may keep it. My darling, the curtain is rising
on your destiny. To dance with Gerald Graham is a
gift. Your reputation will soar, but along with this
opportunity comes responsibility. You must reach
perfection. You understand? Yes?"

I felt like I had been asked to dance for the
Queen. She instructed me to learn everything I could
from Gerald because he was a genius. She was sure
he was going to be a major force in the future of
choreography.

I was dying to dance a love song with him. I
wanted to wear a chiffon gown and be dipped by
Gerald. Instead I got to do a novelty number, "Be a
Clown," wearing a rainbow wig, a nose the size of an
apple, and baggy pants. But it didn't matter how I
looked because the number was a showstopper.

Madame Fouché was right. From then on, I
was known as a "Dancer" with a capital D. We were
the hit of the recital. Myrtle used a whole roll of film
on us. But she never gave me even one picture. I
imagined her sitting at the kitchen table methodically
snipping me out of each snapshot. Go ahead, laugh.
Maybe I am a little paranoid. But she always gave me
the creeps.

I got to know Myrtle when we were rehearsing
for the number. Gerald invited me to his house to
practice. Everyone had heard rumors that he had
his own private studio at home, but no one really
believed it. Then I got the chance to go. Well, lo and
behold, the guest bedroom had been converted to a
rehearsal hall. There were mirrors on two walls and
the carpet had been replaced with wooden flooring.
He had barres for ballet and a shelf lined with records.

On the walls without the mirrors, he had playbills
and photographs and posters of musicals. The only
furniture were the shelves, the table for the record
player, and a couple of director's chairs with "Gerald"
and "Myrtle" stenciled on the backs.

That was when I knew I was not dealing with
an average boy, and Myrtle was definitely not an
ordinary mother. She wasn't even an ordinary stage
mother. She'd always answer the door and usher me
to the practice room, saying something like, "Today
you have one hour and seventeen minutes. Section B
needs work. Set the timer for twenty minutes, break
for five. Then we'll proceed as necessary." Gerald
would be waiting at the barre and we would start. She
never left us alone for very long. Usually, before we
even finished warming up, she'd come in with her tap
shoes on. That was strange enough by itself, but what
made it even odder was that her tap shoes were flats.

That probably doesn't mean much to you, but
flat tap shoes are only for children. Girls can't wait to
get their first tap heels. At thirteen, I'd already had
mine for two years. And here was this uncommonly
tall, graceless, grown woman wearing shiny black
patent leather Mary Janes in what had to be a size
eleven at least. She'd flap across the floor to her chair
where she'd watch us go through our steps, making
notes on our performance. Her feet would be moving
the entire time we were dancing like she was right up
there with us.

She was polite to me, but there was a sharp
edge to her comments. Truthfully, I don't think
she really wanted me to be good. With Gerald, her
criticism was harsh and, I thought, unfounded. He'd
have to repeat steps and segments until she was
satisfied. But the worst thing was when she would try

to demonstrate for us. I was embarrassed watching
her clunking around, but Gerald must have been
mortified. That was his mother up there making a fool
of herself.

Do you have any children? I've heard jokes
that it's a parent's job to embarrass their children,
but I hope I never embarrass Cal the way Myrtle
humiliated Gerald.

It's hard being the mother of a son, especially
when the hormones kick in. You notice him staring
at girls and you know he's beginning to think about
sex. It's rather frightening. Looking back I can
understand why Myrtle probably wasn't thrilled that
Gerald's partner was developing a figure. Or that he
would blush when he talked to me. Compared to what
mothers have to worry about today, Myrtle didn't have
a care in the world. We were so innocent. Both of us
were probably in a state of constant blush.

When most redheads blush, they look like
they've come down with hives, but Gerald's face
looked like he had the faintest tinge of sunburn, not
one that's going to blister and peel, but the kind that's
going to become a healthy bronze. I can still picture
him grinning, all out of breath and happy to be with
me.

We had a wonderful time dancing when Myrtle
wasn't watching. Gerald had a knack for inventive
choreography. I was so small and limber; he could
toss me around like a beach ball. And because
he wasn't a spotlight hog, he created some great
moments for me in that number. He kept saying,
"Show your stuff, Rebecca. Dazzle them with your
dimples. Frazzle them with your fancy footwork. Go
for the standing O." He was so cute going through
his little cheerleading routine. I couldn't help but

be good. At thirteen, dancing with Gerald was like winning Miss America.

When we took a break from dancing, we'd talk, complaining about the usual stuff: school, teachers, homework, but never parents. It was like we thought Myrtle might have the room bugged and if we said anything bad, she might lock us in the attic and tell the world we'd been kidnapped.

We did enjoy each other. There was never the self-conscious boy-girl feeling that usually plagues kids that age. We were at ease. I suggested he come over to my house for supper one night, but Myrtle refused to let him. At least, I think that's what really happened. Gerald made an excuse, but he was awkward about it. That was so uncommon, to see him being clumsy about anything. I knew he really didn't have to stay home because some uncle was visiting from out of town. After our first number together, Madame Fouché said we were to be steady partners, and our friendship grew. At school, we had a few classes together, but not many because he was in the highest levels and I was more of an average student. We both joined the chorus and the drama club.

Gerald was involved in all kinds of activities: student council, honor society, pep squad. He did everything right, but he wasn't a goody-goody. In fact, he loved practical jokes. Every day the music teacher would find Beethoven's bust going around and around on the record player. He did impersonations of most of the teachers. In front of them. Do you think he ever got in trouble? Of course not. To most people, it seemed he led a charmed life.

If he ran for office, he won. He made A's even when he didn't study. The only thing he did not excel in was sports. And I think he could have if Myrtle

had allowed it. Maybe not football, but certainly
basketball or baseball or track. But he never went
out for the team because he might injure his dancing
future. He was popular, but he was different. As I
said, the girls would argue about Gerald being a sissy.
I heard rumors he was queer, a fairy.

I haven't thought of that word in that way in
a long time. We weren't very tolerant of different
lifestyles in those days, were we? Some people still
aren't. Never will be. Our generation was supposed
to change the world. Love and peace. It didn't turn
out that way, did it? I knew a lot of really wonderful
dancers and actors, in college, in the theater
department, who were shunned or mistreated just
because they were gay.

You know, that's what made Gerald even more
of a standout because even if people thought that
about him, it didn't affect his popularity. Gerald was
a bright spot. No doubt about it. Sometimes, though,
I wondered why he was so driven to be everything
to everybody. Maybe it helped him to be so busy he
didn't have time to think about his mother. I think
there was something empty in him that he was trying
to fill up.

He sure poured himself out on other people.
No one ever treated me the way Gerald did, not even
the man I married. Whenever I talked, he looked at
me, and his eyes didn't shift away. I never got the idea
he was watching something else over my shoulder or
that he was waiting his turn to talk. We were in tune,
in step. Maybe it came from the dancing, having to
be synchronized; but whatever it was, emotionally we
were in rhythm. I never had that with anyone else.

Somehow I could tell when he was having
a bad day, and I'd bring him a Butterfingers candy

bar. When I was down, like when he was elected cheerleader and I wasn't, he'd show up with roses for me. Handpicked from Hamilton's garden. Perfect roses. Gerald used to say roses were his father's ballerinas.

Something like that would have sounded mushy coming from most guys, but Gerald could pull it off. I don't know where he got all his sensitivity. Myrtle was about as considerate as a hit man. Hamilton was too passive to show concern. But Gerald would notice when someone needed a boost and he was always available, approachable. He would have really been in demand a few years ago when everyone was searching for the sensitive male. Women would have clamored for a date with him.

If you don't have kids, you probably don't have any idea when they start dating these days. A lot of them are having sex by the time they're thirteen, some even younger than that. I don't know about you, but my parents didn't even allow me to double date until I was fifteen. It was the same for almost everyone I knew. We couldn't solo until we were sixteen.

Gerald and I were such good friends by then that romance seemed goofy. But it also seemed perfectly natural for us to go out. Usually it was to a movie or out for burgers after dance classes. Gerald was at a real disadvantage when it came to dating other girls because Myrtle refused to let him get his driver's license. He didn't have any close male friends that he could double with, but I could already drive and he didn't have to feel self-conscious with me. So I could pick him up at his house and we'd escape from Myrtle's evil eye.

She didn't like me, but I think she felt less threatened by me than some other girl that Gerald

might get starry-eyed over. It was a real turn-around
when I'd go to get him. She would tell me to have
Gerald home at a decent hour like I was the guy and
Gerald was the girl.

Hamilton was different. I could tell he thought
it was ridiculous, but he either felt it was impossible
to change or it took more effort than he could
muster. I wish he had spoken up for Gerald. I wish
he and Gerald could have banded together, could
have united against Myrtle. It was amazing to me
because everyone thought Gerald could talk Dracula
into donating blood, but when it came to his mother,
he was completely at her mercy. He didn't even try
to cross her. Myrtle was like a tidal wave, engulfing
everything in her path.

Not everybody saw that side of her. She was
deviously charming, always laughing and being
helpful at the studio. People loved Mrs. Graham. I
guess Gerald got his personality from the good in
her. When she was out in public, at the studio or the
games where Gerald would cheer, she acted like she
was a normal mom. She was friendly and knew the
kids by name. My mom worked on lots of committees
with her. She could never understand why I felt
uncomfortable, and it wasn't something I could put
my finger on exactly. I couldn't explain what it was
about Myrtle Graham that made the hairs on my neck
bristle. It wouldn't have surprised me if one day she
had unzipped her Myrtle skin and exposed some kind
of alien dance monster. My mom said, "Oh, she's just
a stage mother. She wants Gerald to be famous. She
might be a little pushy, but Gerald doesn't look any
the worse for it."

I don't think anyone ever realized what Gerald
went through while he was growing up. I certainly

didn't and I was his closest friend. Between Madame Fouché and his mother he was controlled by the two strongest women I have ever known. It wasn't until we were seniors in high school that I finally understood. He finally opened up to me. I wish I had known sooner. Maybe I could have made things easier for him. I didn't know Gerald was going to die so young. I thought we still had time to be happy.

You've been a reporter since college? We must have been in college at about the same time. You couldn't have been more than two years behind me in school. Well, those two years made such a drastic difference. It seemed like there was an explosion of reality from the time I finished high school to my college graduation. My teenage years were sheltered. You lost out on the little protected microcosm that was high school. Instead, you were thrown into the turmoil of what was happening in the world. Vietnam. The riots. The drugs. I was back on the safe side of all that, when high school was just high school and on the surface, everything was perfect. We had an ideal life. We had fun.

Status for us came in making good grades and pleasing adults and having school spirit. Everything seemed simple and good. We had all of that and we had the stage. Gerald and I had performed in all of the plays at school. He was a lead and I was in the dance line or the stage chorus. But in our senior year, we did *Oklahoma!* and I was cast as Ado Annie. Lindy was playing the female lead, Laurey, and Gerald was Curly. Lindy still had a crush on him, so she was out of her mind when she realized she would get to kiss him at every rehearsal and performance.

Lindy was a beautiful girl, perfect for a romantic lead. Angelic face. Long blond hair.

Soprano range that was just glorious. She wasn't
as strong an actress as she was a singer, but Gerald
worked lines over and over with her until she began to
sound natural. At times it didn't even matter because
they looked like a storybook couple on stage.

Lindy and I were casual friends. We were in
the same dance company and we had classes together.
We weren't secret-sharing close, but she knew that
Gerald and I were.

Gerald had always been somewhat of a
mystery to the kids at school. Here he was – class
officer, cheerleader, a brain, handsome, funny – but
no dates. Everyone knew that if Gerald went out at
all, it was just with me. But we had always insisted
we were friends. I went out with other boys, but I
enjoyed Gerald's company more. I spent most of
my free time with him. We didn't advertise the fact
that Gerald didn't drive yet, so people didn't realize
that was the reason we went places together. But
truthfully, I think he liked being with me. I was safe
and comfortable and I had already been exposed to
the Myrtle treatment.

Anyway, most of the girls would have killed
for a date with him. There were rumors that he was
madly in love with a ballerina in New York who would
not give up the stage for him. There was also talk that
maybe Gerald was gay. But he had so many friends
and was so well liked that the idea was squelched.
Lindy approached me to ask if I would fix them up. At
least let Gerald know that she would go out with him if
he asked her. She said, "Now if you like him yourself,
of course, I'd never dream of stepping in. But if you're
only friends like you say you are, then I'd really like to
date him."

At the time, I didn't know why that irritated me. My first reaction was to tell her to keep her hands off Gerald. But I just smiled and told her I'd see what I could do.

To tell the truth, I was a little curious about Gerald myself. In all the time we had spent together, he had never even attempted to make a pass at me. We'd hug after a performance, but no kissing, no hand-holding, no longing looks. Nothing. I had been out with enough other boys to know that sex was foremost in their minds. They were driven to some form of bodily contact as fast as possible. Think about what you were like at sixteen. Gerald was definitely different in that respect.

So one afternoon before study hall I found Gerald at his locker. I told him Lindy really liked him and that it might be a good idea to ask her out. He looked at me like I had just run over a puppy. I had hurt him by even suggesting that he should get together with Lindy. He said she was too high pressure for him, that every time he did the love scene with her at rehearsal, she tried to French kiss him. I think he was afraid of her. Most guys would have jumped at the chance to French kiss Lindy Hayes. Actually most guys probably had, but Gerald was not most guys. Then he looked into my eyes and said, "Rebecca, you're the only girl I want to be with. I don't want to be just your friend anymore. I hate kissing Lindy. I want to kiss you." He reached over and took my hand. We had been dancing together for years. He had lifted me and held me in his arms hundreds of times. But that day, when he touched my hand, my stomach flipped. There we were, standing in the hallway with kids changing classes all around us, having a Kodak moment.

We went to rehearsal that night as usual,
but whenever we looked at each other, I'd get this
tingling. I knew something was about to happen. I
drove Gerald home. Not straight home. Behind
Madame Fouché's, between the studio and the scenery
warehouse, there was a small, secluded parking lot.
That was where we went. We got in the backseat,
and he put his arm around me. When I leaned back
against him, I felt his whole body sigh. Mine, too.

It's really strange to hear myself talking about
this, especially to you, a stranger and a man. I never
told anyone the details of my romance with Gerald,
not even my best girlfriend. You know how it was
in those days. Girls guarded their reputations and
if couples were having sex, it was kept top secret.
Maybe the boys talked. You'd know that better than
I would, but girls were afraid of being labeled. Then
after Gerald died, I couldn't think about him without
dissolving into tears much less talk about what we had
shared. Sex meant something to us then. It wasn't
just something you did when you were thirteen.

Remember when it took a guy all night to get
up the courage to put his arm around a girl, when
French kissing was a major commitment? Then
only a couple of years later, teenagers became flower
children and believed in free love and the sexual
revolution. Frankly, I liked it better when life was
innocent.

Sitting in the backseat with Gerald was one of
the most exciting nights of my life. It had to do with
anticipation and discovery and the reward for waiting
so long to find your destiny. I can play back that
scene like it was yesterday, every detail. Gerald was
so tender it made me love him even more. He said,
"I know some people think I'm not normal, and I was

scared they might be right. But then I realized I was watching your lips and noticing things about you – the line of your collarbones, how your hair smells like lemons. And it wasn't just that I hated doing my own love scenes, but I hated seeing you do yours."

I turned around in his arms so that I was facing him and put my fingers on his lips. And I looked at him, so handsome and vulnerable, really looked at him with the electric knowledge that this was the first man I would make love to, that he wanted me. I was in the arms of Gerald Graham and I adored him.

I know when you're a teenager, all those hormones surging through your body enhance your responses, but honestly, kissing Gerald was more erotic than the hottest romance novel you could find. Deep, long, sweet kisses. Like everything else he had ever done, Gerald was good at it. There wasn't any desperate groping and panting. It was a slow motion dance. I was overwhelmed by how powerful the heady feeling of passion was and how it could transform us. So was Gerald. As innocent as we both were, we had an instinct and a natural knowledge of each other that moved us light-years ahead of where we had been just an hour before. We didn't go all the way that night. Probably we would have, but Gerald thought he saw a light in the studio. We got scared. It was getting late and we knew Myrtle would question us.

From then on, you could say we were hearing a new music. We couldn't wait to be alone. When we danced together, it was like foreplay. Gerald and I were hot for each other. The news that we were going steady spread around school within a week, and most people said it came as no surprise to them. We were billed as the perfect couple.

I don't know who was more upset about this turn of events, Lindy or Myrtle. Of course, Lindy got over it as soon as Kevin Brannigan asked her out. He played trumpet in the band, and Lindy had a theory that brass players were the best kissers. So she was satisfied.

How Myrtle found out about us was a mystery for a while. But pretty soon we realized that Madame Fouché had spied on us. She knew we were parking behind her studio. We were pretty sure she told on us. Myrtle was ready to send Gerald to a monastery. Honestly, if she saw us holding hands, she nearly had a hemorrhage. She forced him to go to the doctor for a lecture on teenage pregnancy and venereal diseases. Gerald was mortified. Then she had the nerve to call my mother and warn her that I was not only a danger to myself but to her son as well. Mother was concerned that I might be going too far with Gerald, and she talked to me. But mostly she was infuriated that this woman would insult me like that. I think she finally realized that Myrtle Graham was not what she appeared to be.

Gerald's father made a token effort to keep things reasonable. He would tease me and keep the conversation going when I would come by to pick up Gerald. It helped that he liked me. But I think what really mattered to him was that Gerald was involved with something other than performing, and doubly glad that it was a girl.

As I said, Gerald opened up to me during that year, and he told me he was afraid his father was ashamed of him. That he knew he wasn't what his father wanted in a son. It broke my heart to hear him talk about his dad. He wanted so much to be close to him, but he felt like Myrtle had wedged herself between them from the beginning and by the time he figured out what was happening and why, it was too late to change things. He said he remembered his dad planning fishing trips for the two of them, but Myrtle would schedule a dance class on the same day. Gerald was really torn because he loved to dance, loved the attention he got when he was good at it.

Myrtle made him choose. She was very good at manipulating him. You can make a little kid do exactly what you want if you know how to handle him. She would tell him that he could go fishing. That would be fine. She would just go to the lesson by herself and watch all the other little children dance. And then she would tear up and hug him. She'd say, "I'll be all right. You go ahead and have fun with your father. I'll just stay here alone. I won't be scared."

Can you imagine putting that guilt trip on a six year old? Gerald fell for it when he was little, but he was coming to many realizations about his mother during the last year he lived. I believe he would have freed himself from her if he'd had a little more time.

We learned to be careful about what Myrtle saw of our relationship. In front of her we limited our contact to holding hands. We never said anything private on the phone because we were afraid she might be listening in. The door to Gerald's practice room was always kept open. We made sure Myrtle would have nothing to throw in Gerald's face.

But that didn't keep her from expressing her distaste for me or for the feelings we had for each other. One evening after Gerald and I had practiced and planned the recital numbers for the Petite Tappers Class we taught, he asked me to stay for dinner. Myrtle rarely allowed that and so I was surprised when she consented. But it didn't take long

to discover her motives. She sent Gerald out to the
rose garden to pick some flowers for the table. I was
going to tag along, but she said she had a job for me
too – helping her set the table. She just wanted to
trap me alone. As soon as Gerald shut the back door,
she started. It wasn't only her words, but the way she
said them and the expression on her face that made
me feel I had been slapped. She looked inflamed.
Maniacal.

She said, "Rebecca, dear, I know what girls
like you have in mind. I was your age once myself.
But what you want – a husband, children, split-level
house – those are things Gerald won't be able to
give you. He has another direction to follow. He's
different, special. I'm sure he's trying very hard to be
like normal boys, but there's hurt waiting for him if
you try to mold him to fit into your little dreams. I'm
his mother. I'll love him no matter what. But you,
you're just a little experiment. He's testing himself.
When he fails, and you shun him, I'll have a great deal
of damage to repair. The sooner you quit teasing him
along, the better off he'll be."

I was dumbfounded. I stood there holding the
silverware, my mouth open, while she kept chopping
celery like we were discussing recipes. Gerald came
in with Hamilton and the roses, and we ate dinner.
She never let on that she had said anything out of the
ordinary. From then on I made sure I was not alone
with Myrtle.

I didn't tell Gerald what she said, but I told
him we needed to guard ourselves. That was tough
because we were in the throes of a steamy teenage love
affair. Before we found out about Madame Fouché,
we spent hours parked behind her studio. But of all
those hours, I can count on one hand the number

of times we actually had sex. We were too afraid of
getting caught or getting pregnant. Lots of nights,
we'd just wrap ourselves around each other and talk
about what we were going to do with our lives.

You know how it was when we were kids. The
expectation was that everyone would get married and
have a family, a house, a station, and a dog. Who
knew that we'd all end up divorced and cynical? I had
no idea I'd be a single parent living in the house where
I grew up, making bouquets of flowers that don't
even smell good. And you? How did your dreams
turn out? Did you think you'd be a news anchor in
a big city, expose a major political scandal, win a
Pulitzer? Or did you imagine you'd end up talking to
uninteresting strangers about the dishwasher suicide
of a manic-depressive old woman?

I'm really sorry. I should not project my
feelings of disappointment onto you. It's just that
sometimes when I think about Gerald and what could
have been, I get irritated with life. Things should
have been different. We were going to have the whole
dream, and not even Myrtle was going to stop us.

We wanted to spend our lives together. That
was going to take some working out. Gerald knew
Myrtle wanted him to go to New York. He was scared
she would go with him, just leave his father and head
for Broadway. He didn't want that. In fact, getting
away from his mother was becoming an obsession.
Against Myrtle's wishes, Gerald had decided to try
Nashville. Country music was not very popular
then, and I couldn't figure out why in the world he
was interested in it. But the truth was Gerald was
trying to relate to his father. Hamilton was from
Tennessee and, although he had never been back
there except to visit, he loved the mountains and the

space and the isolation. Gerald remembered going to
his grandmother's funeral there when he was about
seven or eight. He said that even though his father
was terribly sad, he seemed happier than he had ever
been. Gerald said that for a long time he couldn't
figure out how Hamilton could be so glad to be at
a funeral. But he was only a child at the time. He
didn't know the dynamics of his parents' marriage or
the discontent of a man who knows his life is full of
weakness.

That visit to Tennessee when his grandmother
died was the only time Gerald remembered seeing
his father as a force in his life. They stayed in the
old family home place out in the country for about
two weeks. Hamilton's brother, Joe, was there, and
Gerald spent a lot of time listening to his stories about
World War II, something Hamilton never talked
about. Myrtle was miserable, complained constantly,
but Gerald was enchanted by the fields of sunflowers
and scarecrows and trails that led through the woods
to the homes of cousins Joe said were as plentiful as
the bean vines that covered acre after acre. Mostly,
though, Gerald loved it because he got to spend time
with Hamilton. He said the two of them would leave
the house early in the morning before Myrtle woke up
and take one of those trails into the woods for a walk.
If they got back before breakfast, Myrtle wouldn't
realize they had been out. That worked for a few days.
But on one of their little excursions Hamilton was
helping Gerald climb his favorite boyhood tree, and he
fell, breaking his front tooth. Myrtle threw a fit and
forbade any more father-son outings.

Gerald was just beginning to feel comfortable
with Hamilton. Stories of hunting rabbits and deer,
of fishing in the river, of camping out in the forest

had been pouring out of his father like rain after a
drought, and Gerald wanted to get wet. Sitting in
the woods, Hamilton had told him about how he had
grown up idolizing Joe, how Joe had taught him to
read the signs of animals, to shoot, and to clean game.

Gerald said that Joe was gruff and seemed to
fuss a lot, but he was fascinated by his uncle and how
he seemed to blend into the forest. He thought it was
a shame his father almost never saw Joe. There was
a problem between them. He knew Myrtle detested
Joe and didn't want him at their house. But he didn't
know why.

What he did know was that he longed for the
father that had appeared so briefly in the Tennessee
mountains. He wanted to reach Hamilton somehow,
relate to him. He was afraid it was too late, but he
had it in his mind to try. That's why he was going to
Nashville. That's why he chose country music. He
wanted to sing his way into his father's heart.

The last summer Gerald lived, he was taking
steps toward his father. He signed on at that theater
in the mountains because of Hamilton. Telling people
he wanted to hike the Blue Ridge was for Hamilton's
benefit, to try to earn his respect. Gerald didn't
know anything about hiking. He hadn't hiked since
he walked the woods with his father in Tennessee. I
always wondered if Hamilton ever knew how hard
Gerald was trying to be his son.

If he had lived, we would have gotten married.
We talked about moving to Tennessee and opening a
dance school, or maybe teaching English and drama
in a high school somewhere if the country music thing
didn't work out. Gerald wasn't completely sold on a
stage career, although Myrtle had always pushed him
in that direction. She badgered him about New York.

Secretly, we made plans. We loved each other and thought we could be happy anywhere as long as we were together. You know how kids are at that age, hopeful and sure. I guess it doesn't matter what age you are, when you're first in love, you believe in magic. At least we had a little while to be starry eyed before we realized that magic is nothing but trickery and illusion.

Blindly, we imagined our future. Meanwhile, Myrtle tried to break us up. But the harder she tried, the more determined we were to stay together. I think she tried to convince him he was gay. He wasn't, but she confused him. Myrtle did her best to warp him. I have to believe she didn't know she was hurting him. I can't stand to think she would have done it intentionally.

I'm grateful that, with me, he had a few months when he was able to be somewhat normal and that he felt he was breaking away from her. The spring of our senior year was Gerald's beginning. He was starting to transplant himself. He had been root bound for most of his life.

Everything came to a head in May, a few weeks before graduation. We had both been selected for All-State Chorus along with Lindy and one other girl from our school. The concert was in Charleston. The choral director from our school was the chaperone and was supposed to be in the adjoining motel room with us girls. Gerald was rooming with one of the boys from the All-State Band, namely Kevin, who was still dating Lindy. It took Gerald weeks to convince Myrtle to let him go. She didn't agree until she found out that Madame Fouché would be there in Charleston with her ballet troupe. With her spy in place, I guess, she felt secure that she could keep an eye on us.

Our choral director wasn't much older than we
were. She knew we didn't want her hanging around
all the time any more than she wanted us hanging
around her all the time. Besides, she was bringing
her husband, so she booked a room that, as she told
us in our little pre-trip meeting, was actually not
going to be adjoining ours. In fact, it was going to be
in another wing of the motel. She told us she knew
we were old enough to be on our own and that we'd
probably only run into her at the practices. A fact
that would probably get her fired if anyone found out,
but we weren't about to tell. As it turned out Lindy
and I were the only girls who went. The other girl got
mono. We managed to keep all of this from Myrtle.
If she had known, Gerald never would have been
allowed to go.

Lindy and Kevin decided they wanted different
roommates, namely each other, and told us that
on the drive down. Gerald and I never would have
thought of that ourselves, but it was an opportunity
we couldn't pass up. We all swore that no one would
tell. After we checked in, we switched our things
around and we were set. It was pretty exciting
to think that we had the whole weekend to spend
together, that we'd get to sleep in the same bed and
wake up next to each other. But it was scary too. If
anyone found out, even the choral director, we would
be in deep trouble.

The first night was wonderful. We finished
the rehearsal and took a horse and buggy ride around
Charleston, pretending it was our honeymoon. It was still
cool weather, but we went for a moonlight swim in the motel
pool anyway. Then we went back to our room. Our room.
We'd never had the luxury of unhurried sex or even the
freedom to be completely undressed around each other.

Do you remember how difficult it was to find
a place to be alone with someone when you were
dating? The backseat at a drive-in movie was about as
private as it got. Our little weekend in Charleston was
worth the risk of getting caught. Let me put it this
way. That was the best experience we ever had. If I
could have spent the rest of my life in that motel room
with Gerald, it would have been fine with me.

We felt safe. There was no way that we could
get caught. At least that was what we thought. But
Myrtle was more suspicious than we were naïve. The
next day while we were rehearsing, slipping away
at every break and kissing in the parking lot, Myrtle
was packing an overnight bag and leaving a note for
Hamilton that she was driving to Charleston to hear
the concert that night.

To this day, I don't know what alerted her. I
assumed it was Madame Fouché, but since she wasn't
staying at the same hotel, I'm not certain. Whatever it
was though, Myrtle showed up. The concert hall was
packed and we never knew she was there. When it
was over, we raced back to our room anxious to make
the most of our last night.

We'd been back about thirty minutes, so we
were right in the middle of making love, when there
was a banging on the door. Then Myrtle's voice
started screaming like a banshee. I panicked but
Gerald was amazingly calm. He said, "Rebecca, go
in the bathroom and get dressed. I'll let her in." As
I closed the bathroom door, he was pulling up his
pants.

Myrtle barged in like she was raiding the place.
The first thing I heard was a slap, loud and snapping.
Then she lit into him, telling him he was throwing his
life away on a tramp, that she had known I was evil

from the first moment she had seen me. She said,
"That girl is a slut sent by the devil to lure you away
from me. She's after one thing, a bastard child to tie
you down. You're fooling yourself if you think you'll
be happy with her or with any woman." She stormed
at him about betraying her trust. Then she started
pounding on the bathroom door, yelling at me. I
heard struggling and Gerald's voice, gritting out his
words, saying, "Dammit, Mother, shut up. Shut up.
Shut up." Over and over. But she didn't stop.

Gerald never said anything else until Myrtle
demanded he get his things and leave with her. Then
he spoke. In a clear, sane voice, he said, "Mother, I'm
not leaving Rebecca. I love her and we are not evil.
This is what's right. Maybe we should have waited
until we were married. But I'm not sorry. I want you
out of our room."

All sound stopped. For maybe two or three
minutes, it was absolutely quiet. Then she started
moaning, sobbing, "My baby, my baby, my baby."
Gerald told her to shut up one more time and she
did. The next thing I heard was the door closing and
Gerald telling me it was all right to come out.

I opened the door and he was standing there,
his face bleached, but victorious somehow. He had
not put on his shirt and his chest and arms were moist
with perspiration. His breathing was still heavy. He
was barefoot. At that moment I thought he was the
most beautiful, the strongest, the sexiest man I had
ever seen. God, how I loved him. I slept in his arms
all night long. Just slept. We never actually had sex.
We were making love without actually making love. It
was enough that we felt the emotions.

Lindy and Kevin were scared that Myrtle would
tell their parents, but nothing came of it. I think

Myrtle realized that in order to tell someone else,
she'd have to admit Gerald had done the same thing.
In public, she acted the same as always, but at home,
she stayed locked in her room most of the time and
didn't speak to Gerald at all. He said it was like she
had made him invisible. The weeks before he left for
the mountains, Myrtle tortured him with her silence.

Hamilton didn't know what had happened in
Charleston, and as far as I know, no one ever told him.
But he had to know something was wrong. Myrtle
was pouting and crying all the time. One afternoon
when Gerald went out to the rose garden, he talked
with his father, not about us, but about the conflict
between Myrtle's dreams and his own. Hamilton told
him to live his own life, whatever that entailed. He
said regrets would torment you into surrendering to
hopelessness. I don't know if he felt that way about
himself or if he was speaking of Myrtle.

The morning Gerald left for the mountains,
he approached Myrtle. He told her he loved her and
apologized for hurting her. But he also told her he
loved me and that wasn't going to change. What she
said, he didn't tell me in detail, but it was something
like, "Go ahead. Have your dirty little fling with the
slut. Get it out of your system. But you'll be sorry
someday and you'll realize that I'm the one who knows
you best." They came to terms, I guess. At least they
were speaking. I think Myrtle felt being separated for
the summer would put an end to our romance.

We didn't tell anyone that we were going to
elope when the summer was over. Then we would go
to Nashville, find jobs, and start to make our future.
My parents weren't going to be thrilled about the fact
that I wasn't going to college like I had planned, but
I was going to go to business school in Tennessee so

I'd have a better chance at getting a higher paying job and I'd learn skills to run a dance school if we decided that's what we wanted to do. For the summer, I was going to work and save money to help Gerald and me get established in Nashville.

And then Gerald died. It was the worst day of my life. Hamilton and Myrtle and the Overtons were going up to the mountains to watch him perform. Gerald asked Hamilton to invite me along. I was hesitant because I was afraid of Myrtle, but I hadn't seen Gerald all summer and I missed him. I hadn't been around Myrtle since the scene in Charleston. But things had calmed down, and I figured she wouldn't attack me in front of her neighbors. I went and it was okay. She basically left me alone, but to everyone else, she was as jolly as ever, meeting the cast and director who fell all over himself bragging on Gerald's talents. The only problem was that we didn't get a chance to be alone the whole weekend. We had no privacy to kiss or talk or just look at each other.

But it was obvious that Gerald was happy. He was tanned and healthy. His smile was so powerful you couldn't help but feel good around him. When we went to the waterfall, he was like a little kid, splashing and making a spectacle of himself showing off. I hadn't brought my swimsuit, so I had to stay with his parents on the ridge above the pools.

You've never seen such a day, colors so vivid they almost hurt your eyes. It was breezy and warm. There were lots of people, but it was a friendly crowd. It wasn't a day you would pick for a tragedy.

I guess you know how Gerald died. I'm sure you've already done your research on that. It was so unexpected. Gerald wasn't on the lookout for danger. His life was charmed. Who would have thought to worry about poisonous snakes? He never regained consciousness. My sweet, handsome Gerald died.

I don't even remember getting home from the mountains. I went through the funeral in a state of shock. All my plans and dreams were gone. Nothing was ever very much fun after that. I went away to college. Got married. Lost track of Myrtle until I came back here after my divorce.

Do you think about the life you planned at eighteen and how far you are from that now? Sometimes I think I've just idealized Gerald and our love. That if he had lived, we could have ended up unhappy and divorced too. But still, he was my first real love. I guess his death kept our relationship from becoming stagnant. We never had reason to distrust or tire of each other. We'll always be young and happy in my memory.

So here I am, twenty years later making wedding bouquets with artificial flowers. Great metaphor.

That's probably Cal coming in. He knows I dated Gerald, of course. He doesn't realize the depth of the relationship. I think it's hard for a child to imagine their parent in a romantic, sexual situation with the other parent, much less someone else. It would probably be best if you didn't discuss the details of my past with him. I'd appreciate that. I think it's bad enough for him to know that his father isn't the man of his dreams. I'd hate for him to realize that he wasn't the man of mine either.

Cal's a good kid. He doesn't talk much, but you'll like him. I don't have to worry about him, thank goodness. His head is on straight. He's very reliable and works hard. He's a big boy, very athletic. Takes after his father. He doesn't dance at all. Not a step.

YARDBOY CLAIMS DISHWASHER WOMAN

WASN'T CARRYING A FULL LOAD

Chapter 6 - Cal Setters' Story

Man, that Myrtle Graham was a nutjob. I'd see her coming, I'd lose my place in line. Retreat, man. Avoiding her was a major hobby. Her husband, he was okay. But I figured she had probably sucked the life out of him years ago and left him like some kind of zombie.

But what a cool way to waste yourself. If you're into disposal, you might as well do it in a big way. Me, I don't even like to be shut up in a phone booth. Geez, I can't fathom locking myself in a dishwasher and soaking myself down with Cascade. Talk about your total sheeting action.

Think about it. In some parallel universe, she could have been my grandmother. My mom could have hooked up with her son and I could have been a different Cal. Myrtle would have been mixing up Rice Krispies treats for me and the Cub Scouts.

Like I would have dared eat anything she cooked. She was always bringing me these pieces of fruitcake wrapped up in aluminum foil. Concrete, man. The third little pig could have built his house out of those things and not even a nuclear warhead wolf could have penetrated those kickass walls.

And she looked like something out of a horror movie. Like *Myrtle Graham the Thirteenth*. *I Love Lucy* goes ballistic. Her hair was the color of somebody screaming. You expect little old ladies to be all stooped and breakable, but she sort of loomed over you like one of those vultures with the red heads. I've got friends who are baggers at Piggly Wiggly and none of them would buggy her groceries without making sure somebody knew their next of kin.

My mom says I'm exaggerating, but I've even seen her change direction if she saw the old loony tune heading toward her. She would drive blocks out of the way to keep from passing Myrtle's house. When you were talking to Mom, did she tell you that when we moved back here, Myrtle used to call her up? I didn't think so. My mom keeps most of her worries to herself.

She tried to tell me that Myrtle was just lonely and still missed her son, but next thing you know, we've got an answering machine and caller ID to screen our calls. Bring in the rocket scientists to figure that one out.

My mom and I, we moved here after my dad left us. Bunked in with my grandparents. That was five, six years ago. Man, I wasn't even in middle school yet. And I was pretty bummed out about leaving all my friends, not to mention losing my dad. But we made it. My mom does all right. It's just the two of us now. My grandparents died. And my dad, he's, like, out of the picture.

I help out by doing yard work for the blue-hairs. This neighborhood's packed with them. They pay good and they worry about me working too hard. The old ladies, they all knew my grandmother. Since she died they, like, adopted me. Some of them call me Calvin instead of Cal, but I can take it. Most of them are neat old chicks. The old guys are okay, too, as long as they don't try to help me lift stuff. I like the work.

My grandmother started me off mowing lawns. She used to tell everybody at her beauty parlor all about me. Passed me off as a well-mannered, dependable kid, not like the ones they saw on television. But hey, I am a well-mannered, dependable kid. Handsome too. Grab a look at this face. Just kidding, man. You're tougher than the old ladies. I can make them laugh right off. Some of them giggle the whole time I'm weeding their pansy beds. Ruth Overton, though, she's the one that makes me laugh. You met her yet?

She's nutty in a good way. My best customer, especially now that Myrtle's not next door anymore. My mom would say, "Now, Cal, that's not nice." But geez, I used to try to figure ways to get to Ruth's house without being seen by Myrtle. It didn't matter what I did though – cut through backyards, climb over fences, crawl through hedges – she always spotted me.

And here she'd come with that slab of brick she called cake, trying to lure me into her house. Spooky old witch. Man, like she was demented.

Nobody warned me. Not even my mom. I ought to let her hold it on that one. She knew Myrtle was a wackjob from way back. She should have given me one of those "Don't talk to strangers" lectures.

But see, I didn't know. At first, I was, like, blind. So when Myrtle asked me to help her take some groceries into her kitchen, I thought, why not. I was working on the driveway between her house and Ruth's and it was only, like, five steps. I mean, what could happen?

Going inside was, like, next stop, *Twilight Zone*. She takes me into the kitchen and she goes, "Calvin, could you help me change the bulb in the guest bedroom ceiling light?" So I go, "Sure" because, like, how hard can that be. So I follow her into this empty room. No furniture, man. I mean, where do the guests sleep? And she pulls a stepladder out of

the closet. I climb up and I'm unscrewing the bulb,
and all of a sudden there's music playing and she's
twirling around under the ladder like some really
ancient ballerina and she goes, "Do you hear a waltz?"
I notice she's got this record player that's out of some
kind of time warp. And then I notice all these mirrors
on the walls. Beam me up, Scotty.

The coach should have clocked me getting out
of that house. Olympic record, for sure. But after I
get back out in the daylight, I feel real stupid that I
was scared and I figure it's just that her brain cells are
deserting the ship. And after a few days I forget about
it.

So the next time she needs help, I figure, hey,
I'm a big boy. This old lady's harmless. So, like, I go
back in. Major mistake.

This time she needs some boxes put into
the attic. What can happen? Ruth knows where I
am. The attic's got a window. I haven't seen her on
America's Most Wanted, so no big deal. I'm thinking
I'm the only one going up the steps, but I get upstairs
and turn on the light, and the next thing I know,
Myrtle's lugging herself up the stairs too. She's
panting and sweating and I'm going over how to do
CPR in my mind. I go, "Mrs. Graham, don't you think
it'd be better if you wait down there? And her head's
just coming into view and it goes, "No, dear, I want to
show you my Gerald."

I'm thinking, whoa, say no to drugs. My mom
has told me about Gerald. He's been dead a long time.
And I'm thinking if he's in this attic, he's going to have
a major skin problem.

But I decide to humor her. I'm cool. I go,
"Mrs. Graham, it's like a tropical heat wave up here.
It would be really awesome to meet your Gerald, but

perhaps you could coax him down into the den where
he could join us for a Diet Pepsi."

She looks at me like I'm the crazy one and
says, "Don't be silly, dear. All Gerald's things are up
here. Hamilton won't let me bring them downstairs.
I come up here quite often. In fact, I have a little air
conditioner already set up."

Right there in the attic, she's got her own little
hangout. Sofa. Table. Lamp. Man, all she needs is a
television and she could live up there easy. Sure, the
stuff's old and ratty; but put up some posters, get a
decent sound system, and any dude my age would say,
"Way cool."

So the next thing I know, I'm going through
scrapbooks. Here's this little tiny kid in tap shoes
and diapers. A younger version of Myrtle holding his
hand. She's wearing tap shoes, too, and they're both
throwing kisses to the audience or whoever's behind
the camera.

A whole bunch of pictures show him standing
next to a tall woman with slicked-back hair and a
neck so long and curved it looked like a faucet. She's
wearing one of those long Japanese housecoat things.
Everything about her is extreme. She could have
come straight out of a foreign movie, done in black
and white. To talk to her, you'd have to have subtitles.

So I go, "Hey, who's the Russian spy?" And
Myrtle sort of hisses and goes, "We will not discuss
Lily Fouché. She never understood."

Then she snaps back happy and goes, "Let's
visit the animals." There's the kid, solo again, in
every kind of costume you can imagine. Name an
animal, he was dressed like it: duck, chicken, sheep,
dog, mouse, dragon. Man, I would have run away
from home if my mom had trapped me in any one of

those get-ups, let alone all of them. But here's this kid
smiling.

I figure he must have been a child star, making
truckloads of money. Why else would he do it? Plus
he let somebody take a picture of him. I am real sure
a normal kid would never sit still for that. No way,
man. Not unless you're like that dork Beaver Cleaver.
But see, even the Beav was making a ton of bucks by
acting like a dork. I rest my case.

So I say to Myrtle, "Was he, like, one of the
Little Rascals?"

And she laughs and says, "No, he was always
very well behaved, if I do say so myself."

There are more pictures of him like an Eskimo,
an Indian, a cowboy, a knight, a sailor. He's in a
miniature tuxedo with eight or ten little girls in
wedding dresses. He's a dwarf Uncle Sam with eight
or ten little girls dressed like flags. Little Superman
with eight or ten little girls like stars. You get the idea.
Smiling, always smiling.

I'm thinking, what was she feeding this kid? The
only time I ever put on a costume was Halloween and
then it was either my little league uniform or Dracula
or Batman. My mom tried once to get me to be a
shepherd in a Christmas play at church. Even a ten-
dollar bribe couldn't convince me. But here's this boy
all dolled up just asking for his cheeks to be pinched.

While I'm looking at the pictures, Myrtle's
doing the play-by-play on his performances, giving
me snatches of songs, counting out rhythms,
demonstrating footwork, spouting out stuff like
this: Shuffle-ball-change, Fall off a log, Time step,
Typewriter-step, Bell-Irish-pullback. Pretty soon I
realize I'm actually listening. She's got me hooked.
I'm, like, hypnotized.

A one-woman show, she's putting on in the attic. The thing that's weird is that sometimes when I'm looking at her, I'm seeing the kid. Or when I look at the kid, I see Myrtle. I know how kids take after their parents, but this was different. This was like I could almost see him dancing in the attic. See him in her wrinkly old face. See her wanting him so much that she had him there with her.

I've been through death. My grandmother died. Then my grandfather, too. And I miss them. I wouldn't admit that to most of my friends. But what I'm saying is, I could understand that she lost somebody. Everybody goes through that. What made it sad and weird was that she was still holding on after all that time.

That made Myrtle crazy and sort of pathetic. And it made her a little scary. But I stayed.

So how am I going to explain to my mom that I sat in a jumbled, dusty attic watching Myrtle the Maniac dancing? I figure I'm not. So she doesn't know.

That was a while before Myrtle got rid of herself. I thought she was a harmless kind of crazy. You know, like a lot of people that pretend to be normal. Hey, how was I supposed to know? I'm just a kid. Like, maybe I should have called 9-1-1 and put them on hold until Myrtle was ready to rinse herself.

When I heard about her, I was wiped out. All I could think of was sitting in that attic with her. I went more than once, you know.

The first time, I was spooked. For a little while anyway. Then it got to be a hoot. And I was thinking that I'd tell my friends about her and we'd get a laugh. But after listening to her and seeing that kid grinning, I knew I'd keep her secret.

Maybe it was my mom's pictures that drew me back. See, we were going through the scrapbooks by year. While Gerald was a little boy, he was either alone, or with a chorus line, or with Myrtle or that Russian-Japanese Dragon lady. But when he got to be a teenager, the pictures were of him and a girl. Always one girl. The same girl in every shot. My mom.

In some of them I didn't even recognize her. She'd have on wigs and her face would be disguised by a mask or make-up. Man, if there was one word I'd never use to describe my mom, it would be "clown." She's, like, not funny at all. But there she was painted with these major grins and silly poses. Whoa, I am glad she grew out of that phase.

Or she'd be dressed to look like that chick who had the tornado nightmare. You know, the one with the wizard obsession. Or somebody like Snow White or Cinderella, who always had a thing for the handsome prince. And Gerald, he'd be with her in the picture as the prince or that scarecrow dude or matching whatever costume she wore. Sometimes they'd be exactly alike. Twins, only with him taller and smiling bigger.

But what really freaked me out were the shots where I could see for sure that it was my mom in leotards and tights. I mean, she was a babe with awesome legs. My mom. And instead of staring at them, Gerald's focused on the camera. There's no way I'd let any of my friends see those pictures.

Myrtle didn't talk much about her. She'd say, "Gerald's little partner did a split," or "Gerald lifted his little partner clear above his head." I asked her if Gerald ever had another partner because it was beginning to irritate me that she wasn't even saying my mom's name. And she said, "He had dozens."

Yeah, right. Then why weren't there any pictures of him with another girl?

Gerald and "his partner" taught classes of, what Myrtle called, the baby tappers. And of course, she had proof on film. Gerald, my mom, surrounded by a bunch of nursery school types. Okay, they're Mr. and Mrs. Claus and the elves. A magician, his assistant, and tiny white rabbits. Dracula, a witch, and little Jack-o'-lanterns. You get my drift.

And here's where Myrtle starts crying about how Gerald liked children, and how good he was with them, and how he never got to have a family. Then she stares right at me and goes, "You don't look like him at all."

Man, like, I'm supposed to. I think maybe I should set her straight. But what if she freaks, locks me in the attic, and my face shows up on a milk carton? Then we hear Hamilton banging around downstairs and calling her, saying something about her being in the damn attic again. Real nervous-like, she shuts the scrapbooks and stacks them, tells me not to let on to her husband what we've been doing. Or better yet, I should wait a few minutes after she goes down and then I should sneak out the front door when I hear her get Hamilton into the kitchen. Then she grabs my hand and goes, "You will come again, now won't you? I have so much more to show you, and I want to get everything taken care of on time."

Myrtle had a grip like a weight lifter and I actually cringed before she let go. She thanked me for helping her put the boxes in the attic like that was all that had happened. I went out to help Ruth who never questioned me about why I was gone so long. That's weird, don't you think?

When I got home, I found my mom in the dining room
sitting on the floor with fake flowers all around her.
Her hair was messed up, but it was curly and only a
little bit gray. She had on jeans, a ratty old t-shirt, no
make-up, and her favorite earrings that hang down
and are shaped like crescent moons with faces on
them. I tried to imagine her on stage, dancing in the
spotlight, all young and out of breath. She looked up,
told me there was leftover-something in the fridge for
supper. Major reality check.

The next time I go into the attic, Myrtle shows
me Gerald's costumes. Man, there's no way a moth
could live within a mile and a half of the Graham's
house. I'm wondering if mothball fumes can make
a person go all wacko. Maybe that could explain
Myrtle's condition. Every time she opens another
trunk, she gets wackier. We look at his tuxedo and his
first pair of tap shoes. She puts her hands inside the
shoes and does a little dance on the attic floor. She's
pretty good at it, too, considering she's dancing with
her hands. Then she wants me to try it. But I tell her
I'm left-handed, and she seems to think that's some
kind of tap handicap, so I'm safe.

I've never been to a dance recital, but once
when I was little, my mom took me to see, *The
Nutcracker*. Yawn City. You can take my share of
ballet and give it to charity. But my point is, that from
the audience, those fancy costumes look expensive.
What Myrtle showed me was put together cheaper
than store-bought Halloween junk. They look like
they'd fall apart if you wore them more than once.
But Myrtle had them folded in tissue paper and zipped
into plastic bags.

She had one trunk with nothing in it but hats.
Sombreros, space helmets, Indian headdresses, top

hats. Hats for sailors, cowboys, firemen. You name
it, she had it. And on the lid of the trunk she had a list
of everything inside, inventoried and alphabetized.
She could look at a pair of shoes or a hat or a shirt
and tell right away exactly what dance and song it was
for. Of course, she sang a little of each. It reminded
me of those greatest hits commercials, like "For only
fourteen ninety-five, you get all these unforgettable
Gerald songs recorded by his ozone mom, Myrtle the
Maniac."

Most of what I saw I recognized from the
pictures. By the time we got to the costumes Gerald
wore as a teenager, I was, like, bored out of my mind.
But then Myrtle decides I should try them on. The
left-handed routine doesn't work, so I find myself
standing in the attic wearing a pirate shirt with a
patch over my eye. I draw the line at the pants. I'm
thinking it would not be cool to be caught up here
with my own pants off, wearing satiny knee britches.
Myrtle's okay with that, and she's having a party
pulling out wigs and swords and a stuffed parrot to
perch on my shoulder. She laughs and pulls out a
top hat and ruffled shirt. I put that on with a black
and red cape and a cane. That's cool, too. I realize
that I'm kind of getting into this. Next she hands
me a really fancy cowboy shirt and hat. I'm already
wearing jeans, so this outfit's the best yet. She even
has the lasso that's wired to stand out in a circle and
some boots only they have taps on them. Still I look
great. Myrtle's talking nonstop about how this stuff
came from Oklahoma, and I'm wondering why they
sent all the way out there for a costume. You can get
Western stuff at Wal-Mart.

Then she steps back to look at me and she
starts to cry. She turns around and is down the stairs

before I know what's happening. I'm thinking, "Oh my god, she's going to fold up the attic door and I'll be trapped." But the door stays open and she doesn't come back. I take off the cowboy stuff fast and get the hell out of Dodge.

All the way home I thought that maybe I should tell my mom or somebody about Myrtle, but I never did. Working with Ruth in her yard, I'd come real close to talking to her about Myrtle, but then I'd feel like I was being watched. I was too scared to look up and check the attic windows to see if she was spying on me. One night at supper I got my mom to talking about high school, thinking I could bring up Gerald and maybe work the conversation around to Myrtle. She had told me years ago about dating Gerald and how he died and all, but I didn't pay a lot of attention at the time. But being around Myrtle had made me curious about a lot of things.

I asked her, "Mom, when you were going with Gerald Graham, what did you do for fun during your free time?" Geez, you know how my mom always talks in complete sentences, like she wrote the paragraph first and is reading it to you. She said, "Well, we went to movies, but most of our time was spent either teaching dance classes or in rehearsal for something. We didn't have much free time. Take *Oklahoma!* for example. We rehearsed every night for four months, but we loved it. That was our fun, the highlight of our senior year. It was a huge production, the best thing Gerald ever did."

Whoa. Major stupid attack. It didn't take Sherlock to figure out Myrtle didn't mean the state when she was carrying on about Oklahoma. I was wearing a dead boy's most important costume. Man, was I bummed.

My mom's sitting there, her eyes all watery. I'm wiped out about an old psycho lady and her dead son who might have married my mom if he had lived. And if he had lived, I wouldn't even be sitting at the table hating my meatloaf.

Then my mom said, "I used to sing you the songs from *Oklahoma!* when you were little to rock you to sleep. Your favorite was the one about the surrey with the fringe on top." She got up, started clearing the table, scraping dishes into the sink, loading the dishwasher. And the whole time, she sang that song about chickens and ducks and riding in a surrey. Dude, I know I must have been real little when she sang that to me, and I don't even know what a surrey is exactly, but it was, like, too familiar.

Wouldn't it be weird if Myrtle was singing those *Oklahoma!* songs when she loaded herself into the dishwasher.

When she died, right after it happened, my mom and I went over to the house to see Hamilton. My mom felt, like, it was her duty or something. She's real proper about weddings and funerals and stuff like that. So she bought one of those hams that's already sliced around in a circle and a couple of loaves of bread, and we went over. Man, I had to wear a suit.

Most of the time, after somebody dies, there's a ton of people all over the house. Men in ties and women in black dresses. Everybody's whispering and carrying around wadded-up tissues. But when we got to Hamilton's, it was, like, uninhabited. Nobody was there except him. And he was in faded pants and one of those thin cotton shirts that old guys wear. You know, the ones with the little pleats up the front and back. The ones they don't tuck in. My grandfather used to have a blue one and a white one and a tan one.

We sat in the living room, and my mom turned into this little restless kid who couldn't sit still. She'd cross her legs and swing her foot back and forth. She fiddled with her ring and kept checking her watch. It was like she was being punished. They tried to talk, but nobody could think of anything to say. Finally, I go, "So, Mr. Graham, my mom says she used to sing and dance with your son."

That kind of woke him up, and he started remembering Gerald and my mom when they were teenagers. Then he said, "Come here. I want to show you something." And I thought, "Oh my god, we're headed to the attic."

But it turned out that we went into Gerald's old bedroom. On the wall was a giant photo of the *Oklahoma!* cast at the end of the play when they come out for the last bow. There was Gerald in the middle like he was the star. Next to him on one side was this knockout blond babe holding a bouquet of red roses like a beauty queen always does. But he wasn't looking at her. He was zooming in on the girl on the other side of him. My mom. And she was scoping him out, too. She also had roses, but hers were in a bunch and they were all colors. Roses right out of a garden.

My mom gets all weepy and she turns around and hugs Hamilton for a long time. It was more like Gerald had just died, instead of Myrtle. I went back into the living room and sat on the sofa. I've never been so glad to get out of a place. From where I was sitting, I could see into the hallway. Man, the whole time we're there, I'm staring at the pull-down chain for the attic door. I'm totally freaked.

Before we leave, Hamilton decides to, like, cleanse his soul. He tells Mom that he doesn't have a clue about why Myrtle killed herself. Then he goes,

"She was barefoot in the dishwasher, you know. But she had a pair of shoes with her." My mom stands there, nodding her head, being sympathetic. Then he looks at her like he's doing a scene from a TV movie and goes, "Tap shoes. She had tap shoes with her." That's where you'd hear some kind of dramatic music and they'd break for a commercial.

I am blown away because a couple of weeks before Myrtle died, I was outside helping Ruth clean out the driveway bed. We had finished. Ruth had gone inside and I was putting things away. Myrtle sneaks up behind me and she goes, "Happy birthday dear." She's got a box wrapped up in comic strip newspaper.

I try to smile and wipe my hands off. "It's not my birthday," I say, but she gives it to me anyway. Man, you won't believe what it was. A framed picture of Gerald and his last pair of tap shoes. She tells me she thinks it's right that I should have them.

I thought that was weird enough by itself. Then I find out that she dies with her tap shoes like one of those Pharaoh dudes that buried the stuff they thought they'd need in the next world.

I'm stuck, big time. See, because I felt like I was about six years old and I wanted to tell my mom so she could make it all better. But the problem was that I hadn't told her that Myrtle had given me those things when it happened, so I sure couldn't tell her, like, after the fact.

The box is in our garage. I'm paranoid that my mom will find them or, like, maybe they're cursed. I'm thinking that maybe I should take them over to Ruth's and bury them in the driveway flowerbed. I've seen guys do that on TV. Problem is, I'll have to wait until the season changes and we dig up that pink stuff.

Another problem is, the guys on TV who bury that stuff, they always get caught. Man, every time.

So what I'm wondering is, since you're so fired up over this dishwasher story, would you, like, take those shoes off my hands? I'm, like, having nightmares about *Night of the Living* Dead dudes tapping down the sidewalks and Myrtle and Gerald are right in front wearing top hats and tails and carnations in their lapels. Not a pretty sight.

Chapter 7 - Madame Lily Fouché's Story

You are one of my former dance students, yes? No? Thank God. When you entered into the room, I say to myself, "That is not the walk of a dancer. An accountant, perhaps. A house painter. But not a Lily Fouché dancer. If I taught this man, I should die at this moment, be banished to a hell where I am glued into a dress of checked gingham and forced to square dance throughout eternity.

But you are not one of my students, so death brings no fear. Now the question is, why did you lie to the nurses in order to get in to see me? You, with your walk of the damned, are nonetheless, blessed with a face for romance. But I am an old woman, still graceful and wise, that is true, but I am much too old for you to be a suitor. Thus, the reason for your visit lies cloaked in mystery. You toy with me. I like you right away.

There is no time, however, in my life these days for the games of youth. The point of your visit should be revealed before I tire of you and slip in one of the convenient little naps I find so delightful. So it is best, my darling, to tell me why you have come.

Ah, so it is the unseemly demise of Myrtle Graham that brings you. I should have guessed she would haunt the peace of my last days. That woman had more tragic flaws than a local festival of bad Shakespearean actors. She should never have been allowed to live as long as she did. The guillotine should have been used to sever her feet from her body. She was to dancing like ketchup is to filet mignon. Thank God I rescued Gerald from the clutches of her cursed tutelage before it was too late.

The boy, ah, he was a miracle in tap shoes with more rhythm in one strand of his glorious sunrise of hair than you, my darling, have in the whole of your incredibly asymmetrical body. The most heart-wrenching decision I ever had to make was whether to concentrate on tap or ballet. He could have done both, you see. Any major ballet company would have signed him to play leading roles, even though he did not have the tortured soul of a Russian. No, despite Myrtle's efforts at entrapment, Gerald's soul was freer. American. "Yankee Doodle Dandy" all the way. And so, we chose tap. There was more potential for fame. It was right for Gerald. It was what Myrtle wanted from the beginning.

To agree with her was a heartburn for me. She wanted tap. She wanted Broadway. I hated to help her get what she wanted. But the little boy needed me to channel his talent, to bless his feet with the gift of my knowledge. I was good fortune for his life. I was his light and he, my sunflower.

It was not always so. My dancing past was filled with the pain of what could have been. The story I like to tell is one in which I dance on the great stages of France. A tale of France before the war. I regale you with glittering details of standing ovations and roses thrown at my feet, of handsome suitors in tuxedos wooing me with Champagne and caviar. Then the bombing comes and the invasion, the occupation, the resistance. I break your heart with how I starved and used my body to coax secrets from the enemy, how I faced danger and death every day to bring my beloved France the freedom so cruelly stolen from her people. With tears in my eyes and yours, I recall the arrival of the Americans, how I helped care

for injured soldiers, how stories the young officers told
of their wondrous country convinced me to journey to
New York, where I fought to regain my strength. But,
I tell you sadly, my youth had vanished, and though
desire to dance for the masses still smoldered within
me, I knew I could not rekindle the fire. I felt instead
a longing to share my great love with the children of
America. I became a teacher.

A lovely story, yes? Too bad none of it is true.
But it gave me students and a business and respect in
a Southern society that doted on a history of sacrifice
and loss. Life on the stage is a life of pretending. That
is what I had. No great harm done. I smile at how
a string of clichés tied in a pretty bow made such an
irresistible package.

But I am not what you would call a con artist.
I fulfilled my promises. The children danced with
passion and with charm because they wanted to please
Madame Fouché. They danced with beauty and skill
because I was truly a gifted teacher.

My darling, you should forget Myrtle Graham.
Perhaps your great story lies in exposing the mysteries
of Lily Fouché. A legend revealed. You are intrigued,
yes?

A fine ear you have. The accent is real enough.
You are accurate in your hearing. I am French,
though only half and only from Canada. Imitation
French, but a very good one, yes?

My father was an unexceptional man.
Uneducated, un-French, and uninterested in marrying
my mother. It was, to be sure, his greatest mistake in
life for she was a most exquisite woman, the kind that
would have been painted by Monet. Men clamored
for her, and she lavished them with attention.
Important men with much to lose dared to risk it all

for their time with my mother. Those men she never compromised. Their secrets and their wallets were left unopened. The men who would see her only once, she felt deserved less.

She was a woman of extraordinary talents, mostly involving illegal endeavors. Unfortunately, her talents for eluding the law were not as finely honed, her little crimes always discovered. Thus we found it necessary to leave our various homes rather quickly when I was very young, not even in school yet. Midnight, for me, was the hour of rapid packing and shadowed departures.

America was a ripe plum, my mother felt. And so, when I was seven, we approached New York as if we were invited. We found a room near an elegant gentleman's bar. In no time at all, my mother was making very close friends. Oscar Cleveland was her favorite of all, and when she became his, there was no longer a need for other lovers. A laughing, freckled man with a generous heart and a love of malted milk balls, Oscar was the owner of a vaudeville theater. He told my mother she should be on the stage. With her face and her legs, she would be a star.

Oscar Cleveland flattered my mother into becoming a magician's assistant. Soon no one cared to wonder how the silly rabbits came to be in the top hat. All eyes were on my mother. But that was only the beginning. She charmed the audiences every night until she had worked her way up to having her own name on the billboard. She was known as "The French Kiss," the most erotic stripper in the business.

Meanwhile, I became quite the showstopper myself, learning tap dancing and singing and comedy from the headliners. You could not ask for better training. But ballet was different. I went to the best school. It was a source of pride for Oscar. He paid for my lessons from the time I was nine until I was old enough that he thought he could buy me as well.

But he was wrong. I loved my mother dearly, but the desire to emulate her life was the last thing I wanted. I knew it would crush her to think that Oscar would betray her, especially for her own daughter. I felt I had no choice. When I was seventeen, I went on the road with a chorus line of six beautiful young women, five of whom did not have among them the combined talent to dance their way out of a paper bag.

For traveling troupes, frustration was a way of life. Discomfort dogged our every step. The trains were hot and crowded and the hotel rooms were dirty. My loathing for those five girls multiplied with each mile. In Detroit, I left them. Show business was not for me. But I was so very young and so very poor, and I had to do something. I found a dancing school run by a shrewd woman named Madame Clarisse Fouché. At first, she did not believe one so young as I could have the skills to teach, but she liked my accent and decided to pass me off as her daughter. We were very much alike in that we understood the need to create illusion, and so a story was concocted about how I had been trained in France. And voilà, Lily Fouché was born.

My mother had no problem accepting my deception, even though it meant she had been replaced. She found my new identity wickedly amusing and delighted in the fact that dozens of Detroit's finest families were being duped into believing their tiny spoiled daughters received dance instructions from an authentic French ballerina.

The trick, of course, was on me for I found that I truly enjoyed teaching children to be graceful and

poised, showing them how to smile and leap and spin
and bow. They adored Mademoiselle Lily. And why
not? At the barre, they stood like whispers while I
glowed.

I was not yet twenty years old. There was still
time to perfect the details of my image. Madame
Clarisse could see that, even though I could not. In
her effort to make me believable, she ordered me to
study the subjects she thought a real French ballerina
would have been taught. Each morning I would read
the dictionary, choosing twenty words that I wrote in
a notebook for the evening practice session where she
would quiz me on the meanings. I spent hours in the
library poring over huge volumes of French history
and art. Music of the great composers was what I
hummed as I moved about my bedroom at night.
My mind was very quick. I inhaled the knowledge.
Madame Clarisse was most pleased with me, her own
Eliza Doolittle.

Part of my role, she felt, was to create an air
of mystery. I was to be a dramatic moment, a head-
turner, a showstopper, a work of art to be observed
and adored from afar. Though she allowed me to
continue teaching the children, I was to be sterner
with them. I was to hold myself back from getting
personally involved. People were to stand in awe of
my beauty. She wanted for me to become more aloof,
more set apart from others. It was important to me
that I please her, so I did not mingle socially with
people my own age. Though I longed to go out with
young men, I kept to myself and discouraged advances
of would-be suitors.

Ah, you have the foolish courage to interrupt in
the middle of my history. Others have allowed you to
control conversations. Others are not as interesting as

Madame Fouché. But while I do not reward impolite
behavior, I do relish a man who propels himself
forward to reach his goals. You want to know the link
between my past and the truth of Myrtle Graham.
You shall have it all in good time, my darling. You
must learn to listen between the words, to hear what
is not being said. I tell you my story as a prelude
because my life had music and orchestration. Myrtle's
had only the broken record sound of a woman who
could not proceed, and the dependence on a small boy
to lift the needle.

   You can be forgiven for your desire to hasten
my tale. Your life moves like a gust of wind. You want
to lift everything up, shuffle it around, and move on
to disturb the peace somewhere else. But what you
must consider is that old women enjoy the undivided
attention of a handsome man. Any woman does. You
could coax syllables from a statue. All you need do is
patiently give the brown of your eyes. You will hear of
Myrtle, but you will hear of Madame as well. What a
shame you were not present in the romantic youth of
a French ballerina.

   Alas, there was no one that left me breathless.
The men gazed at me and tried clumsy approaches,
but their awkwardness only made me more resolved
to follow Madame Clarisse's bidding.

   And so it was. Madame Clarisse and her
beautiful daughter bestowed grace upon the heads of
the moneyed children of Detroit. I became a legend, a
strict and demanding mistress of ballet. To be in my
class was an honor, and parents paid the extra tuition
to be assured of a place at the barre.

   It was during my reign in Detroit that I
received word about the death of my mother. The
time of plenty was ending. Oscar Cleveland had lost

his fortune, and with it, his mind. He took my mother to the theater that was no longer his on the pretense that they would pack important papers, memorabilia. There in the dressing room that was once hers, he shot my mother and then himself. So, you see, this is not the first time I have faced the violent death of a woman.

It is not possible to compare the good-hearted dishonesty of my cheerful mother with the hurtful imbalance that skewed Myrtle Graham; nevertheless, in their endings, they are alike. They relied on the happiness men can bring; my mother on Oscar with his shiny shoes and malted milk balls, Myrtle on the clicking heels of a winsome boy. A woman can gift wrap her despair, but in the end, she is left with nothing but torn paper littering the floor.

Myrtle's death to me was a settling up for all the pain she had caused. Accounts were balanced. I did not mourn. With my mother, it was a different story. There are some who would scoff at the idea that Madame Fouché had a heart at all, much less one that could be broken, but you are trained to probe, to observe. You can see more. You have the eyes of a writer, eyes that listen. You are hearing and sorting the trues of a story. To you, people reveal themselves. I am no different.

My mother's death left me with a guilt that I could not shed. I felt, somehow, I had made her smaller. The joy that came from my mother, that part of me, I had crammed into the furthest corner of my life. I had stuffed it into the dusty trunk and forgotten it was there. More and more I had become the fictional character that Madame Clarisse had imagined. I missed my mother and I missed myself. I was consumed with grief.

Madame Clarisse worried so about my state
of mind that she suggested I go away for a while.
The winter was dismal enough to convince me that I
should, indeed, seek warmer surroundings.

Florida seemed the ideal locale for a young
woman to remove the coldness from her life. I
boarded the train and spent the majority of my
journey alone. Then in the middle of the night,
somewhere between South Carolina and Georgia,
the train stopped unexpectedly trying unsuccessfully
to avoid a cow that had wandered onto the tracks.
Everyone in the Pullman car was thrown from their
berths, and I landed in the arms of James Allen
Stevenson.

What I knew about the charm of Southern
gentlemen came from legend. He was everything I
expected him to be. Mannerly. Courteous. Witty.
The rest of my trip was spent in the delightful
company of James, who convinced me that I should
abandon my plans for Florida and choose, instead, to
vacation in the true flower of the South, Charleston.
His family was untouched by financial strife and, he
assured me, would be ever so pleased to entertain me
in gracious fashion.

I could not resist his sincere invitation but
insisted that I stay only two nights at his family's
home. After that, I would book a room at a hotel in
the city. James, like you, had a face for romance.
Unlike you, he had the style to go with it. Dashing and
handsome. He was quite my undoing.

When he asked about my life, I told him my
French ballerina lie. His mother, overjoyed that
James had found a lady with a European education,
wasted no time in introducing me to the cream of
Charleston society. My visit was filled with afternoon

teas and evenings of theater and small dinner parties.
James and I spent hours walking through the cobbled
streets, holding hands and aching for a private place
where we could kiss and make lovers' promises. I
was careful not to go too far. Madame Clarisse had
schooled me well in knowing the value of my virginity.
And I had seen the mistakes my mother had made,
what she had gotten for giving herself unwisely to a
man. I wanted more. I wanted true love before I gave
my all.

The time came too soon for my return to
Madame Clarisse, and, as I had come to realize, my
stiff Detroit life. I dreamed of the moment when
James would ask me to stay, but instead he told
me I should go home while he made plans for the
future. He had some considerations to make, some
alternatives to ponder. I thought he meant he needed
to prepare for our life together. I was a fool, yes?

Back in Detroit, I again became Lily, alone and
silent. No word came. No calls. After many weeks,
I surrendered my hope. Madame Clarisse, seasoned
to the ways of the world, comforted me but gave me
no encouragement. She said for me to make James a
memory.

Then one morning in June, finally a letter
came. In it, James said he loved me and missed
me. He was sorry it had taken so long to make
arrangements, but now we could be together. Would I
meet him, not in Charleston, but in Savannah? There
was a ticket in the envelope. One way.

What ecstasy I felt as I read his words aloud to
Clarisse. She beseeched me to stay, to guard myself
against this man whose love had taken so long to
surface. But I was not dissuaded. And in the end,
she gave me her blessing. The last time I saw her, she

stood on the platform at the station, arms by her side
while I waved good-bye from inside the train.

When I reached Savannah, James was waiting.
His arms were filled with bouquets of lilies, long-
stemmed and exotic. Calla lilies in one arm and tiger
lilies in the other. He was even more handsome than I
remembered. I felt radiant. I felt that everyone on the
train should be watching as the elegantly dressed man
and the enchanting young woman approached each
other and revealed their love in passionate embrace.
It was a grand entrance. It should have been filmed.

James took me to a very expensive restaurant
where I could not eat even a bite of my meal. I was
that happy and nervous. It was not a time to speak
privately with the waiters bustling about, constantly
in attendance. So it was not until afterwards, when
James had checked me into my room and the bellboy
had left, that we were alone. He took me in his arms.
Ah, the passion of a young woman who thinks she is
in the caress of the man who loves her truly. I gave
myself completely. It was my first time. I was naïve.
A foolish, foolish girl.

Take care to use your power wisely. Your face
gives you leverage. With it, you can pry a woman's
heart from its foundation. So do not pretend to love.
A woman often cannot tell the difference.

It was after the lovemaking, as I lay in his
arms and prattled on about being married, about
starting a family, abut life with him in Charleston,
that the plans he had taken so long to make were
revealed to me. You have already guessed, yes?
I was to be his mistress. To live in Savannah, far
enough from Charleston to stay safely hidden. Close
enough to allow frequent visits. He had done some
investigations, he said, into my past. I was not what

I had led him to believe, yet he loved me still. But he
had an image to uphold. Charleston would not accept
the daughter of a stripper, a common dancer, a liar.
I could not, he explained, expect him to subject his
family to the embarrassment, to the scandal if anyone
were to find out the truth.

But he loved me still, he said. He did not
want to live without me. I should be happy with this
arrangement. I would be well taken care of. There
would be no worries for me. A woman such as I should
be grateful for this chance.

It was a good thing that Madame Clarisse had
forced me to pretend aloofness, to hold myself apart, to
feign detachment. I was able to rise from James's arms
and wrap my robe around myself with dignity. Then I
told him to remove himself from my room and from my
life. It was only after he left and I lay alone in the dark
hotel room that I cried.

I felt very stupid for a very long time. Sometimes
I still do. Women make great fools of themselves for
men. We mask their faults. They do not deceive us. We
deceive ourselves.

It is the same story regardless of the leading lady.
Madame Fouché or Myrtle Graham. My mother or
Gerald's sweet Rebecca Montgomery. When a woman
bases her life around a man, she bases her life on ice.
When the ice melts, she has nothing but cold water.

So there I sat. What was I to do? I could go back
to Madame Clarisse. I loved her. That was true. But life
with her was destined to be one of isolation. And while
James had left me devastated, he had, for a short time,
wrapped me in warm affection. I desired that feeling
again. I thought, perhaps to start over in a Southern
city where hospitality was tradition, would be the best
idea.

Fortunately, my mother had left to me an amount of money, small, but enough to finance respectability, at least until I could find proper employment. In the days of the Depression, there were not many who could afford dancing lessons. But in the South, families like James Stevenson's continued to move in a world set apart. Culture was mandatory and the arts, they believed, were the salvation of society. I was quite lucky to have been heartbroken in a place where gracious living survived, at least for a few.

Madame Clarisse was not as fortunate. She struggled for many years until the unrelenting curls of Shirley Temple again brought children into her classes. Parents desperate for relief pinned all hopes of recovery on their children's potential to be a star. During the time that her studio was empty, I was able to send her some assistance. She had given me the ability to be Lily Fouché. And she had taught me well.

I located an exclusive private school where I interviewed with the headmistress in hopes that she would give me an introductory letter reference. I was quite charming, but to no avail. Society's children, it seemed, were not in need of a smiling Cinderella or a generous fairy godmother. What their parents wanted was the swanlike, elegant taskmaster who would demand excellence and discipline. I realized that I must yet again abandon warmth. I was perfect, yes?

I placed an ad in the newspaper. "French-taught ballerina seeking gifted students. Excellent opportunity for the serious minded. Previous training not required, but must show potential in audition to be accepted. Contact Madame Lily Fouché."

I had rented the upstairs rooms in the home of a respectable widow who was the seamstress for many

of Savannah's fine ladies. Her address was listed in
the ad, and it also helped me to become accepted, to
be sure. She allowed me the use of her parlor for my
auditions, which I scheduled for Thursday afternoon
and Saturday morning of the first two weeks in July.

The response was quite amazing. Altogether,
I auditioned thirty-four children and eighteen
teenagers. I knew that to seem credible, I must turn
down a proper percentage of students. The ones
accepted would then feel they had achieved an honor.
Those rejected were encouraged to take a class in
tap. I made it clear to parents that my classes would
be small to allow personal attention but that I would
require practice at home and dedication to the art and
image of ballet.

I presented myself with regal bearing. My hair,
I wore in a severe bun to match my posture and my
facial expression. I allowed no speaking in class, no
gum, no street clothes. Promptness was expected and
the door was locked after class started. If a student
missed two classes in a semester, her place was given
to one on the waiting list. Praise was given when it
was earned, and no one was coddled.

I was a tremendous success. Before the first
year was over, I had expanded my classes to the extent
that the parlor could no longer accommodate them.
Madame Fouché's teachings were quickly becoming
a rite of passage for girls who would be accepted into
society. That was, of course, not unexpected.

What most surprised me, however, was
the popularity of the tap classes. These small,
well-mannered young ladies were thrilled with
the boisterous rhythm of their feet. The need to
offer more classes forced me to search for a more
satisfactory studio.

It is safe to say that I came through the Depression much better than most people. The dance has brought me much good fortune, though no partner of merit. A woman is doomed to repeat her mistakes with men. It is like dancing a familiar pattern of footsteps painted onto the floor. One-two, fall in love, three-four, break your heart. Without fail we dance ourselves into disaster.

In the midst of my Savannah success, I found it necessary to leave. I fell in love with the father of one of my students. He was not married. That is what you are thinking, yes?

But no, his wife died of tuberculosis. I was not the maker of scandal. I was, after all, Madame Fouché. This man would come to my studio to pick up his teenage daughter, one of my longtime students of unexceptional talent. In the waiting room he would stand, leaning against the wall, wholly uncomfortable in a feminine world. And I would appear after the class, to acknowledge the parents and make myself visible to thunderstruck students who took their lessons from the assistants I had hired to teach beginners.

Stares were customary, but this man would gaze at me as if he hadn't the ability to blink. Yet it was not a wide-eyed wonder that stood behind his concentration. I was the focused obsession of his thirst. Aware, ah yes, I was very aware of him. Week by week, year by year, he stood in the same spot waiting for his daughter, never speaking. Then one evening, when the class was finished, he stood there, yet again. The same but different, for his daughter had been absent. He was there again when the last class for the night had been dismissed, and I came to turn out the lights, to lock the doors.

"Lily," he said, "dance for me." You, my darling, have a face for romance. James had a face for romance. This man had romance in his heart. A man like this is most dangerous of all for a woman. A man like this can make her believe.

I should have run that very moment. I should have banished him from the room and locked myself away. I should have screamed and struggled and kept him back at all costs. Instead I danced for him. For him, I danced.

I had the same dream as Myrtle Graham. We both wanted a change of life. For Myrtle, it was the longing for the stage and the applause of thousands— if not for herself, then certainly for Gerald. Through him she could be on the cover of magazines, be recognized, win honors. Through him, she would no longer be ordinary. She was waiting for him to change her. Her life was eroded by hope. She stood in the wings. She sat on the front row, waiting for the curtain to rise on the new improved life of Myrtle Graham. She was no bigger fool than I.

This man can change my life, I thought. I was consumed with hope, eaten alive. My life was void of passion and I longed for someone to desire me as a woman. I wanted to exit the stage. It was a life like Myrtle's I coveted. Husband. Family.

It is impossible for a woman not to hope. We lash ourselves to reality with ropes of thread, because, my darling, we do not really want the knots to hold. We want to be free to run to a fantasy, blind with stupid hope.

What happened in Savannah was truly a sinking for me. The man's daughter was his commander, as is often the case with children who have been led to believe the world is their personal gift. We began a courtship, first in secret because the greed of our entrancement was so powerful that we felt the urge to keep it all for ourselves. Later when we wished to establish a foundation of propriety, we began to make public our relationship. He was well respected in the community and I was known and admired by all. It should have been an accepted match.

But the daughter would have none of it. She didn't relish the idea of being overthrown. Quite an uncommon number of feminine wiles had been learned by one so young, and she used them all to keep her father to herself. In the end, we parted, not sweetly, for I was livid that he allowed the spiteful, spoiled girl to ruin my chance to change my life.

As the whole city knew of my rejection, I felt I had no choice but to leave. It was a great loss to Savannah, and well they knew it. I disappeared for a while, brooded and enjoyed, what I felt was earned, self-pity. It was good to be away from silly, clumsy children and parents who had no understanding for the art of the dance. After my period of mourning, I realized I had nowhere to go. Madame Clarisse had been dead for some years. I was stranded with only myself for company.

This was a fearful time for everyone. We were fighting the war, you see, and life became fragile. So many men were gone from the small towns and cities of the South that there were many jobs open to women who would step in and claim them. In Atlanta, I found a position in a movie house at night and on the weekends. During the day, I worked in a shoe store. I knew about running a business, you see, and I was most helpful to the owner who allowed me to make decisions that would have ordinarily been handed over to his son who had sailed away to fight the war in the Pacific. I did not dance with children during the years of the war. I put away the tap shoes and the ballet slippers and instead held in my arms countless boys whose lives were speeding beyond their grasp.

You think it is coincidence that my life made this parallel with Myrtle Graham's, yes? Perhaps it is more than that. Perhaps, fate had drawn a line between the two of us, tying us together in a slow dance of tragedy. Think, my darling, what would have been if only Hamilton had ended up in my embrace instead of the clutches of that woman. If I had my life to do over again, I would not have kept myself at arm's length from those young men. I would have flung myself willingly into their small-town stories. I would have found the happiness that Myrtle took for granted, that she did not deserve.

I was older than most of those boys, but it made no difference. I was a woman, beautiful enough to be a touchable fantasy. I was real and imagined. At the time, it was most satisfying to me.

When the war was finished, the shoe store owner's son came home. The thousands of men who had traveled through Atlanta settled back into their regular girls. And I was left again, unanchored and alone. There was too much competition in that big city for me to open a dance studio. I had heard many times from many soldiers about Columbia where they trained at the military base, so I decided I would begin my life all over again here. And here is where I stayed.

Once again my hair went into a bun and I resumed my teaching. I was quite established by the time Myrtle Graham first entered the doors of my business. I will never forget how she looked.

It was summer in the afternoon, the time of
the year when I held auditions for fall classes. Almost
always there is a thunderstorm to cool off August's
rage against Columbia. That day was no exception.
The rain had come irate against the heat, the steam of
its anger still rising from the streets. I thought, when
I looked up to see her standing there, that she must
have been caught in the middle and still was reeling
from the fierce argument going on outside.

She was as unfeminine as Milton Berle in drag.
Surely you know him from your childhood. You are
not that young, I do not think. Look him up and you
will see how Myrtle appeared. She was tall with pale,
yet splotchy skin. Her face and her hair were in direct
disagreement, and even as I watched her, more of
the frizzy strands escaped from the ponytail that held
them hostage on her head. The color could only have
been the result of torture. Her lips were painfully red
and had the harshness of being slammed in a car door.
She smiled, but it did nothing to soften her jutting
edges. With no style, she wore a drab raincoat that
hung almost to her ankles. Umbrella in one hand,
small boy in the other, both dripping excessively onto
my floor, she held onto them as if they were weapons.

But it was not her looks that gave me an instant
distaste for Myrtle Graham. I often considered why
the reason my loathing was automatic, and it pained
me to realize the truth. Perhaps it was because I
recognized in her what I most despised in myself. She
was a falsehood, the product of invention. You have
heard the expression "She speaks out of both sides of
her mouth." Yes? To me, Myrtle Graham looked out
of both sides of her eyes. It was as if she had a double
eyelid like some animals have. At times she would
forget to guard herself, leave the inner lid open, and

one could see what she truly set her gaze upon. It was not the rapt expression of a mother on her child. No, she was looking through the boy at what he could bring her.

Knowing her was like being on a raft in the ocean. There is peace in the floating, but beneath you are the stings of jellyfish, the dragging undertow, the barging hunger of the shark. And always, there is the threat of the breaker that comes from nowhere to send you flailing into what you most fear, the unknown. All of this I did not know immediately, of course. I learned by testing the water.

At first, it was just a woman in my doorway, and on the end of her arm, a dangled boy. Seeing him, one could almost forget the shock of the woman. Almost. You could forgive Myrtle most of her sins when you realized that she was the beginning of this beautiful child. What you could not forgive was that she had imprisoned him in one of those hateful yellow slicker coats that steam a child like a bowl of squash.

Myrtle said, "We are here to audition for your classes. Gerald, introduce yourself."

The boy needed no prodding. He stepped forward, put out his hand, and announced that he was pleased to meet me. "I am Gerald Graham and this is my mother. We know how to soft shoe. Can you do that?"

Imagine a tiny boy asking the great Madame Fouché if she could dance. Myrtle's smugness settled on her face like a yellow cat on a sunny porch. The confidence I saw in Gerald was extraordinary, not unlike the faith you carry in yourself. We three are much alike in that respect, but for Gerald, it was not manufactured.

He carried with him a small plaid valise. "Do
you have a dressing room where I can prepare?"
Again the boy surprised me with his words. He was
most self-composed. There was no sign of the usual
restlessness of the preschoolers, yet it was obvious he
was no more than four years old. I stood and came
around the reception desk to confront him. Almost
everyone, including my longtime students who had
known me over the years, was somewhat cowed by my
direct inspection. Even you, savvy reporter, you who
are paid to bombard others with questions that shake
foundations, even you are intimidated by Madame
Fouché.

But not this boy. He merely turned his face
upward to me like a little sunflower and smiled. I was
most intrigued by Gerald.

I was not in the habit of accepting students
under six years old. It was a waste of money. Parents
got only cuteness in exchange for their dollars, not
real dance training. I was prepared to turn Gerald
away, but my instincts told me to give the boy an
audition.

We went into the studio where Gerald took
from his valise a record. He then excused himself to
change clothes. While he was in the dressing room,
Myrtle began her nonstop barrage on the talents of
her son, her hours of training, her own dancing past.
She told me she had already spent months preparing
Gerald for his future as an entertainer, that she could
give him the proper lessons. What she felt he needed
from me were the contacts that could be established
through a real dance school. She wanted to be
discovered, to go places.

When the boy returned, he handed the valise
to Myrtle and then positioned himself in the center of

the room. He wore what was obviously a homemade costume: shiny black pants and white shirt, an ill-fitting tuxedo, and glittered top hat. Myrtle was behind me, and as I was intent on watching and listening to the boy, I was unaware of her actions. While Gerald rattled off a list of the steps he would include in his dance, she was preparing herself.

I heard tapping behind me, turned to see Myrtle. Her raincoat was gone, revealing an identical costume, equally as homemade. Approaching Gerald, she said, "We're ready for our audition, Madame Fouché."

Those two people astounded me more in fifteen minutes than in the whole of my life to that point. Never before had I been subjected to the audition of a parent, or any adult for that matter. They were always content to let their children impress or disappoint me in the tryouts. Many could not even bear to watch and would wait in the reception area until it was over.

But Myrtle was there to dance, to dazzle me with her stage presence. I was flabbergasted, and immediately, I felt an overwhelming sympathy for Gerald, whose own mother desired to dance rings around him. I should have thrown Myrtle out into the rainy street and slammed the door, but my interest was piqued. I had to see what she would do next. Also, for the first time in my life, my maternal instinct surfaced. I had an intense urge to reach out and protect the boy.

I started the record. What I witnessed was at once demoralizing and exhilarating. Gerald showed the kind of talent that adds proof to the theory of reincarnation. A boy that small could not have possibly learned to dance the way he did in four years, some of which he had not even the capacity

to walk. It was as if his feet had been brightened in
some other lifetime. But there was still more to cause
wonderment: the way he moved, the facial expression,
the grace. Gerald was the dancer I had been born to
hone.

But a hurricane in tap shoes, that was Myrtle.
Total destruction of lives and property. Winds to blow
off a roof. Power outages. A tidal surge to drown the
defenseless. It was devastating to watch, dangerous to
stand too close. For Gerald, it was deadly.

The boy danced with snap. He was clean
and sure. Myrtle's steps sounded like a blind man
wielding a jackhammer who hits his own feet and
jumps about in pain. Rhythm was a foreign language
to her. And her singing voice? Flat as a tire.

When they were finished, Gerald approached
me. "Madame Fouché," he said, "I like dancing in this
room. My feet can hear what they are doing."

Then Myrtle, not even winded for all her
stamping and bellowing, said to me, "When do we
start? We're willing to pay extra for private lessons.
I was thinking of twice a week, once for Gerald alone
and once for the two of us."

When Madame Fouché explodes, it is best
to seek cover. Often it was to enhance my image as
temperamental artiste. This time, the first in a long
line of barrages against Myrtle Graham, I was truly
livid.

How dare she presume that the incomparable
Madame Fouché would deign to accept the
gracelessness of a full-grown toad disguised as
a woman. I could feel a match ignite my fuse. I
could hear the hissing crackle as it burned toward
detonation. I knew I must place Gerald in safety
before I blew her into unrecognizable pieces, so I sent

him to the dressing room.

Then Myrtle felt the power of Madame Fouché's dynamite. "If it were not for your son, I would have you arrested for impersonating a dancer. You are suffering from delusions of grandeur. You should not even be allowed to park in the lot of my studio, much less enter the building. God would strike me dead if I even entertained the idea of showing you how to shuffle-ball-change."

Myrtle puffed herself up, glared at me. "My father taught me to dance. During the war, GIs lined up to spin Myrtle Graham around the floor."

"War often causes men to do things, horrible things, they would not, in times of peace, accept," I said.

Suddenly, her inner lid closed and she pulled herself back. "Very well," she said. "Take Gerald, alone. He will be your student until he is discovered. Twice a week to start. More when he is older. It is for him that I accept your scorn. My day will come." She liked to believe she controlled me. Ha! Madame Fouché was the only one she did not control, the only one she did not destroy.

I would not have chosen a dishwasher for Myrtle Graham's tomb. I would have selected a very large Cuisinart with three speeds, a wide variety of chopping styles and the option to dump her in all at once or feed her slowly into the blades. Feet first, of course.

I took Gerald not twice a week as Myrtle dictated, but three times. We started in September, the same month he turned five. In those days kindergarten was not so important as now, so Gerald was free to come in the mornings. On Monday, Wednesday, and Friday, we worked from ten until eleven. Myrtle was banned from the studio, forced to wait in the reception area with my secretary standing guard. She would not be offered coffee, and I had all the magazines removed from the tables while she was there.

You would call that petty, yes? I call it assurance. I didn't want that woman to feel comfortable in my place. She was like a bird that takes over the nest of another, making it her own, claiming residence. I could not afford to give her an inch. Perhaps you think I feared her.

No, I detested her. An eyesore to my soul, a blight on my spirit, she was. But worse, so much worse on the boy. On him, she was a plague.

I would watch from the window upstairs as they would arrive. She would wait in the driver's seat for Gerald to come around and open the door for her. I expected to see him bow. Then she would march him across the parking lot like a drill sergeant and an errant recruit. I could not hear her words, but they fell nonstop from her lips as the boy nodded and shook his head in whatever response she demanded. At the end of the lesson, again I would spy on them. Gerald would stand on the pavement performing new steps and combinations I had shown him, and she would copy his movements. Badly, I might add. It was quite bizarre and quite sad.

The lessons, however, made me gleeful, a feeling I seldom experienced and did my best to conceal. It would not do for Madame to giggle. Gerald learned quickly, and on the rare occasion when his feet made a blunder, his charm eased away any tension and the dance continued. Because he was only five, he was far from perfect, but there was plenty of time. No one was in a hurry, except Myrtle.

Often she would assail me with questions about his progress, ask if he were ready to make a debut on the local theater stage.

It was not enough for her that I featured him in every recital. For years he was the backbone of every program I produced. Her craving was quite unhealthy. She wanted him to be consumed with performing, and every performance consumed by him. Part of her regimen for him was a journal, a log of practice hours and steps perfected. He would bring it once a week for me to initial. I began to ask what else he had done during the week and discovered there were no accounts of baseball or birthday parties, only dance.

I watch you as I speak. You nod and smile as if believing every word, encouraging me to give you more and more. And I look into your eyes to find you sorting the facts, placing truth in small packages to open later and examine. You can see what is real and what is created to fill a need or gap. You would have known, as I did, that Gerald was being created, in much the same way Madame Clarisse had created me. Myrtle was giving him an image, a persona. As badly as I wanted the boy to dance, I could not bear to think his life was being artificially formed.

Remembering the solitary pain I bore when my life was blocked from all except dance, knowing how I longed to do ordinary things, I began my own campaign to cheer Gerald's afternoons. By this time, he had been my student for several years, and since he was in school all day, I taught him from four to five o'clock each weekday except Friday.

The lessons were supposed to be private, but I started putting Gerald in group classes just to place him with other children. He had no trouble

interacting. In fact, the little girls adored him. Alas,
there were very few boys in my classes, and those were
older than Gerald and rather dull. Already, he was
nine or ten years old, and I knew that soon people
would no longer think a boy in dance class was merely
cute. They would speculate that the boy was growing
up to a homosexual lifestyle.

To me that was not a problem. I had
been around theaters since my childhood, had
been surrounded by people of every sort. Sexual
differences, to me, were a matter of privacy. But for
most people, things were more narrowly defined in
those days. There was much stigma attached to any
difference. I did not want Gerald ostracized.

I could not detect any outward signs that he
was gay, but because he was so immersed in dance,
I was afraid he would be labeled. Real or imagined,
I began to see some traces of strain on his wonderful
face. Most children go through an ugly, awkward
stage when their permanent teeth are too big for their
faces and their arms and legs stretch out of control,
but Gerald was untainted by the usual physical
pressures of growing up. His tensions came from
pleasing his mother and realizing he was not typical.
In early childhood, awareness is blurred. Children
don't comprehend their shortcomings until they are
pointed out, usually by other children. This boy was
not made for worry, but he was beginning to see that
his afternoons spelled a difference that other boys
couldn't understand.

One September, after our summer break,
Gerald returned to class, tanned, more robust, and
beaming with pride over a broken tooth. He was
bursting with an idea for a recital piece. He had been
to Tennessee, to the mountains, and he wanted to

base an entire act on the life of Daniel Boone, with
rifles and Indians and coonskin caps.

"I have to be rugged, Madame Fouché," he said.
"I have to be strong. Only the strongest men survived
in the wilderness. There was no room for sissies."

I wondered who had called him a sissy, but I
did not ask. Instead we choreographed a recital piece
called "The Pioneers." It was the only time I saw him
dance for revenge.

At the end of that year, I decided to speak to
Myrtle about the wisdom of continuing with dance
every afternoon. I thought perhaps it was time for
Gerald to explore other aspects of his personality. She
would have nothing to do with it.

"If you will not teach him every day," she said,
"then I will find someone who will. We have not come
this far to have our dream crushed simply because you
say Gerald is not meeting his full potential."

"I am saying that Gerald has more to offer in
other areas besides dance. But more importantly, I
am saying that Gerald needs to have friends. He needs
to get dirty and bruised. He needs to laugh and make
rude noises with other boys. He needs to be normal."

Myrtle glared at me. She pointed her finger
at my face and gritted her words. "How dare you tell
me what my child needs. You are not a mother. You
have no idea about raising a child, especially one as
gifted as Gerald. You would delight in seeing him
rolling in filth and using vulgar language. You can't
accept his talent. You're jealous that he's better than
you are. You and Hamilton are just alike. We should
leave you both." And with that she stomped out of my
office.

I had met Hamilton Graham only a few times
over the years. He seemed wholly uncomfortable
even visiting the dance world. That is not uncommon
with fathers. Fathers of little girls are more pliable
to the idea of tutus and toe shoes because their little
princesses share joy with their exuberance. It is
contagious.

Fathers of little boys can accept it up to a
certain age, as long as the boy grimaces at the thought
of lipstick and jumps in a mud puddle on the way to
the car. But Hamilton's stress was so great that asking
him to sit down was like forcing him into the stocks.
In so many ways, Gerald was a punishment for him.

The next September when Gerald was
supposed to start classes, there was no call from
Myrtle. I saved the spots in my schedule that had
been Gerald's, but I began to wonder if that stupid,
spiteful woman would actually allow her son to be
taught by someone other than the best. Then on the
last day of registration, it was Hamilton who brought
Gerald in. It was late on Friday afternoon, and I was
alone in the reception area. Gerald came in first. His
eyes were almost as red as his hair, and there was a
deep sadness settled over him. His lips trembled as
he asked me if he was too late.

I thought he was alone, and I was nearly
around the desk on my way to gathering him up in my
arms, to surrounding my little sunflower with light
and warmth when Hamilton opened the door. The
two of them looked as if they had suffered through
the damage and shock of a murdering tornado. They
looked as if they had narrowly escaped disaster and
were rummaging through what was left of their minds
for something they could hold onto.

I was halted in mid-step. Hamilton stood next to his son. He cleared his throat. "My wife was unable to make arrangements this year for Gerald's lessons. If you have no more room, I understand completely, but Gerald wanted to try."

Gerald looked at me right in the eyes. He was never afraid of the great Madame Fouché. He gazed at me, and suddenly his face was free of distress. He knew me too well, you see. He knew his place with me was safe. "Everything is okay, Dad. Madame Fouché didn't give up on me. She knew I wouldn't stop dancing with her."

Hamilton seemed relieved but not happy. He had resigned himself to his tapping son. Have you ever seen a man in a hospital, a man who is not accustomed to wearing pajamas but must put on a new pair with a new robe and slippers and face the hateful fact that he is sick and out of control? That is how Hamilton looked. Disgusted and embarrassed. Defeated.

He told Gerald to wait in the car. The boy didn't question his father. After he left, Hamilton said, "I am grateful that you reserved Gerald's space. Dancing is not what I would choose for him, but it seems I have no say-so. I'm sorry that we are so late in registering. My wife wanted to explore some other options regarding Gerald's training."

I felt I had to ease Hamilton's discomfort and let him know that I was aware of Myrtle's unpleasantness, so I said, "Mr. Graham, from time to time a parent must question the directions a child's life takes. That is understandable. I am the best teacher for Gerald. That is undeniable. Wisely, you have realized that.

"What you may not realize is why. It is not because I am the best. It is because I feel that Gerald is a special child with abilities that go far beyond dance. That is why your wife wanted to sever ties with Madame Fouché. She is focused on dance, on success, on pushing Gerald to achieve her dreams. I am blunt, perhaps, overstepping, but this you should know. I believe the boy should broaden his horizons. I believe he needs more influence from you. He is your son."

You would think the man would be relieved to find that the dance teacher would suggest other avenues, yes? No, he looked all the more devastated. Perhaps he knew that he was not strong enough to battle Myrtle.

Week by week I worked on Gerald himself, encouraging him to try new activities at school. I told him cheerleading would help his projection and physical strength. I suggested he run for office because, I told him, social and political contacts were necessary for the arts to survive. Friends, I told him, would enhance his audience appeal and encourage more people to attend theatrical events. Shamefully, I used my influence to maneuver him to extend himself into other directions. I was right in doing this, yes?

Over the next years, there was more joy in Gerald, but not, I am sad to say, because of Hamilton or because of my efforts. It was because of Rebecca Montgomery. She was like a daisy worn on the lapel of a clown's oversized coat, the kind that squirts water into your face. She made Gerald gasp and jump back and laugh at himself.

Pairing them was an act of genius. Gerald had always been a favorite with the other students. They admired him for his talent, and they enjoyed his personality. Still they remained apart from him, star-

struck by the charming presence he possessed. But
Rebecca was different. She would pretend innocence,
but she encouraged him to play jokes on people, to get
into harmless trouble, to be naughty. She was quite
charming in her own right.

I waited for them to discover each other in
a more romantic way, and I wasn't disappointed.
I knew for years before their first kiss, they were
destined for love. It was what I would have wanted
for myself.

The French long for romance, yes? Even, my
darling, the French-Canadian. I was swept with desire
for them to be lovers. Not as silly teenagers, but later
as young people who deserved beauty and poetry
and passion. As their feelings for each other grew,
I watched. Many nights, I would stand at my office
window, peering down at Rebecca's car parked behind
the studio, imagining the soft kisses and the whispers
of future dreams.

I thought of myself in the arms of James
Stevenson and of the sweet pain of first love. How
I wanted those two to find the happiness I had been
denied.

Myrtle could not abide the thought of Gerald
loving Rebecca. For a while I thought it was jealousy,
that in her twisted mind she had a perverted desire
for him. But that wasn't it. What she wanted was his
fame. And Rebecca stood in her way. Her life was
based on Gerald's future on Broadway. She lived for
the day when they would leave for New York, just the
two of them.

I think she wanted Gerald to be gay. Her
biggest fear was that the love of a woman would
dissuade Gerald from what she felt was his purpose
in life. Myrtle hated Rebecca. I kept my contact

with Myrtle at a minimum. I allowed her to serve
on committees for refreshments or scenery or
fundraisers, but I never gave her welcome in my
private offices or classrooms. So I was quite surprised
when she came knocking on my door. She was
distraught, almost to the point of tears or rage. I
am uncertain which. She said she had reason to
believe that Rebecca was trying to trap Gerald into
a compromising position. She felt that Rebecca
wanted to get pregnant so that Gerald would have to
marry her. It would ruin her plans for him, she said,
Gerald's future would be jeopardized.

What she wanted was for me to spy on them,
to try to catch then and report back to her so that
she could stop the little schemer before Gerald was
damaged. My first instinct was to scream her out of
my sight, but I instantly realized that if I did not aid
her, she would find someone else less sympathetic to
Gerald and Rebecca. After years of acting, it was no
great feat to pretend an alliance. What I really tried to
do was protect them. I told her nothing.

I was in Charleston, but not to spy. Charleston
was, for me, the city of love destroyed. I did not want
the same for Gerald. As witness to their romance, I
once again felt the awakening of old emotions I had
thought to be dead. I had strong ties to the boy, of
course, but it was with Rebecca that my heart aligned.
I shared her radiance and her awe whenever I watched
her gaze at Gerald. It was joy and sadness that I
observed the dancing of their souls. The sadness was
for me, all alone in the city of James Stevenson.

You, young man, with your face of perfection,
wield a mighty power. You and Gerald and James
and all the rest. You steal our sleep, give us vanishing
hope, and when you have gone, the haunting vision

of your face cruelly reminds us of what we have lost. A woman aches for a man such as you.

Charleston was a place of pain. When Myrtle caught them there, it was none of my doing. In fact, she confronted me afterwards demanding to know why I had betrayed her. She tried to have me banish Rebecca from my studio, called the poor girl a slut and a tramp. But I stood up for Rebecca. "Leave them be," I told her. "Let Gerald be happy. Let him live his life. You have wasted yours."

She turned and stomped out of my studio. That was the last time I saw Myrtle until Gerald's death.

I regret that I even went so far as to play along with her selfish plan because it hurt Gerald. He came to see me before he left for the summer. "Madame," he said, "since I was a little boy, I have relied on you to teach me, not just about dance, but about life. You have given me success and attention and praise. I thought you had feelings for me. I thought you looked beyond dance at what would bring me happiness." He hung his head, dejected. I told him that was true. And then he lifted his head and gazed at me with a look of heart-crushing pain. "Then, why," he said, "did you tell my mother about Rebecca and me?"

I walked to the chair where he sat, kneeled down in front of him, and for the first time ever, I put my hands over his and then I touched his cheek. "My darling, I would never join in a conspiracy with your mother to hurt you. She asked for my help, but I never intended to give her the ammunition to bring you or Rebecca down."

He heard me, and he knew what I said was true. He even apologized for doubting me. He said to me, "I should have known my mother couldn't control you. You are the great Madame Fouché. No matter where I go, I'll never forget what you have taught me."

And then he was gone, my little sunflower
that I had taught from my soul. When I heard he
was dead, I mourned for the tiny boy who tapped his
first audition, for the beguiling child who entranced
the audience with his songs, for the handsome young
leading man who won the hand of the girl he loved
and the world he believed in. And I mourned for
Madame Fouché.

The funeral was like Myrtle, self-conscious and
overdone. She had Gerald's pictures on the walls like
it was an opening night. The poor boy was laid to rest
in white tie and tails. The dance students were asked
to walk in behind the casket. The spray was made of
white roses surrounding a top hat, a cane, and a pair
of his tap shoes. Hamilton sat like a dead man himself
while Myrtle sobbed for the world to hear. Rebecca
was not allowed to sit with the family. Instead she sat
between her mother and me, shredding a tissue into
pieces as tiny as the tears that streamed down her
cheeks. The girl was never the same after Gerald was
gone. Laughter was forgotten. She smiled and she
danced but with no joy.

Too soon after the funeral, it was time to make
preparations for fall classes. My heart was not in it,
but Madame Fouché had learned to continue in the
presence of pain. The show must go on, yes? Very
early on the first morning of registration, I came to the
studio to gather my thoughts. I unlocked the door and
went directly to my private office. Within only a few
moments, I heard footsteps in the waiting room, but
not just ordinary steps. It was tapping that I heard. It
was hours before the students were to begin coming,
but the steps were there. Madame Fouché would
not make a mistake when it comes to identifying the
sound of tap shoes.

I listened as the steps came closer, up the stairs
and down the hallway until they stopped outside my
door. Expecting a knock, I realized I was holding
my breath. An uneasy feeling slithered up my spine.
Madame is not one to be frightened, but there was
something in the sound of those feet that gave me a
sense of dread. The knock did not come. Instead, the
steps entered my classroom right across the hall from
where I waited.

Your eyes have become quite large. Perhaps
you think Madame Fouché is going to tell you she saw
the restless spirit of Gerald Graham performing an
endless time step. Perhaps you think the pirouettes
of an elderly ballerina have made her dizzy and
confused, yes? No. Ballerinas always return to the
ground. They are much too disciplined for the flight
of fancy. But I must admit that, for a moment, I
almost hoped it was my little sunflower returning to
dance for me once more.

As I stood, frozen and still, in my office,
the steps began to flap across the floor. Clumsy.
Disjointed. Bulky. And I knew it was Myrtle.

I opened my door, crossed the hall, and
watched as this buffalo stamped her hooves in a futile
attempt at dance. She wore a leotard and tights,
black as death itself and, what seemed to be, a pair
of Gerald's tap shoes. As I looked closer, I realized
they were strapped, so they had to be her own. It
was obvious she had not brushed her hair in days. It
seemed to be in a state of chaos, rioting against her
head. Around the room she spun and crackled, one
foot unaware of what the other was doing. Finally
she ended with a bow to the mirror. Her smile was
nothing more than a slash across her face. It was only
then that she seemed to notice me.

I do not know what I expected her to say
when she finished, but it was not what I heard. She
catapulted herself to where I stood, positioning her
body so closely in front of me that I see the tiny red
veins like latticework in her eyes. "You must be
Madame Fouché," she said. "I am Myrtle Graham.
I'm here to register my son, Gerald. He's changing
for his audition. Oh, but wait till you see him. He's
a dancer. Already, he's a dancer and not even one
formal lesson. Forgive my bragging. You don't mind
my warming up, do you? I must work very hard to
keep up with my son. We're a team, you see."

I was stunned into silence, and so she rambled
on for a few more moments before I was able to gain
control of the situation. "Myrtle," I said, "Gerald isn't
here. You must go home." I thought I would be able to
bring her to her senses, but suddenly she flew down
the hallway, opening doors and shouting Gerald's
name. "Oh, my god," she said. "He's not here. I've left
my baby at home alone, and he's so little. What must
you think of me?"

Before I could stop her, she was down the stairs
and out of the door. I followed her in the parking lot,
but already she was in her car. She didn't even back
out of the space but drove over the curb with a terrible
scraping noise and into the street. I went into the
studio, sat in my office and cried, not the expected
behavior of the great Madame Fouché. My condition
and hers, I passed off to grief, convincing myself
that time would take care of my tears and her erratic
behavior. I did not call Hamilton to warn him. A
mistake, yes?

For months I did not hear anything from
Myrtle or about her. I was relieved and thought all
was as well as could be expected. Then after the

Christmas program, I got a phone call. At first no one
spoke, but as I was about to hang up, Myrtle's voice
presented itself, hostile and irate. "How dare you not
list Gerald's name in the program. He was the star,
the best thing on the stage. Without him, your little
show would be nothing more than a cattle call of no-
talent brats. His heart is broken. He's in his room
right now, crying his eyes out. Look what you have
done to him. Just look." And with that she slammed
down the phone.

I was at a loss as to what I should do. Several
times, I dialed their number, hoping to speak with
Hamilton, but each time Myrtle answered and I hung
up. Days passed with no more incidents, and once
again I did nothing. After that, I had no more direct
contact with Myrtle for a long time. However, the
next August, my receptionist came into my office, her
face bleached. She closed the door, approached my
desk, and in a startled whisper, told me that she had
gotten a disturbing phone call from Myrtle reminding
us to save Gerald's space for private lessons. The poor
woman was quite distraught. She said that before
she could answer, a man's voice had come on the line,
saying he was sorry and to please forgive the call. It
was Hamilton, she was sure. I reassured her that
Hamilton would take care of Myrtle. I, too, felt great
relief that he was aware of Myrtle's actions.

Over the years, there were a few other strange
happenings with Myrtle, but none as alarming as
those. Once in a while, I would see her car parked
across the street from the studio, but she didn't
venture in. Almost every Christmas, a bouquet of
flowers would arrive at the theater. The card would
be written out "To Gerald, Break a leg." I thought
of it as a memorial. The year that I announced my

retirement, I received a letter from her. In it, she
accused me of sabotaging Gerald's chances of making
it in New York. She said I had vile designs on him
and had tried to turn him against her. She finished
by saying she was glad I would no longer have the
opportunity to corrupt young minds. It was the
closure I would have expected from Myrtle Graham.

That was the last I heard of her until I read of
her death. But there have been many times that I have
thought of her, for you see, I cannot remember Gerald
without being reminded of his mother. No matter how
hard I try. My little sunflower turned to my light, but
Myrtle, with the blackness of a solar eclipse, made him
hang his head and languish. If only I had been able to
shine brightly enough to save him. Ah, once again, the
great Madame Fouché has the unexpected tears.

So you have the damp eyes, too, my handsome
young friend. You see the pain of love. You feel what
others feel. Perhaps that is why they tell you secrets. It
is quite the burden, yes?

Do you feel what we weep for? It is not the
death of Myrtle, not the life of Myrtle. And certainly
not the love of Myrtle. No, my darling, she was a
reason for pain. She was a cause of hurt. Perhaps that
is what she finally realized. Perhaps that is why she
ended her life.

I wear regret like an overcoat, too heavy for my
rounded shoulders. An old woman, such as myself,
can also wear memories like a flowery perfume. Just
a touch at the pulse point and the fragrance of the past
gives the illusion of youth. But a dousing spray causes
the head to throb from the cloying scent of mistakes
and lost chances. Old women should remember this
when they try to catch the attention of a young stranger
with a heartbreaking face, yes?

DISHWASHER WOMAN STEAMS
BROTHER-IN-LAW

Chapter 8 - Joe Graham's Story

I don't give a good goddamn that Myrtle's
dead. Who the hell does? You drive two hours to talk
to me about her. It's obvious you didn't know her. If
you did, you wouldn't be wasting my time or yours.
Woman did nothing in her life but seek and destroy,
pretending the whole time that she was Harriet
Nelson. Made my brother's life a living hell. Gerald's,
too. Turned him into some pretty-faced mama's boy.

No, I didn't like her from the get-go. Scary
looking but so damn bold, it was like she was daring
you to keep looking at her. You ever see people slow
down or stop to stare at a wreck on the highway? The
bloodier the better. Or kids staying after school to
egg on a fight, cheering the punches. That same urge
made people notice Myrtle. Everybody wants to see
something horrible. Come face to face with terror, but
stand far enough away so that it don't touch them.

Never had any patience with rubber-neckers.
Don't get my kicks from somebody's misery. I put
myself the hell away from Myrtle and her kind. Damn
woman was bad news. Dumb ass brother of mine
wouldn't listen. Told me to mind my own business. I
shoulda busted his ass and dragged him the hell away
from her. But no, I left him to fend for himself. Both
of us lived to regret it.

Damn woman got under my skin like poison
ivy. The second I laid eyes on her, I knew she was
a trap. It was the Saturday afternoon of my first
weekend pass in Columbia while I was stationed at
Fort Jackson. Me and some buddies were down on

Main Street, hanging out at a soda fountain. Through
the window we see Harry Malone drive up in his
convertible. He was a low-key kind of guy, not a lot of
brains, but decent. Plenty of family money poking out
of his damn pockets. Hell, enough to own a car and
have the means to get it to Columbia where it would
be available for him to drive while he was stationed
there. That's how we knew him. A recruit with a car.
Goddamn, his name was as famous as General Ike's.

Everybody knew about Harry, liked him, too.
He didn't lord the fact that he had money. Just acted
like your regular Joe, the kind of guy a fellow could
count on.

Another thing about Harry was he could have
turned the ladies' heads if he had wanted to, but he
was the type who would stand around in the shadows
and never be noticed. Didn't like to call attention
to himself. Harry was ahead of us and scheduled to
be shipped out pretty soon. He only had a couple of
weeks left.

Anyway, we see him, and he ain't alone. He's
with a skirt. All us fellas start to feeling horny and
jealous, but then we get a close-up of the dame. In he
comes with this goddamn tree of a woman growing
out of his side. At first I think she has measles or
something broken out all over her face and arms,
but hell if she ain't splotched with freckles, blotchy
and inflamed like she had a rash. Harry, he has his
hands stuffed down in his pockets, and his head and
shoulders look like they were stooped from the weight
of her hanging onto him. Her arms are twining
around him like one of those vines that reach out
to the closest tree trunk, gentle at first, then finally
grabbing on and squeezing until the whole damn tree
is choked dead.

He introduces her as Myrtle, his beautiful
fiancée. Damn, we could have shit a brick. Hell, she
looked like a goddamn brick. But she was purring and
giggling and making eyes at him like she was stuck
on him for life. So we figure if love is fucking blind
enough to keep Harry from seeing what she really
looked like, then he'd be happy.

Next few days, we see Harry at the fort. He's
talking about coming back from the war and settling
down with that frizzy-headed dame. Got that moony
look on his face, sighing and talking mushy about
her like she was some kind of Rita Hayworth or Betty
Grable. Never had another woman that makes him
feel so alive, he says, so willing to take a chance of life.
Buddy of mine even catches Harry staring at himself
in the mirror. Harry gets real embarrassed and tells
him Myrtle thinks, that with his looks and her talent,
the two of them could make it big. My buddy comes
back and tells me about it, says he didn't have the
heart to laugh at poor Harry. But we think his brain is
in his damn dick.

On Harry's last weekend, he and Myrtle are
out at the USO club dancing tight. She's taller than
he is and has wound her smothering self around him
in tangles so snarled, I think he's dead already and
just don't know it. Inside me, there's the urge to chop
her down at the base, destroy the whole damn root
system. Why I was having that reaction to her, I sure
as hell didn't know. Some kind of sixth sense.

Why Harry was having his reaction to her, I
sure as hell didn't know either. But we were headed to
war. Funny things happen to a man when he knows
he's going off to kill other men, that maybe he's going
to die himself in a country where nobody will even be
able to understand his last words. Some guys need to

know there's a woman longing and praying for them.
Maybe they need to leave a heart that will grieve for
them if they don't make it back. Some men, like me,
have an awakening of sorts, get the ability to see right
down into the soul of a person. All of a sudden, you
know their motives, whether a person has goodness or
evil inside them.

I ain't saying I was some kind of magician or
fortune teller. I'm just saying that sometimes, when a
person's faced with the hard truth that he's probably
going to die, then he looks deeper and longer at what's
happening around him. Clearest goddamn vision I
ever had was before I went off to war.

How about you, son? Did you do your duty
for your country? Tour in Nam, maybe? No? Hell,
I ought to know better than to ask. That's what the
hell's wrong with this country. Men don't feel the
obligation. Don't get the military experience that'll
grow them the hell up either. You go to war, you get
your priorities straight. Pronto. None of this living
at home till you're thirty shit. None of this touching
your feminine side garbage. Worst thing that ever
happened to this country was when they did away
with the draft. Worst thing that happened to men,
too.

I was a recruiter. Hell, I've seen our army
forced to its knees. We're reduced to making
promises to little girls that they can be officers.
What's happened to the masculine side of the United
States? We ain't got the balls left to say that all you
soft young men owe the country for the rights and
the freedom you take for granted. Payback ought
to be demanded. Give the country what it needs.
Patriotism. Loyalty. Give the men what they need,
too. Self-respect. Dignity. Confidence. Pride. You

give that some thought before you write me off as a
goddamn relic from the past.

Maybe I'm old-fashioned, but when I was
young, we had what this country was built on, the
willingness to fight for what was right and put our
own lives on the line to keep what was important.
We were glad to fight for America. We thought she
was worth it. Values. That's what we had. People
nowadays got shit for values. Take a whiff, son. That
smell in America, it sure as hell, ain't perfume.

In my day, we knew what had to be done and
we did it. We knew we might die, but it would be an
honorable death, not in some yellow-bellied drive-
by shooting or by putting drugs in our veins. When
we left for the front, we had our lives in order. It
was important to do things right. Whatever the hell
mistake Harry was making with Myrtle, I couldn't
fault him. Just like the rest of us, he was going to war
to fight for the right to have his dream when he got
home. If his dream was Myrtle and making it big,
then more power to him.

The last time I spoke to him, he was setting
up a portion of his paycheck to go to Myrtle so she
could start buying the things they needed to set
up housekeeping and start a nest egg. Said he was
leaving her his car so she would have it easier while he
was gone. He had bought her a ledger to write down
expenses and the amount they had in savings. Poor
son of a bitch trusted her to love him.

Anyway, Harry leaves. We figure that's the last
we'll see of Myrtle, figure she'll be at home moping
over him. But goddamn, the very next weekend, she's
back at the club, swinging all around the floor, flirting
with the new guys. By the end of the night she was
latched onto one. I went over to her, grabbed her arm

and dragged her away from him. "What the hell do you think you're doing?" I asked her. She shrugs me off, twitches her hips at me, says, "Insurance, Joe. Harry's a nice guy, but he may not be back. A smart girl's got to cover her ass."

Scheming little bitch. I never in my life hit a woman, but goddamn, I wanted to flatten her every time I saw her. And I saw her lots. Saturday afternoons, she'd be driving up and down Main Street in Harry's car, backseat loaded with packages, stopping at the drugstore for a soda. On Friday and Saturday nights, there she'd be getting off the bus from town, coming out to Fort Jackson to dance with the GIs. Here's all these flowers of the South, you see, dainty and fluffed pretty. Put the horns on a priest. You could hear the giggles coming from that bus before the door was even open.

Anyway, me and my buddies always lined up outside the club deciding if we were going to send out the scouts or attack full force, picking out the likely targets and ready to fire our bombs. Damn full of ourselves, acting like jackasses. Of course, we quieted down some once those pretty little things started towards us.

Truth was, most of us were fresh out of hometowns smaller than Columbia. We were nothing but farm boys. And these sweet girls could have been our sisters or the girlfriends we had left crying for us. Those guys pathetic with homesickness took out after the pale and breakable-looking ones. Most of those girls looked like they were scared their little tits would fall off if a man stared at them, much less got a feel. Then there were a few of what you'd call real lookers, had an air about them that scared the living daylights out of us. Swayed when they walked, tilted their

heads. Cocky as hell and out for fun. We thought
they'd fuck us to tears. Hell, you could trust those.
They wanted what we wanted, a good time and a roll
in the hay. No secret plans. It was all up front.

Then there was Myrtle. Tall. Good god
almighty, the woman was sticking out over the tops
of those other little ladies like an advance warning.
Hair looked like it had been hit by a damn grenade.
Unrecognizable. Scattered in ruins. And holy shit,
the mouth on that broad was big enough to house
a torpedo. Bigger than Martha Raye's and Judy
Canova's combined.

You ain't ever heard of Judy Canova? Well,
look her up, son. Don't expect to be able to talk to old
people unless you got a frame of reference. Hell, all
you know is what you didn't sleep through in history
class. Tell you what. I got me the whole set of *Time-
Life* videos on World War II. Got the cassettes of all
the big bands we danced to. Take them. That'll get
you a frame of reference, I'll guaran-damn-tee you.
Send them back, though, once you're done.

Anyway, getting back to Judy Canova. She and
Martha Raye both were smart enough to know that
with mouths like theirs, you're better off making jokes
instead of expecting to be kissed. But that goddamn
Myrtle had a hell of a high opinion of herself, playing
her deceitful little game, thinking she could dance
her way into a man's heart and end up with a ring on
her finger. I was stationed at the fort for more than
six months, longer than most of the trainees, so I had
plenty of time to watch her, to hate what she was up
to.

Every weekend, there she'd be, laughing and
rubbing her shoulder against whatever man she was
standing next to. Most of the fellows got a kick out

of her with her flirty winking and her sassy remarks, thought it was funny that a girl who looked like her had the brass to think she was the cat's meow. She was a joke on herself. Lots of the guys would dance with her once or twice, and there was enough of them to keep her on the floor. Fact was, most guys were safe for just a dance or two, if you weren't the one she locked her sights on. My buddies had a running bet. They'd try to pick out the one that Myrtle would draw a bead on. Then they'd bet on whether or not she'd get her hooks into him. Me? Hell, I never saw any humor in the situation. I just kept my eyes open and stayed the fuck out of the way.

How she'd operate was like this. She'd dance her way around the room, examining the stock, as I called it. Before too long, she'd latch onto one GI, one that was real green. Those guys stuck out the same way poor Harry had. They wouldn't drink much, and they had that "I sing in the choir" look about them. You know the kind of guy I'm talking about. One that would wind up taking a bullet his first day on the front or else saving the whole goddamn platoon by accidentally falling on a grenade.

Poor sucker wouldn't even know he was her target. Anyway, she'd make an approach, like dancing over close to him and then asking her partner to go get her some punch. While he was gone, she'd start up a conversation with the target. That was pretty predictable. A lot of guys managed to sidestep that routine, so Myrtle had to come up with a more clever strategy.

You've had your share of modern women. I'd bet on that. From what I see on television, women don't wait around anymore for the man to make the first move. They're brassy and horny and full of that

equal rights bullshit. Putting notches in their bra
straps for all the men they've screwed. But hell, at
least, they're open about it. Scary maybe, but could
be exciting as hell to have a woman coming on to you.
Maybe you'll tell me some war stories of your own,
how you're winning on the fucking battlefield these
days. Make an old soldier happy.

Women in my day pretended to be innocent
and uncomplicated. But most of them were busier
than the top generals, making plans and deciding
where to strike next. Women ought to serve in the
military, all right. But not on the front lines. Put
them in as spies and strategists. They can sure as hell
trick you into thinking you're the most important
thing in their lives to get you to give them what they
want. And they can come up with a thousand ways to
twist you around their little fingers. Myrtle could have
been one of our most dangerous weapons.

Her best battle plan was to let the guy think
he was making the goddamn moves. She'd pick out
her mark early, just wander by, make a comment,
innocent and casual and off she'd go. She'd be all
over the floor, pretending to be interested in whoever
the hell she was dancing with. All the time, though,
she'd be making eyes at the victim, real easy like and
bashful, until he'd start to move towards her. Then
she'd let go of her partner and stand stone dead
still, big mouth dropped open, eyes blinking like she
couldn't believe what was happening. Stupid jackass
would walk right into her arms. But she wasn't
finished yet. Most times on the first dance with one of
those girls, you kept a polite distance. Hell, it was for
our own good. We didn't want them to know we were
sporting a hard-on that could hammer a nail.

But Myrtle would get herself situated in this poor guy's arms, look straight into his eyes; then her hand would ease up his shoulder to the back of his neck, and her fingers would start to rub along his hairline. Next thing you know he had pulled her close like it was his idea and they'd dance themselves into a shadowy part of the room.

She played the same fucking game over and over, trying to trap some dumb ass that was stupid enough to fall for it and marry her the hell away from small-town life. Local gal, name of Esther or Ethel or something like that, told me she was writing to at least a dozen boys all over the Pacific and Europe, banking on the chance that at least one of them would live through the war and come back for her. I figured she was keeping Harry on a chain with the rest of them, spending his money and driving his car.

Esther, Ethel, whatever the hell her name was, said that Myrtle didn't want just any ordinary GI either. She was looking for one with a face that had heartbreak potential. He had to be handsome enough to make women stare. Goddamn bitch told Esther that she wanted one to set off her own looks, make people comment on what a striking couple they were. Had to be tall. Had to be able to dance. Had to be pliable. Myrtle wanted someone who would take her to New York or California. Thought she had a chance at being a movie star.

We all thought that was one hell of a laugh, remembering Harry gazing at himself in the mirror. But Esther said Myrtle was serious. Said she had made her father take her to Atlanta to try for Scarlett when they were searching the country for the perfect woman to play in the movie. Came home and told people she would have gotten it too, if she hadn't

been so young. One thing for sure, she was one hell
of a conniver, same as that *Gone with the Wind* bitch.
Esther thought Myrtle had one hell of a nerve. I
thought she was fucked up.

But hell, as long as she wasn't hurting any of
us, we didn't do anything to keep her from getting
what she wanted. Let her have a go at it, everybody
said. Couldn't stop her anyway. Damn woman was
like a tank.

And who fell for her scheme? That goddamn
son of a bitch brother of mine. Danced himself right
the hell into her plot. What really burned my balls
was that she picked him out as a sucker. My buddies
were all over me about that one. "Hey, Joe," they'd
say, "what's the matter with your brother that he's got
to get his rocks off rubbing against Myrtle? Ain't he
ever had a piece of ass before?"

I tried to tell him the very first night what kind
of woman she was. I told him, "Stay the hell away
from Myrtle. Poison. She's poison, Ham. She's a
cocktease, a deceitful bitch. I've seen her with other
men. I've seen how she works. All my buddies
know what she's doing. They'll think my brother is a
goddamn fool."

Hamilton said to me, "Lay off, Joe. I'm a big
boy now. Hell, I'm a soldier. I don't need you to look
out for me anymore. Besides, you're wrong about
her."

I tried again to tell him about the other men
she was writing to, tell him she was using him to get
what she wanted. But this goddamn look came over
his face like he had been brainwashed, and I knew I
had lost him to her already.

Then he got mad, accused me of being jealous.
Hell, the last thing in the goddamn world I wanted

was Myrtle. "What's the matter, Joe? You can't take it because she fell for me instead of you? Is that it? Stay the hell away from her," he said, "and out of my business."

Just as I thought he was going to haul off and slug me, his face changed. He starts talking again, real quiet. "You gotta understand, Joe," he says with this dopey expression, "something happened to me when I danced with her, even before that. When I first looked at her. She's so alive. She's electric. I can't believe I'm this lucky, but I feel it deep inside; something's telling me that Myrtle was meant to be mine."

Son of a bitch sounded like he was a damn poet or something. Said he saw the way other men looked at Myrtle, how everybody wanted to dance with her, how she was what fighting this war was all about. That's when I knew how powerful that damn Myrtle really was. She was dangerous, and I couldn't do anything to save my own brother.

All I could hope for was that some other dumb ass soldier would come back and marry Myrtle before Hamilton had a chance to throw his life away. I prayed that Harry Malone would take the bitch away from my brother.

Women will fuck up your life if you let them. I had a girlfriend back in Tennessee before the war. She pretended to be in love with me until I joined up to fight. Hell, as soon as I was gone, she was giving it up to goddamn flat-footed 4-F Anderson Davis. Got herself pregnant and married. Wrote me a letter saying how sorry she was, asking me to be happy for her. Trust a woman, show yourself out to be a fool.

So I go off to war, leaving Hamilton in the clutches of Myrtle. Nothing I could do. By the

time the war was over and I got leave to go home to
Tennessee, Hamilton was in Columbia and getting
ready to marry her. He calls me up. Hell, you could
tell he had a shit-eating grin on his face just from the
sound of his voice. Says, "Hey, big brother, whatdaya
say you hop on a train so you can stand up for me at
my wedding?" I said, "Tell me you're not marrying
Myrtle and I'll crawl on my hands and knees to get
there. But goddamn it, Ham, I can't stand by and
watch you land yourself on that Venus's flytrap."

Hell, that was the nice part of the conversation.
Ham and me, we were never the same after that. She
stole my brother away from me. He hated me for
hating her and later he hated me for being right. Now
that she's dead, maybe he'll stop hating me. But hell,
I've got one whopper of an "I told you so" rumbling
around inside of me. Now, goddamn it, I haven't got
the spirit left to let it out.

Years went by without the two of us seeing
each other. I stayed in the army, was stationed all
over the world, from the most godforsaken hellholes
to the easiest paradise tours in Hawaii. Ham, he was
stuck in Columbia. Whenever I got leave I went back
to Tennessee to see my mother. My father died before
the war even started, and since me and Ham were
her only two children, she was living alone in the old
farmhouse.

There were plenty of other relatives close by to
check on her and give her company, but every time
I went back she spent hours regretting over the fact
that she never got to see her only grandson. She'd
show me pictures of Ham's kid dressed up in those
goddamn sissy-pants clothes, posing for the camera.
All over the damn house, she had photographs of him
stuck up. But the picture that burned my balls was

taken right after Ham's wedding. In it he and Myrtle
are about to leave for their honeymoon. They're
standing at the back of a car all decorated with old
shoes tied to it and signs saying, "Just Married." And
goddamn it, if it ain't Harry's car.

I figured old Harry must have bought the farm
somewhere in France. Goddamn sucker would never
know how lucky he was to get killed fast and easy in
a hero's war instead of dying a little every day with
Myrtle.

Damn shame that all women can't be like my
mother was. Hell, probably all men say that. You
think about it, son. You ever had any woman compare
to your own ma for goodness and love? Hell, no.
Nobody's going to treat you like your ma. At least that
was true of the old-fashioned mothers. Of course,
these days things are different. Shit, you probably
can't name five women who stay at home with their
kids. Damn women out in the world trying to act
like men. Maybe the next generation won't have
such a hard time finding a woman to compare to the
perfection of their mothers. Maybe it'll be easier for
them to be happy with a wife. Their expectations
won't be nearly as high.

My mother. Hell, she was a true saint, never
had an unkind word to say about anybody. Did
her good works for the church and didn't complain
when life showed its mean streak. And when she
talked about not seeing the kid, it was herself that
she blamed. She thought she hadn't shown enough
kindness and hospitality to Myrtle, didn't know how
to make it up to her. She wrote letter after letter
appealing to Myrtle, begging her to let the kid come
for a visit. My mother went to her grave thinking she
had offended that bitch.

When the kid was born, my mother wanted to
come to Columbia so she could help out. Ordinarily,
she wouldn't have considered it, thinking Myrtle's
mother would be there for her daughter. But during
Myrtle's pregnancy, her parents had been killed in
an accident, so my mother was worried that not only
would Myrtle have a new baby to deal with but also
would be grieving still.

She had written to both of them, Ham and
the bitch, but Ham wrote her back telling her that
Myrtle wasn't up to company, so Ma let go of the
idea. My mother was not one to stick her nose the
hell in somebody else's business. Then about a week
after the kid's born, she gets a phone call from Ham,
telling her that Myrtle's crying constantly and the
baby's crying constantly and he's losing his mind. My
mother takes the next train to Columbia.

When she gets there, all the blinds are closed
and the house is dark. She's about to knock when
Ham opens the door. He looks like he's the one that
had the baby, circles under his eyes and hair hanging
down. The house is filthy and his clothes are wrinkled
and dirty. My mother said she was shocked to see him
so thin and drawn, but she tried not to let on.

Myrtle, he said, was asleep and so was the
baby. He said it was the first time since they got home
from the hospital that at least one of them wasn't
screaming or crying. He said Myrtle hadn't allowed
him to ask anyone for help, not even their best friends,
and that he was about to collapse. Within a couple of
hours, my mother had the house looking straighter
and was at work on the kitchen. Ham was dead to
the world on the sofa, and she was thinking that any
minute the baby would be waking up and ready to eat.
She finished drying the dishes and was on her way

to look in on the kid, when Myrtle's bedroom door opened.

From what Ham had told her, she expected that Myrtle would be weak and distraught from childbirth and grief over her parents. And judging from the way Ham himself had appeared, she knew Myrtle could only look worse. But what she saw was more shocking than anything she could have imagined.

The door opens and there's the damn giraffe woman. Her nightgown was low-cut and made of satin, too tight over her bosom and stomach. My mother thought it was indecent for a woman, especially a new mother, to show cleavage. From what I gathered, even the cheapest fuck-the-fleet-on-a-group-rate hooker would have been embarrassed to wear it. The shoes she wore were heels and had puffy things on the toes, not what my mother called sensible shoes. They made Myrtle wobble even when she was standing still.

Her hair looked like it hadn't been combed since the baby came. It was in tangles and knots, the way field mice would build a nest. But Myrtle had a red satin ribbon tied into a big bow around all that hair like she had spent hours styling it to be perfect. My mother said it reminded her of the red fox that had gotten caught in some leftover pieces of barbed wire fencing and had twisted himself tighter and tighter until his fur was matted, and he died snarled in his own coat.

Myrtle's face was floury white and her freckles were like splatters of mud. But what scared my mother was the gash of red lipstick that followed the natural lines with the precision of a damn surgeon's scalpel. And the eyes. My mother said Myrtle's eyes were too bright. They were shiny from fever or sickness deep in the soul. She had them lined too, with thick black slants that pointed to herself.

Still my mother thought this was the result of all the damn stress and was feeling sympathy for the bitch. But then Myrtle starts talking, hissing out the words like she's spitting anger. She says, "What are you doing in my house? How dare you come here uninvited to try to take control of my husband and my child." Ma stands there too shocked to speak. Myrtle's voice gets louder and louder saying, "You won't take them from me. I have the power here. Things will be different now that I have Gerald. You'll see. You'll all see."

By now, of course, all her goddamn yelling has the baby crying and Hamilton's busting his ass to get to the hallway. Mother watches him try to calm Myrtle down, but the bitch is flailing her arms, hitting at him. She even bloodied his lip in the struggle. Ma can't stand to watch and besides the kid's wailing like a damn air raid siren, so she goes to the baby's room. But she can hear Myrtle threatening Ham that he better get my mother a ticket on the next train out of town or they'll all be sorry.

After a while, things get quiet. Ham calls the doctor who comes over and sedates Myrtle. Ma stays the hell out of the way, mostly in the room with the baby. Later that night Ham comes in to tell her she better go home to Tennessee. He says Myrtle's not herself, but the goddamn truth was that Myrtle was always her same evil, crazy-as-hell self. My mother doesn't ask any questions, just takes her little suitcase that she hasn't even unpacked yet and calls a cab.

And goddamn if my sweet mother didn't regret until the day she dies that there wasn't something she could have done for Myrtle. That stupid ass brother of mine didn't have the decency to keep that bitch from worrying my mother sick.

But at least he had the balls to stop her fucking Hollywood idea. That must have really pissed her off. Ham probably turned out to be more of a man than Myrtle wanted. She could manipulate him to a certain point; then his stubborn streak would kick in. At least I know she didn't get everything she wanted. That's some consolation to me. Goddamn, I hate to think of her being happy.

Hell, when I think about it, she couldn't have been too happy or she wouldn't have killed herself in the goddamn dishwasher. Fucked-up woman couldn't leave Ham in peace even when she died. Had to go and kill herself in a way that would get attention. That's why I think she did it. Wanted people to notice her. She did some god-awful things to Ham while she was living. Why couldn't she leave him the hell alone when she died?

The worst thing she ever did to Hamilton was to ruin his son. You know about Gerald, I guess. Maybe that was her revenge against Ham for destroying her chance to be a star. But whatever the hell it was, she turned that little boy into the biggest goddamn sissy you ever saw. First time I was around the kid was when my mother died and Hamilton brought his family to Tennessee for the funeral.

Here was this dressed-up little pussy prancing through the house before the services offering to help with the dishes and setting the damn table. All the other children there, cousins and what have you, that had grown up around my mother, sitting in her lap and loving the daylights out of her, were having one hell of a hard time keeping still and quiet like normal kids. Then along comes little prissy pants who hadn't

even spent a good goddamn on a stamp to mail her
a card, and he's so damn long-faced, so composed
and grief-stricken, they could have lined him up with
the pallbearers. A little soldier of death standing at
attention for a grandmother he hardly knew.

But he was only following his mother's lead.
Myrtle's got herself draped in black like she's the next
of kin. Church people bringing covered dishes were
met at the door and ushered into the kitchen by that
bitch. She's dabbing at her eyes with a wadded-up
handkerchief, got her hair pulled back into what, I
guess, she thought was a dignified bun. Looked more
like gnarly, rusted wires spiking out and ready to
snag into your skin. I thought again about my mother
comparing her to that mangled-up red fox.

I kept my distance and my peace, didn't want
my mother's funeral marred by a scene even though
I was throbbing to kick her ass out the backdoor and
all the way down the mountains. We got through the
services without any trouble between the two of us.
And it would have been all right if Ham had taken his
family home as soon as the funeral was done. But he
had to stay on until my mother's business was settled.

For a few days the house was filled with
relatives, and men and women separated themselves
so I didn't have to see her up close, only hear her voice
grating against Ham and the kid when she hollered
orders for them. She didn't want the boy too far out
of her sight, didn't allow him to get ten feet away from
the house without calling him back. It wasn't much of
a problem anyway; the kid looked like he didn't even
know it was possible to walk on grass, much less sit
down on it or pull off a piece to whistle through your
thumbs.

Hell, the kid didn't even own a pair of blue
jeans. Only shoes he had were the kind you wore
to Sunday school. All his cousins living around the
farm steered clear away from him. As far as they
were concerned, he had the damn cooties. Mostly the
kid sat on the porch swing or stood at the edge of the
men's circle while we talked baseball and cars and
fishing or told a few dirty jokes. Damn little shiny
clean boy flinching whenever somebody cussed. And
the whole time, Hamilton's so embarrassed that he
wouldn't even acknowledge the kid was there.

I couldn't stand to watch my brother's
humiliation, so I went to one of my relatives and
got some play clothes for the kid. Even managed to
find an old pair of high-tops, still had some wear in
them. I never said a word, just left them on Ham's
bed. Thank god, my brother still had some sense.
Next day, the kid's wearing the hand-me-downs and
Myrtle's pouting in the bedroom. Right off the kid
looks normal enough that one or two of the cousins
start playing with him.

Late that afternoon I was out in the barn, I
thought, by myself. But I keep hearing noises in
the loft. Goddamn mice, I think. But the noises get
louder, so I look up and there's the kid. Scared the
shit out of me to see this pale little face staring down.
"Damn, kid," I said, "what the hell you doing up there?
Ain't you afraid you'll get dirty and make your mama
bust a gut?"

"Damn, hell," the kid says, "a little dirt never
killed nobody. What the damn hell you think water's
for anyway?"

Damn hell? Where'd he get that damn hell
shit? I laughed so hard my fucking side was hurting.
Kid had balls after all. He thanked me for the play

clothes and said he wanted to go off to the woods with
me the next morning. Hell, how did he know I walked
in the woods every day? I sure as hell ain't about to
babysit no little scaredy-cat mama's boy in the woods
where he might see a snake and piss his pants, so I
tell him he can't go unless he gets his father to come
along. Kid says, "Damn hell, Uncle Joe, what do you
think I am, a miracle worker?"

But the next morning before sunup, Gerald and
Ham's stealing out of the house, eating last night's
biscuits, and hoping the fog don't beat them to the
edge of the woods or else Myrtle might spot them and
make them come inside and read some damn poetry
or something. The kid, he keeps looking back over his
shoulder, like he's afraid she's going to reel him back
in. But they make it to the trail where I'm waiting,
and the three of us do the things men are supposed to
do.

We spook a doe and two fawns. Kid's so
excited he almost shits his pants, but he keeps quiet.
Keeps quiet when he falls down, too, and I think
maybe he's not all pussy.

Ham's the one that acts most satisfied though.
Goddamn shame that Myrtle kept those two from
being a real father and son team. That night after I go
to bed, I hear Ham and Myrtle arguing, hear the boy
crying. I expect that the bitch is laying down the law,
but, shit and all in it, the next morning there they are
waiting for me on the trail. For a few days Ham and
the boy spent hours in the woods, sometimes with
me and sometimes not. Down at the creek's the first
time the kid gets to swim in a place where he can't
see the bottom. He's starting to get some color to
his face. Ham and me, we even get him to climb up
twelve feet to the old deer stand. He's scared shitless,

hyperventilating all the way up, and face whiter than a
nun's belly, but he makes it. Then the three of us just
sit there and grin at each other because it's so damn
good to be a man. Hell, kid even farts a couple of
times. Doesn't even say, "Excuse me."

Everything seemed to be going along smooth
if you didn't mind the silent treatment from Myrtle,
which nobody seemed to give a good goddamn about.
Then the kid fell out of a tree. Busted his lip. Broke
his front tooth almost to the gum line. Goddamn,
those two were afraid to go home. When we got there,
I found out why. Myrtle acted like it was the end of
the goddamn world. She cried and screamed that
his beautiful face was ruined. Damn woman threw
my mother's favorite flower vase across the room at
Hamilton. Said she was going to break his tooth just
like it said in the Bible. She's screaming, "An eye for
an eye, a tooth for a tooth."

I stood on the front porch watching through the
screen door, listening to her crazy raving. She's going
on about how Hamilton did this on purpose to destroy
her dream. Said it was a conspiracy to keep her and
Gerald off of Broadway. She said he had defeated her
once, but he wasn't going to do it again. That bitch
threatened to kill Hamilton if he tried to stop her
plans. And the whole time, Ham don't say nothing,
not a goddamn word.

I listened until I couldn't stand it anymore.
There's Hamilton like a damn henpecked coward bent
down over the pieces of Mama's vase, trying to pick up
the damn sharp edges of yellow and pink, and Myrtle
reaching for Ma's ceramic calico cat. Before I can stop
the goddamn she-devil, the cat's flying through the
room and connecting with Ham's forehead. Hits him
hard enough to make him lose his balance. One hand

goes to his head. The other hand, he jerks toward the floor trying to right himself before he falls. Damn if it doesn't land right in the middle of the broken glass from the vase. He lets out a holler about the same time that his ass hits the floor. Damn fool sits flat down on the ceramic cat, which crunches like bones. If he hadn't had on a thick pair of old hunting pants I'd loaned him, he'd have been picking glass out of his ass for weeks. Even so, he's bleeding from his head like a goddamn son of a bitch. Gerald's crouched in the corner of the sofa, mewling like a snared rabbit. His top lip's swollen out and his eyes are scared wide open.

Myrtle's still exploding, pieces of her temper shooting out like damn shrapnel, and still bombing the room with my poor, sweet mama's lifetime treasures: her collection of china cats, twelve painted butterflies of the world, and her imitation Wedgwood blue tea kettle. She's cleared the mantel and has her hands on Ma's "Mares Eat Oats and Does Eat Oats" music box that I sent her myself from California. That's when I jerk open the door, feeling pretty goddamn crazy myself by this time and mad as hell that this bitch is trashing my mother's house and breaking my brother's balls.

"Damn hell, Hamilton," I yell, "get up off your knees and tell her to go fuck herself. It's bad enough she's turned your kid into a sissy, but goddamn, she's done it to you, too."

Gerald's head jerks over to look at me; then he jumps up and runs crying from the room. What the fuck came over him, I sure as hell don't know. He cowers through the whole ugly scene with his lunatic mother, sitting tight and taking it; then I come in and he runs for cover.

Anyway, I throw myself across the room like
I'm diving for a foxhole, trying to knock the legs out
from under Myrtle. She won't go down for nothing,
but I destroy her aim so the music box lands on the
sofa. It starts playing the damn song like we're at a
party, getting ready to dance. Myrtle and me, we're
locked together tighter than a damn tango. Her, not
giving an inch.

Then I feel a damn woman's most clever and
damaging defense, fingernails. Myrtle uses hers to
bite into my arms, hurts like the devil and I'm just
about to surrender. We're staring eye to eye and I
can tell she knows she's about to win. Then I kick her
hard in the ankle, and when she starts reacting to the
pain, I use my other foot to slam down hard on her
instep. She lets go and my arms are free. For a split
second, I think I'm going to slug her. But I don't. I
just get the hell away from her.

I look at my brother still sitting on the floor,
Myrtle towering over him, and I know it's no use.
Can't save a damn fool from drowning if he won't give
you his hand.

Good thing we're about finished conducting my
mother's business because I sure as hell didn't want
to be around Myrtle, or Hamilton, for that matter, any
longer than I had to be. When you ain't married, you
don't have to put up with women, their snippy little
moods, their attempts to maneuver you, their selfish
demands. When you ain't got no wife, you don't have
to kowtow. Your bread ain't buttered by the little
bitch. You know what I'm talking about? You ain't
married either. You're young enough, though, that
you're still thinking someday you might.

Take it from me, son, no woman is worth
the pain she'll put you through. Best advice is love

a woman for a little while, during the time when
she's still trying to impress you with how sweet and
considerate she is. But don't go getting crazy with it.
You go and get in, what I call, stupid-love and you're
sunk. Leave her while you're still in one piece. She'll
call you a lowdown son of a bitch, but what the hell,
you won't be there to hear it. No skin off your balls.
You know what I mean?

It ain't right to hit a woman, but Myrtle made
me want to slug her. It didn't have to come to that
because I could walk away from her. I didn't have
to live with my stupidity, have it stare me in the face
every time I looked in the goddamn mirror. I could
walk away. Ham, he had to wake up with his mistake
every morning of his shitty life.

A couple of days after Myrtle's fit, they left.
Kid's back in his sissy-britches clothes. Ham's lugging
boxes and suitcases out of the house and packing the
trunk. Funniest damn thing of all is that all those
boxes were filled with what my mother left Ham and
his family, her legacy to them.

My mother was one hell of a precise woman.
She had put coded stickers on everything in the house
so we'd know who got what. She left Ham some
books and fishing equipment that belonged to our
father. And she left Myrtle almost all of her little
knickknacks, including the goddamn flower vase, the
calico cat, and all the other pieces the bitch threw at
Ham. Left her everything that sat around the living
room except the damn music box. That she left to me.
That's it over there on the bookshelf.

That night after the fit, I waited until everyone
had gone to bed. Then I packed the last cardboard
box myself, wanted to be sure nothing was left out,
that Myrtle got what was coming to her. I went to

the trash can and took all the shattered pieces of my
mother's treasures, wrapped them in newspaper,
labeled them "flower vase" and "calico cat" and so
on. Then I arranged them, side by side, the way my
mother would have done herself. When I was done,
I stuffed more paper around the bundles so they
wouldn't rattle and shift, taped the box shut, wrote
Myrtle's name on it, and put it beside the others
to be packed in Ham's car. Got a lot of goddamn
satisfaction every time I pictured Myrtle opening that
box and sticking her hands into all that glass.

     Those last days, the kid kept out of my sight.
But after they were gone and I had the chance to
go walking in the woods, I found what, I guess, he
meant to be a message to me. Up in the deer stand,
in black marker like I had used to label Myrtle's
box, were the words "dam hell." Over and over
again, "dam hell dam hell dam hell." He had gone
to the woods alone. Climbed up the twelve feet
alone, just so he could tell me to go to man hell. He
wasn't as much of a sissy as his dumb ass father.

     What do you think of that? Do you
remember the first time you told someone where to
go? Made you feel like a man, didn't it? Especially
if you knew you were right. Nothing more satisfying
when you're pissed off than letting somebody have
it. If you can't, you just keep getting pissed-er and
pissed-er until you back up on yourself like a damn
septic tank.

     My advice to you, son, is to piss your anger
the hell out of your system. Then zip up your fly and
walk away. That's what the kid did that day. That
had to grow him up some, show him he had balls.

     One thing about family, it's damn impossible
to forget about them completely. A few years go

by, you blur out the bad stuff, think maybe you try
again. Drink too much and start feeling sentimental.

You don't know what I'm talking about. Do
you? Well, wait until enough birthdays go by that
nobody remembers or some Christmas Eve when
you're all alone, and then see whose phone number
you end up dialing.

Whatever the hell the reason was, I called Ham.
Told him I was coming through Columbia on business
and wanted to see him. "Sure, sure, come on over," he
says. "We're looking forward to it," he says. "Problem
is, we don't have a guest room," he says.

That sounded like a piss-poor excuse to me.
"I've already booked a damn hotel room," I told him.
Shit, I would've gotten a better night's sleep in the
castle with Macbeth's old ball and chain than in the
same house with Ham's bitch.

What the hell kind of look is that You don't
think an old army lifer from the back mountains
of Tennessee is smart enough to know about that
Shakespeare crap, do you? Hell's bells, the old fart
can read. What do you think of that?

Open up your eyes, son. You're a reporter.
Ain't you supposed to be observant? Take a look at
that bookshelf, the one with the damn music box.
That's loaded with every goddamn collection *Time-
Life* has put out. I like to keep my mind sharp. I get a
lot of satisfaction out of my reading. Books are better
company than most people; that's what I've found
out. When I retired, reading made a hell of a lot more
sense than spending time watching those money-
hungry idiots on game shows or those holier-than-
thou talk show hosts who ain't happy unless they're
jerking out somebody's god-awful secrets or taunting
the audience into a slugfest.

I'm a goddamn self-taught man. Got me a
complete set of classics. Read them all, except for
that sissy *Little Women* story. Hell, I can sweep any
literature or author category those damn *Jeopardy*
big brains can come up with. Ask me anything.
Shakespeare. Dickens. Chaucer. Goddamn, you've
got to hand it to a man who writes about people farting
and gets it printed in a genuine leather, gold-embossed
collectors' edition.

But that's all beside the point. The point is that
I wasn't about to stay in Myrtle's house even if they
did ask me, which they did not. It was summer the
first time I went to Ham's. We cooked steaks outside
with their neighbors. Hell, it was fine with me to have
other people around. I figured it might keep Myrtle
from stabbing anyone or putting poison in the drinks.
Besides, I remembered Henry Overton. I knew we
could talk about the war and I could block Myrtle out.

The kid was older, but not much different. A
pretty boy still, but easier to have around because the
Overtons seemed to like him. With them, he acted
more normal. Myrtle was the one that was odd. One
would have thought she was entertaining the goddamn
President. She was bustling around, bringing out
trays of cheese and dips and snacks, refilling my
glass, smiling so wide her damn cheek muscles were
beginning to twitch. I wondered if Ham had taken her
in for shock treatments to make her more agreeable.

Overton's wife talked nonstop for the first hour
while she stood guard over the table with a fly swatter
in one hand and her drink in the other. Ham and
Overton both sweating bullets trying to grill a damn
perfect steak. The bitch flitting around like a goddamn
wacko Betty Crocker. Family life in the suburbs.
Hell's bells, you can keep it.

Then the phone rings. The kid breaks his
neck getting in the house to answer it. Myrtle's right
behind him. Overton's wife finally stops talking for a
minute when she hears the ringing. Damn, she was
like a prizefighter going to her corner after the bell.
That was my chance to get away for a few minutes.

I went inside to take a leak, walked in on Myrtle
lecturing the kid. At first they didn't realize I was there,
so I heard how she hadn't changed one damn bit. She's
giving him up the country about putting his damn sissy-
pants dancing lessons ahead of everything else. Kid
looks like somebody dished up a plate of shit for his
supper, told him to eat every bite, and enjoy it or else.
He says, "But, Mother, it's a birthday party and it's at the
skating rink. Please."

Damn, I hate to see anyone beg. Kid was
practically on his knees. I realize he's got the phone
receiver in his hand, so the other kid is probably hearing
the whole humiliating scene. Myrtle says something
stupid like, "Dance is your life. The answer is no, and
that's final."

With that she turns to find me standing in the
doorway, makes a shrill giggling noise, but glares at me
like she's expecting a fight. Hell, I ain't getting involved,
so I just ask where the bathroom is. She goes outside
and I start off through the house, leaving the kid to finish
his phone call.

I went down the hallway toward what I thought
was the john, but I opened the wrong door. Damnation,
but Ham wasn't lying. They didn't have a guest room.
They had a damn ballroom. I was standing there
remembering Myrtle dancing during the war with poor
old Harry Malone and thinking how sick she was to have
this place where she probably made my brother practice
with her, when I heard the kid behind me.

"This is where I dance," he says like he's
apologizing. "My mother always wanted to be a
professional dancer, but then the war came along and
she couldn't put her desires ahead of the country's
needs. One day I'll be dancing on Broadway and
everything will be right."

Kid sounded like he'd been brainwashed and
programmed by the damn KGB. Desires ahead of the
country's needs. Hellfire. Myrtle never put anything
ahead of her desires. Here she was with her tap-
dancing, prissy-britches robot son still trying to get
what she wanted.

I looked him straight in the eye and said,
"Listen, kid, you may not want to hear this, but your
mother has shit for brains. You ain't a total loss. Not
yet, anyway. Today it's only a birthday party, but
who knows what the hell she has in mind for you
tomorrow. Back in Tennessee, you had the guts to
fight for your manhood. You can still win the war, but
you're going to have to face the fact that the enemy is
your mother."

Kid stood there, flinched a few times while I
was talking. Then he took a deep breath and fired at
me. "You're wrong about her. She's good and smart
and unselfish. I owe everything to her. And we are
going to be famous. Just you wait and see."

Kid was as big a dumb ass as his father. I
ate my steak, drank my beer, and got the hell out of
Myrtle's territory.

I didn't go back to that house again until the
kid died. Talked to them on the phone a few times.
That was enough for me.

When Ham called me about the accident, I was
real sorry. But I didn't plan to go to the funeral. I was
halfway across the country and didn't figure anyone

would be comforted by my presence anyway. But then
Henry Overton called me. He said that Ham was in a
bad way and that Myrtle wasn't acting normal. Said
he was calling me on the sly and that I shouldn't let
Ham know he had contacted me. The arrangements
were getting out of hand and nobody seemed to be in
control.

I flew in the next day. Henry was right. It was
as if Ham was shell-shocked. Walked around the
house like a goddamn zombie. Then he'd disappear
and I'd find him out in the garden staring at the
roses or holding one up to his mouth like a damn
microphone. I expected any second that he was going
to start singing. I'd no sooner get him back in the
house than Henry's wife would be going after Myrtle.
She kept locking herself in that damn dancing room,
turning the music up full volume, and throwing things
at the mirrors. Broke them all. Every last damn one
of them.

I got the doctor over there, pronto. We sedated
the both of them. Had to do it. They were both so
drugged I doubt if they even remembered the funeral.
Myrtle was calmer, but all the fucking drugs in the
world couldn't keep her spiteful nature from showing
through, even at the services for her only son.

The goddamn bitch had to have her way, had to
have control of him even after the poor kid was dead.
I don't know if the kid was as crazy as Myrtle was or
not, but shit and fall in it, he did have a girlfriend. I
met her at the funeral parlor the night before the
burial. Henry Overton's wife and I had driven over
early to check on a few details and receive friends.
Henry was supposed to bring Ham and Myrtle later.
The place was packed, and the funeral director said
there had been a steady stream of mourners all day

long. I thought for a sissy-britches kid, he must have been damn well liked.

Overton's wife placed me next to the casket and kept introducing me as Gerald's favorite Uncle Joe. We hadn't been there long when she grabbed my arm and whispered, "Gerald's dear, sweet little girlfriend, Rebecca, just came in the door. He was head over heels in love with her. Such a pretty little thing to have so much sadness."

The fact that the kid had a girl was surprise enough, but when I looked across the room and saw her, it was a goddamn shock. There was an openness about her face that reminded me of my mother. A face that couldn't lie. Everything she felt was right there for the world to see. And I could see that she was battle scarred. She had the same expression I had seen on young, green recruits who had witnessed the most horrific tragedies of war. Her devastation was so damn complete that she had to be held up. She was flanked by two women; one of them was an older, happier version of the girl. I figured it had to be her mother.

On the other side was another woman, a tall jolt of a broad who looked as stiff as the last cup of black coffee in the pot. I found out later that everybody called her Madame. Hell, she didn't look like any fucking madam I ever met. She was about as sexy as an enema. She had on black like everyone else, but on her it seemed to sink all the way into the skin. People parted for her to pass and practically bowed when she walked by. In her arms she carried two flowers. One was white and long-throated, like an Easter lily but without the hope. The other one was a huge yellow sunflower, the kind you see by the hundreds in fields in Kansas. She headed straight

for the casket, straight for me, and when she got
there, she lifted the kid's hands and tucked the two
flowers in between them so that they rested against
his chest. Then she stroked his cheek with the back
of her fingers, turned, and held out her arm like she
was granting permission for the kid's girlfriend to
approach.

The girl left her mother and sort of trembled
across the room. With every damn step, her face lost
more color until she was as white as that death lily
in the kid's hands. When she was close enough to
touch the Madame's fingertips, she lifted her arm.
For a minute, I thought she would allow herself to be
steadied by the woman, but instead, she turned, and
I watched as she changed her focus to the kid's face.
Then she put her arm down and stepped up to the
casket.

How do you react to a crying woman? Most
men feel their balls turning to jelly when a woman
starts that boohooing shit. Me, I get mad because
I figure she's trying to get you to feel sorry for her.
That's when I stonewall her. Hell, I usually end up
slamming a door.

There have only been three women in my
whole life who have gotten to me with their tears. My
mother, of course. Hell, that goes without saying.
Second one was Marilyn Monroe. It didn't matter
how sexy she was or how many people were watching,
when that little lady's heart was broken, she let the
world see her cry. Her weakness was so goddamn
beautiful I couldn't help but feel sorry for her. Made
me want to punch whoever had hurt her, especially
that DiMaggio fool

And then there was the kid's girlfriend. When
that clear-faced little girl looked down for the last

time on the kid, when her shoulders started to shake and the sobs shuddered out of her, I couldn't swallow worth a damn. Lump in my throat big as a baseball. Most pathetic sight I ever saw.

Everyone was so taken with watching her and crying in sympathy that no one realized Ham and Myrtle had arrived. The only noises in the room were the sounds of sniffling and people shuffling around in purses and pockets for handkerchiefs.

All of a sudden, the peaceful grieving was shattered by a shrieking wail. The damn bitch, Myrtle, was making her entrance. Everybody turns to the door. Myrtle screams, "My baby, my baby" and lunges across the room like she's been shot out of a bazooka. The Madame and the little girlfriend are frozen in front of the casket like a shield for the kid against the onslaught of the bitch. But she's coming fast and the devil himself can't stop her.

She gets to the casket, glares, first at the girl, and then at Madame. Then she takes her arms and pushes them both away like she's saying, "Out of my way. I'm the mother here. I'm the one that's important. The pain belongs only to me."

The Madame recovers, pulls herself up and exits with her head so damn high I almost applauded. But the girl's not so composed. She loses her balance and causes one of the flower arrangements to topple over, clattering down and sending petals flying through the air. I'm close enough to reach out and steady her, and Overton's wife sort of steers her out of harm's way. But Myrtle's forgotten about the girl, at least for a while, because she's in the middle of a badly acted scene, moaning and draping her damn self over the body of the kid.

People are either trying to get the hell out of there
or else they're glued to their spots, so shocked by the
goddamn ravings of a crazy woman that they can't budge.

Then without any warning, right in the middle
of a goddamn word, she goes silent. Bang, no noise at
all. People are shifting their eyes at each other, a few
start edging to the door, but they only take a step or
two before there's a new sound in the room.

It's a low humming, then an ahhh-ing. Louder
and louder, until everyone in the room has once again
focused on Myrtle because that's where the goddamn
ahhh-ing is coming from. She turns around and looks
out at all the faces. The ahhh-ing stops. She spreads
her arms open, points her gaze at the ceiling like she's
waiting for an angel to swoop down, and then, shit
and fall in it, if she don't start singing. "Sonny Boy,"
that's what she's singing, and goddamn if she ain't
trying to sound like Al Jolson himself.

Starting out, it was soft enough that people
were straining to hear, but by the end, she's belting
the notes so loud that the funeral director comes
hot-footing it from his office to see what the hell's
happening. He's stopped dead in his tracks at the
doorway. I'm still holding up the little girlfriend,
who's trembling in my arms and close to passing out.
I look over and try to find Ham, wondering why the
hell he's not doing something to stop the bitch, but
he's backed himself up to the wall and has slunk down
into a damn fetal position. And still she's singing like
a nightmare.

She gets to the end. By this time she's down
on one knee, arms wide apart, voice blaring out.
When she finally lets go of that last note struggling to
wrench itself away from her, the goddamn bitch pulls
her arms in and crosses them in front of herself real

fast and dramatic, jerks her head down in a bow, and
waits about three seconds, for the applause to start,
I guess. Then she lifts her head, and the look on her
face was the goddamn scariest thing I've ever seen.
She was enjoying herself. She was in damn ecstasy.
She stands up and bows again, this time from the
waist. Hell, I don't even think she realized no one was
clapping. In her mind, I think she heard them.

Over and over, she's bowing and saying,
"Thank you. Thank you." People were staring at
her like they were afraid of her, but nobody was
doing anything to stop her. Finally Henry Overton
steps forward. He picks up a basket of flowers
and approaches her like he's going to present an
award. "What a performance," he says and hands
her the flowers. Then he puts his hand on her back,
looks at the people and says, "Because of previous
commitments, Mrs. Graham will not be able to
give autographs this evening. I'm sure you all
understand." And with that, he guided her out of the
room.

Nobody moved a damn muscle until Henry and
Myrtle were out of sight. Then the girlfriend's mother
came and collected the poor little thing from out of my
arms. By that time, Overton's wife was trying to pry
Ham off of the floor, so I went to help her with what
was left of my brother.

We got him in the car and I went back in to
let the funeral director know we were leaving. That's
when he told me there was a slight problem with the
limousine and seating arrangements for the next day.
Earlier Overton's wife had given him a list of who
should ride in the family car and sit in the reserved
section. The girlfriend was included.

The director said that not only had he received
an irate call from Myrtle but also was cornered in his
office by her before she, as he put it, paid her unusual
last respects. The cause of her distress was the
presence of Miss Montgomery's name on the family
list. He said that Myrtle refused to allow the young
lady anywhere near the beloved relatives of her son.

His problem was that he had already
notified Miss Montgomery of her preferred seating
arrangements and didn't know how to tell her of the
changes. The damn little coward wanted me to do
it for him. It didn't take long to figure out who Miss
Montgomery was or why Myrtle didn't want her
around. But goddamn, it seemed to me that the kid's
girlfriend ought to be given special treatment. I had
held her while she cried for the kid. I felt her grief.
And here I was going to have to be the bastard that
booted her out of the family limo.

When we got Ham and the bitch back home,
I decided to have a go at changing Myrtle's mind. I
figured, what the hell, she already hates me and I
hate her double, so I didn't have a rat's ass to lose.
Overton's wife was the one who had actually made out
the list, but Myrtle must have approved it before the
funeral director saw it. What I had to do was get her to
see things the way she did at first. But I might as well
have been bottling shit and trying to sell it as perfume.

Ham was no help at all. He sat on the damn
sofa, practically had his thumb in his mouth. Wouldn't
even answer when I spoke to him. Made me want to
shake some goddamn sense into him. I knew he was in
a bad way, but I was losing my patience with him all the
same. I am not a person to sit around feeling sorry for
myself. And I don't feel sorry for the people who do.

A real man won't stand still and let somebody
beat up on him, even if he's his own victim. Hell,
especially if he's his own victim. Get off your ass and
fight back. Ain't that the truth?

You're a fighter, aren't you? I can tell by the
way you look me dead straight in the eye. You're the
kind of man that will punch someone out if they even
dare to think you're an easy mark. You got something
to prove. Hell, that's the way it ought to be. Stand up
for yourself and don't back down for nothing. Keep it
that way, and you'll always be able to respect yourself.

Self-respect. Damn that stupid brother of mine
for losing his self-respect. It's like a woman losing her
virginity. She sure as hell can't get it back. But the
fact is, she only has to lose it once. Ham kept losing
his self-respect over and over to the ball-breaking
lunatic he married. He could have spoken up, if not
for himself, then for the girlfriend.

But he never said a word. It probably wouldn't
have helped if he had, but it would've made me think
better of him.

I said to Myrtle, "The funeral director has some
questions about the seating tomorrow."

Before I could go on, she started raving. "What
possible question could that idiot have? I, personally,
went over the arrangements with him this very
evening. The man is, without doubt, ill-prepared,
inept, and totally inconsiderate. He should not be
dealing with persons during their time of grief. I'm
going to see to it that his employer make the necessary
changes so that no one else will have to suffer through
his bungled attempts to be a consolation."

Goddamn, she was the biggest bitch I ever
knew. I told her that the man only wondered about
the change concerning Miss Montgomery and that I

was sure there had been a misunderstanding because
I was sure that the girl was supposed to sit with
the family. But as I talked, I noticed Myrtle's face.
Blotches started appearing, around her neck first, and
then spreading up her cheeks and onto her forehead
until they matched her hair. She looked like the damn
devil himself had rubbed her face in the dirt from hell.

Then she yanked herself out of the chair and
stamped around the room, swearing and yelling about
the girl. She said, "If that little trollop so much as sets
one foot anywhere near the family, I will see to it that
she is publicly humiliated and labeled for the slut that
she is. She tried to ruin my boy with her evil wiles,
tried to lure him from me. But no more.

"I know what she has done. She's flaunted
her body in front of the funeral director, rubbing
herself against him like she did to my Gerald. She'll
do anything to get what she wants. They're plotting
against me. They want the people of this town to see
Gerald as unsure, to think that he needed a female to
satisfy his desires.

"But I'll not have it. Gerald needed only one
female in his life. Not Madame Fouché, as she would
have you believe. Not that little Montgomery tramp.
Me. I was what he needed. And I'll be the only
woman of honor at his farewell appearance."

There was nothing I could do. The bitch
was farther gone than I ever suspected. So the next
morning I called Overton's wife, and the two of us
went to the Montgomerys' house to break the news to
the girl. Funny thing was, the girl wasn't surprised.
Seemed relieved that she didn't have to be that close
to Myrtle. I was sorry as hell that the kid hadn't lived
long enough to marry the girl. She was a goddamn
good little soldier.

We went to the funeral hoping it would go off without a hitch, but Myrtle had one more shitty surprise for us. The minister makes his opening comments, reads some verses, prays a couple of times. Everything pretty normal up to that point, then his whole damn demeanor changes. He starts clearing his voice, shifting his eyes around. I was wondering if he was sick or something. Then he says that we're going to break from the traditional manner of conducting a funeral because someone very close to Gerald wanted to speak about him.

Shit and fall in it. Myrtle stands up and practically dances up to the pulpit. If it hadn't been so god-awful, it would have been funny watching the faces of those same miserable people who had witnessed her singing show the night before. Hell, nobody knew what to expect. Even the man of God was at her mercy.

She positions herself like she's going to preach the sermon, even adjusts the damn microphone, reaches inside her purse and pulls out her written speech. Crazy bitch went on for thirty minutes at least. She started from the day the kid was born and included every event in his life that she considered herself to be a crucial part of. She told about how she taught him to dance and sing, about how he adored her. She told stories about how he used to say he was going to marry her when he got bigger, and how she knew that, of course, all little boys said that. But, she said, the truth was that she knew Gerald would never have left her. She finally finished with the information that if the accident had not happened, the two of them had plans to leave for New York where he was already signed with an agent who had auditions scheduled and dancing opportunities in the works.

It was a wagonload of bullshit. I knew it; so
did Ham and the Overtons and the girl. Maybe a few
others. But for most people, it gave the idea that the
kid was a sissy-britches mama's boy too light in the
loafers to have a life of his own. And as far as Ham
was concerned, the impression it left people was that
she was leaving him for a younger man, her son.

I left Columbia two days later. Glad to be out
of that crazy bin and away from the bitch's demonic
ideas. I called Ham a few times, but only at his office.
He sounded hollow, but there wasn't a damn thing
I could do to fill him up. After a while though, his
attitude changed. His voice was surer, sturdier. He
even laughed and told some dirty jokes. This was the
Ham I remembered. There was an old Tennessee
woods freedom and contentment in his voice. The
man was feeling like a man. From our talks over the
phone our relationship was beginning to grow again.
It felt damn good to have my brother back.

Well, I could have shit a brick when I get a
phone call a few months later from Myrtle. My first
thought was that Ham was dead and I'd have to battle
through another funeral. But it was better news than
I ever expected to get from her.

She's blubbering that she thinks Ham is having
an affair and that she's losing him to another woman.
She wants me to talk some sense into him. Hot damn
and fuck me to tears. After all those god-awful years,
Ham was finally showing some signs of life and some
guts.

I unloaded both barrels on the bitch, told her,
in no uncertain terms, that I hoped he was fucking
a twenty-three-year-old, sweet-pussy blond five
times a day and that he would father a whole brood
of beautiful, normal children. I told her that maybe

Ham would finally be happy and dump the pile of garbage he had been lugging around on his back since World War II. She slammed the phone down so hard my ears rang. Goddamn prettiest sound I ever heard.

I couldn't have been happier if I had been fucking a damn twenty-three-your-old blond myself. My first thought was call Ham and congratulate him, send him a telegram. Hell, hire one of those airplanes that fly a message across the sky to let the world know that my brother was getting a piece of ass and making a fool of Myrtle. But, hell, it wouldn't do me any good to tell him I knew. Ham ain't the type to entertain the guys with war stories. He'd probably deny the whole damn thing and then end it because he'd been caught. So I kept my mouth shut, for a while, anyway.

Brothers ought to confide in each other. You got any brothers, son? Hell, if you do, call him up and tell him one of your darkest secrets. There ain't nobody else in the world that will guard a confidence the way a brother will. You can tell a brother anything, no matter how bad. The bond will only grow stronger. Ham should have let me in on his life with Lydia. She was the other woman.

I found out about her, not from Ham, but from Myrtle. She called to gloat when she got Ham back into her clutches again. She told me that she had true friends who had been willing to save Ham from his sins. Someone had thought enough of her to rescue her husband and return him to the path of righteousness.

Goddamn bitch made me so angry, if I had been face to face with her right then I would have slugged her for sure. I told her to go to hell and hung up. I called Ham and told him I was coming to Columbia, that we had some talking to do.

We talked for hours. Me, trying to convince Ham to leave the bitch and run away with Lydia. Ham, repeating over and over how guilty he felt and how sorry he was to have caused so much pain. I kept telling him that it was Myrtle who had caused all the pain in his life and in the kid's. He deserved happiness and he should grab the chance to find it. Then I asked him to tell me about Lydia.

Goddamn, you should've heard the way he went on about her. She was beautiful. She was an angel. She was sexy and gentle and loving and funny. Ham was like a damn teenager in love for the first time. I told him he was a fool to choose Myrtle.

But he didn't listen. I tried for weeks to convince him, but he had sold his soul to Myrtle. If I couldn't make him reconsider, I thought maybe Lydia could, so I went to see her. Ham was right. She was a looker. I sure as hell wouldn't have kicked her out of my bed.

It turned out that she was a decent woman, too, and as much in love with Ham as he was with her. I gave her the rundown on the bitch, told her that Ham's decision to go back into that marriage was going to kill him. I used all my recruiter techniques trying to fire up her enthusiasm, make her want to fight for what she believed in. And I didn't let up either. I must have called her twenty times, but I couldn't shake her. She was determined to let him go. Guilt was eating up her damn insides. Hell, sometimes you got to screw morality and do what will make you happy.

Long story short, Ham stayed in a godforsaken marriage, Lydia faded out of sight, and they all lived unhappily ever after.

There's one more connection I had with Myrtle
that nobody knows about. You might call it a dirty
trick. People might call me a cold-hearted son of
a bitch for what I did, but I never let name-calling
bother me. Anyone who really knew Myrtle would
understand that sometimes you've got to get even.
You've got to have satisfaction, at least in a small way.

It was years after Ham went back to her. I
hardly ever spoke to him. Myrtle had managed to pry
us farther and farther apart. I blamed him for being
stuck and miserable. He couldn't face my disgust. It
was easier to be brothers if we didn't have to see each
other. So that was how it went.

Then a few years ago I got an invite to a
reunion of some of the old units from the war. Big
damn deal in Washington. Roll out the red carpets
for us vets before we all die. Hell, I went. There'd be
plenty of free beer, red meat, and I'd be comfortable in
a room full of old smokers instead of a bunch of damn
goody two-shoes waving their hands in front of their
faces and holding their noses.

Second day I'm there I'm scheduled to take
the special vets' tour to Arlington. Shit and fall in
it, if I don't get on the bus and spot Harry Malone.
Goddamn, we all thought he was dead. Turns out he
was on the beach at Normandy and spent the rest of
the war in France where he met a little mademoiselle
and ended up bringing her home with him.

Hell, we all thought since he never came back
for his car and his money, he must have bought the
farm. Harry got a good laugh out of that. What we
had forgotten, he reminded me, was that he had
family dough. A car and a couple thousand dollars
didn't amount to a damn load of shit to Harry. He
said he felt bad about leaving Myrtle at the altar, so

he figured he'd just trade off the car and the money
for his freedom. It eased his conscience and let her
remember him as a sweet dead hero instead of a
bastard who jilted her. Who the hell was going to
know?

Of course, he didn't have any bad memories of
Myrtle. He was stupid in love when he left. I didn't
tell him the truth about her either. Goddamn, how
would that have made Ham look?

Before we left Washington, he wrote his name
and address down for me, said to keep in touch. That
night I got good and damn drunk. That's when the
idea came to me. I'd have a little fun with Old Harry's
signature. And maybe one of those ghosts like Mr.
William Shakespeare was so fond of writing about
would pay our crazy little bitch a visit.

Hell, I was so drunk I don't even remember
exactly what the letter said, but it was brassy and
demanding enough to scare the shit out of me, and
I even knew it was a fake. It was pretty damn short,
just a few sentences. "Where is my car? What did you
do with my money? It's payback time. What will your
husband think? Love, Harry." Something like that.

I practiced Harry's name a long time before
I wrote it on the letter. Dirty trick? Hell, yes, and
damn well deserved. I had a good laugh imagining
Myrtle's face when she opened the envelope. Blame
it on the booze, but I mailed the damn thing that very
night. Didn't even wait until the next morning.

Oh, I see that goddamn self-righteous look on
your face. You're thinking you'd never stoop so low
even to get back at a bitch like Myrtle. Hell, yes, you
would. You ain't fooling me and you, sure as hell,
ain't fooling yourself. I know you. You'd do it in a
damn heartbeat. And you know why? Because you're

a man, and a man's not going to let somebody steal what's his without getting some damn satisfaction. I couldn't slug her. What the hell damage could a few poison pen letters do?

Yes, I did send more than one. I don't know how many, exactly. I lost track. Maybe a dozen. Shit, maybe twenty. And they were beauties. "Dear Myrtle, I'm coming to see you. Love, Harry." "Dear Myrtle, when you remodeled your kitchen, did you pay for it with my money? Love, Harry." My favorite was, "Dear Myrtle, We could have made it big in Hollywood. You wouldn't have needed a little boy to do your dancing. Love, Harry."

Ham doesn't know I wrote those letters. Hell, he probably doesn't know about them at all. But I don't give a rat's ass if he does. Not now, anyway. She's dead and he's free. Maybe I did help push her into that dishwasher. She was a goddamn crazy bitch from the get-go.

You want to know why my hate for her was so intense? Well, I always said she was like poison ivy. You don't have to touch poison ivy to feel the pain. Hell, all you have to do is run over it with the riding lawn mower, think you're ridding the yard of the hateful stuff. But the oils fly up in the air, land on your clothes and your skin. Pretty soon you've got the blisters and the itch and the rash just the same as if you had picked out a nice patch of it in the woods, dropped your pants, taken a dump in the middle of it, and wiped your ass with the leaves.

Want some advice from an old soldier? Find out quick who your enemies are, hate them for all you're worth, and don't ever stop, even after they're dead.

EVEN DISHWASHER CAN'T REMOVE
WOMAN'S INDELIBLE WORDS

Chapter 9 - Myrtle Graham's Story

When Myrtle Graham died in a dishwasher, the police found little information upon which to base her motives. The clues in her final note, as Ruth Overton said, disappeared down the drain, leaving many in doubt and wonder and anger. But there were reasons and secrets that Myrtle held to herself from childhood, reasons that multiplied with every year and every disappointment, real or imagined. Myrtle Graham's papers came in cardboard boxes, in tattered envelopes, and on dog-eared index cards. They don't tell the whole story, only Myrtle's distorted view from the cramped cube in which she spent her life.

From the diary of Myrtle Reed Graham, the child:

1 -- When I grow up I will dance forever and audiences will applaud. Father says I am much more talented than any other partner he has ever known. "Even mother?" I ask him, and he pretends to think for a long time before he winks at me and whispers, "Yes." Mother can only do slow dances, you see, not the fast tap steps that Father says are rootin'-tootin' crowd pleasers. We practice, practice, practice. "Dance with personality," he says, and I slam my feet down hard and make lots of snappy noises. It makes me feel like thunder.

2 -- Here are the places I will dance: the deck of an ocean liner on my way to Paris, a bridge at midnight when all the city traffic sleeps, in a mint green chiffon evening gown on the lawn of a country club in front of a lake with swans, Broadway, on

a float in a parade, in a hospital ward for people
who cannot dance for themselves, for kings and
handsome strangers and laughing children and movie
producers, in a room with mirrors on all the walls,
and everywhere, everywhere, everywhere.

 3 -- Cooking makes me want to throw pots
and pans and smash my mother's hateful brown eggs
against the kitchen window and hope they splatter on
her ruffly blue curtains. I hate and despise being sent
to the sink to scrub potatoes and cut a chicken into
wings and thighs and breasts and legs. I would hate
it if I were a chicken with chubby legs that couldn't
dance a single step. I would hate having feathered
breasts too heavy to carry, breasts like my mother's
stuffed so tight behind her bib apron as if they should
be lying in a huge roaster pan waiting to be basted.
My mother's hands are cracked and rubbed raw like
those clumsy potatoes. I complain the whole time I
am helping her, but she complains right back, even
worse than I do. She says I had better learn to cook
all the poor man's foods because I'll never be a rich
man's wife. She says I had better learn to stretch a
chicken down to the boiling bones because there won't
be any steak on my table. Women like us, she says,
are destined to be dishrags for men with silky voices.
The only man she says I'll be able to interest is a man
with an appetite for flat biscuits and potato soup. She
makes me repeat her recipes again and again like I am
saying the times tables. They are more important to
my future than numbers. That's what my mother says.

 4 -- According to my father, there has never
been anyone famous or musical in my family, unless
you count my Aunt Eulenia who plays the piano at
funerals in a place that is too small to even be called a
town. She knows only four songs by heart: two for the

weeping part of the service and two for, what she calls, the Glory Ever After in the Great Beyond celebration, ending part of the funeral. My father says she plays like a cat being thrown on the keys and would not get the chance to play at all except that her husband is the undertaker. He says that all my family will someday stand in admiration and awe of my talents as an entertainer and we will have to hire a full-time seamstress to sew on the buttons that keep jumping like crickets from the vests and coats and dresses of proud relatives and strangers alike.

5 -- There are two girls at school who won't play with me because, they say, I look like a red-headed woodpecker and sound like one, too, with my constant stammering feet. They say I am about as charming as a cactus and that I probably have sharp, stinging barbs under my clothes. They also don't like me because I am much taller than anyone in our class, even the boys, even the teacher. During lunch they get the other girls to cluster in a tight group. Then they whisper and giggle and stare at me. But I show them. I don't even stop eating my apple. I take a bite and start tapping closer. Take a bite. Tap closer. Take a bite. Tap closer. And all the while I am singing and chewing. Closer and louder I come until they run screaming away. Then I laugh and laugh. Someday they will be sorry they treated me so mean. I will never invite them to Hollywood or New York or Paris.

6 -- Making my father proud is the most important thing in the whole wide world. I will do anything to see his lips tilt into a smile and his eyebrows stretch way up his forehead giving him that glad-faced clown expression that makes me feel as happy as a circus. But sometimes I know I disappoint him when my steps aren't just so and my timing is

lazy. I hate myself forever when that happens. He stops talking and only nods or closes his eyes, refusing to watch me. He calls my feet, "the assassins of the dance." I promise I will get it right if it takes forever and I beg him for another chance, but he goes into the kitchen and tells my mother that they should go out dancing the way they used to before they had responsibilities.

We have a secret dream, my father and I. We will audition for a movie producer and become the only father/daughter song and dance team. Of course, my mother will probably have to come along with us even though she tells me daily that I am a silly, foolish girl to believe in fancy thoughts. She clucks her tongue and predicts that I will grow up to be miserable and sadly lacking for love, that I will drown in a sea of high hopes. Promises are like puffy clouds, she says. They seem soft and you would like to lay your head on them and drift along on their delicate, shaped dreams. But clouds are just close-packed water that changes to rain when real life heats up. Then you will find yourself plummeting to earth and landing rock-hard on bruising pieces of wishes.

7 -- My mother asks what if I had polio like President Roosevelt and couldn't walk anymore, much less dance? What if my legs were bags half-filled with wet sand and my feet were hard red clay bricks? What if, when I listened to music, the only movement left to me was to drum my fingers on the kitchen table? What if my father then had to take out an ad in the newspaper requesting little girls to be his partner? My mother serves me a new question every morning with my oatmeal. The answer is always the same. I would kill myself.

From the diary of Myrtle Reed Graham, the young
woman:

1 -- Something terrible and wonderful has
happened. My father has lost his job. I know I am
awful to be happy about that but, to me, it means we
have no reason to stay here anymore. We can leave
for Hollywood right away. In a few days my father
will realize this and we'll be laughing and packing and
practicing and talking nonstop about our first audition
and how we'll take the city by storm. But right now
my father is sitting at his bedroom window staring
outside at nothing. My mother is banging pots in the
kitchen. I hope I never become so old that I can't tell
when something perfect can happen just when we
don't expect it. My dreams are coming true. I know
it. I know it. I know it.

2 -- Tell me how I can be the child of such
uncreative, unimaginative parents. I always knew my
mother was dull and tired of life and that somehow
joy was stolen from her and she was left with an
empty chest of dreams. But I thought my father was
different. Didn't he promise me music and magic?
Didn't he know I believed him? I've been preparing
myself for our future. My future. Myrtle Reed, the
idol of millions of fans. Myrtle Reed, the miracle. My
father planted those dream-seeds. He watered them
and turned them to the sun until they became lush
and green. And now when they are ready to bloom, he
has tried to break the stems so they'll wither and die.
But I won't stand for it. He won't kill the life I was
meant to have. Let him die on the vine. I am stronger
than he is anyway and younger and more talented. I
don't need him. I have outgrown my father.

3 -- Atlanta can burn again for all I care. Hours
and hours driving there with my father complaining

the whole way and then standing in line more hours
for a few minutes of their precious time. The gall
of those no-talent casting idiots shooing me away
without so much as a chance to read the lines. How
positively stupid they are to deny that I am the most
perfect Scarlett in the whole United States. "Wrong
hair," they said. "Wrong type. Too large." And all
those mousy small-town girls behind me in line,
nodding their heads and snickering. It was just like
being in school when those hateful, jealous little
snippets refused to acknowledge my talents. And my
father was no help at all. He seemed to get smaller
and smaller, dripping and melting down into himself
like a candle. Well, I showed them who can act and
who can't. A stroke of genius it was to scream and
pretend to faint. Why, it's something Scarlett herself
would do. They were mesmerized by my domination
of the scene. They snapped to attention then, carted
me inside where the big shots were interviewing the
candidates. "Wait here," they said. "We'll get you
some water and you can rest before you leave." As
soon as they were out of sight, I recovered from my
swoon and swooped in on the auditions. Well, let me
tell you, I was a Scarlett they'll never forget. I flung
open the doors and flounced my Southern self right
up to their highfalutin faces, spouting Scarlett lines
the whole time. I made my mark. But those idiots
missed their chance to discover greatness. "So sorry,"
they said. "What's wrong with me?" I demanded,
slamming my fist on the table the way Scarlett would.
They were intimidated; I could tell by the way they
were looking at each other and stammering. Then
I said I was not leaving until I got an answer, and I
stretched myself out on the floor, crossed my arms
over my chest, and started to count. They bunched

themselves together and discussed me, glancing over
their shoulders now and then for another look. Before
I got to seventy, I had my answer. A scrawny, pale,
tight-faced man sidled over and asked if he might help
me to my feet. I very coyly extended my hand, and
for a moment thought to yank him down to me, but I
decided to be gracious. And when I had straightened
my skirt and shaken my hair into place, I gazed at
him and waited. "We very much regret the fact that
we cannot cast you as Scarlett, especially in light of
your most extraordinary performance; however, we
find that you are simply too young," he said. I did
not even give them a word in reply. No, I tipped my
nose higher than his little pea-head and made an exit
worthy of Bette Davis. I did it alone, with no help
from anyone. And where was my father, the man who
was supposed to be my champion? Outside on the
sidewalk in Atlanta with all the other losers.

4 -- Life has turned so dreary with the war and
the rationing and the solemn faces. It's like the entire
country is attending one big funeral. The Depression
was bad enough, but now every day we have to hear
about men who are missing and cities being bombed
and war orphans and a thousand other horrors. I
am so tired of everyone being poor and sad and
hopeless. I am sick to death of my father dragging in
every afternoon and complaining that we don't have
enough money and how things will never be like they
were when he had a good job and the respect of the
community. I understand his dissatisfaction with
being a grocery store clerk, but he had the chance to
leave, to experience the thrill of reaching for stardom
and he chose not to try, so I am not sorry for him. I
hate scrimping and getting by on secondhand dresses.
These are my most beautiful years. I crave starlight

errad

and wind and low-cut gowns and men in white dinner jackets. My plan was to have been out of this uncultured, unadorned town by now. By now I should be making my grand entrance onto the movie screens all over America. Where are the dreams my father and I imagined? The glittering, alluring Myrtle Reed has been trapped like a prisoner of war.

5 -- I have lost all hope for my father. It's like the war has bombed out his dreams and he is empty and ruined. All he does is sit by that depressing radio and listen for news. Once in a great while he will dance with me, but he is tarnished. My mother talks to him through tight lips and serves his meals on a tray like he is an invalid. I am sick of it all.

6 -- There is one good thing about the war. I get to meet lots of handsome and charming young men who are dying to dance with me. My father chides me about putting my arms around strangers who care nothing about my future and only want to touch a girl's body with their trespassing hands. But every weekend I feel beautiful and exotic with a magnolia behind my ear or my hair swept up on the top of my head so that my neck is exposed to the warm breath of a man who might die next week. Imagine that he might remember the fragrance of my skin and the twining curls of my hair as his last thought. I could keep one of those sweet-speaking boys for my very own and we could elope to Hollywood and be the toast of the town. I have waited forever to be transported to the kind of life I deserve, the life I've been training for. All those hours of practicing until my feet burned with the heat of the steps will pay off and I'll be recognized and idolized.

7 -- My behavior is shocking. Threateningly beautiful, that's what I am. Bette Davis is an angel

compared to me. I have power to make men plead for
my attentions. It's as if one touch of my fingertip can
cause them to forget their silly girlfriends and throw
themselves at my feet. I see them gazing at my legs
so finely formed from the years of dance. I know they
want to run their hands up the curve of my calves.
Pressing my body against a fast-breathing, young man
when he least expects it gives me the most delicious
power. I am enticing. I am Myrtle Reed. They won't
forget that name.

     8 -- It's so simple. I don't know why I didn't
think of it before. There are thousands of men
coming through the fort. Even if only a tenth of
them have star quality, that still leaves hundreds
to choose from. My ticket to Hollywood is dressed
in a uniform. America clamors for the heroes and
the women who love them. All I need to do is find
the handsome, warm-eyed soldier who will fit into
my dreams. We could be the true-life, wartime love
story couple whose amazing talents and personalities
couldn't be dampened by circumstances, but rose to
be all America's ideal. Our beaming faces will gaze
at each other on the covers of movie magazines, so
much in love and so joyful to have found each other
in the midst of strife. All I have to do now is find my
complementary man, the one who can chauffeur us to
Hollywood. All he has to do is hang on and I'll see to
the rest.

     9 -- People think women are the innocent ones,
but they are incredibly wrong. It's so easy to fool
men. They want to believe in the delicate, guileless
nature of the female. Manipulating them isn't even
a challenge. I can do it blindfolded. Acting comes
easily for me anyway. That is why I will be great
on the screen. I play the part of the homegrown

sweet, adoring girl with the wholesome ideals and undying love for the man of my dreams. I even take my mother's gummy fruitcake and pretend I spend hours mixing the batter and blending secret spices to concoct just the yummiest homemade treats for our brave boys in uniform. They can't imagine how I do it, what with all the sugar rationing. I tell them not to worry their handsome little heads about it, but to just enjoy my secrets. And those poor trusting boys fall under the spell of Myrtle Reed.

So far, I have three men writing to me from overseas, all of them planning a paradise life with the incredibly charming Myrtle Reed. A life away from hopeless towns and tired washed-out people. In my letters to them I paint pictures of the two of us bursting into Hollywood and exploding into movies. I tell them how easy it will be because of our magnetism and our natural winning personalities. They write back sweet, compliant letters saying how wonderful it will be to make our life together. This is the easiest thing I have ever done. All I had to do was nudge them with a few kisses. Maybe it's the fact that the war has taken them into danger and they want to believe that magical dreams come true. Or maybe they long for a crystal bud vase, sterling silver, Champagne, tuxedo, Paris, and the kind of long-stemmed life that I want. All I know is that my talent will drive us forward and whichever man I choose is in for the ride of his life.

10 -- My mother has noticed that I am getting letters from more than one soldier. I heard her talking with my father, discussing my morals, speculating about my virginity. My father was boohooing about how I wasn't his adorable little girl anymore. Well, he's not my adorable little daddy anymore either.

All he does is sit and mope about how he can't go to
battles to keep the world safe, how if he were younger
he would be leading charges and fighting for freedom.
He barely gets out of his chair anymore. What makes
him think he could muster the energy to lift a gun?
Anyway, I've decided to get a post office box. Then no
one will be snooping around my mail and I can have
as many sweet-dreaming soldiers as I want writing to
me. That's important because I need assurance that
when this youth-stealing war is over, there will be a
man coming home to me, that my plans will not fall
through again like they did with my useless father.

11 -- Every weekend I scan the crop of new GIs,
culling most of them until I select the best. I capture
him with my eyes and then I dance with him, using my
internal rhythms to lure him closer until he is a dizzy
victim of my enchantment. I make him feel special
and comfortable and brave and strong and irresistible.
He laps up the love at first sight routine and when I
touch the back of his neck with my fingertips, he is
mine. And all the while he is led to believe that he
has drawn me to him and I am powerless to withhold
myself from him. After he leaves I get romantic letters
full of promise. The best was William Jackson Nevers,
a tall and gloriously handsome, smiling charmer with
an innocence that made him boyish and eyes that
America's women would have left their husbands
for. Unfortunately, he died somewhere in the Pacific.
His friend wrote me a pitiful letter telling me about
his last moments and how he longed for me. I don't
let myself get carried away by any one of them. No
time to be heartbroken. I'm not doing this so I can
be miserable. I give them the hope of pleasure and,
after this war is finished, one of them will give me the
pleasure of my hopes.

Harry Malone is rich. And I have him. He has
everything that Nevers had plus money. Our move to
Hollywood will be so much easier without financial
concerns. Harry has said that he'll leave me his car
and have his pay come directly to me. Myrtle Reed
has scored big this time. Myrtle Malone. Harry and
Myrtle Malone, America's sweethearts. Yes, this could
be the one. I look gorgeous driving Harry's car.

12 -- I picked out a new man last night, a pilot
named Hamilton Graham. He's better looking than
Harry, but below average in the money department.
I think he has star potential. I'll have to be careful
though because he's got a watchdog brother who can't
stand me in his sight. I'm sure it's because I never
gave him the time of day. I wouldn't ask him to dance
if he were the last man on earth, much less run my
fingertips on the back of his neck. Anyway, Hamilton
and his friend are so cute with their Tennessee
accents and their thank-you-ma'am shyness. I'm
giving Hamilton the whole treatment: lunch with the
parents, Sunday afternoon swing, kisses much too
deep for a first date with a decent girl but much too
delicious to deny. Oh, yes, Hamilton, hold on to your
Tennessee hat; Myrtle Reed has a surprise for you.

13 -- Harry's checks have stopped coming. I
guess he's dead. Oh, well. If he were only wounded,
he would have written. A simple wound would be
okay, if it didn't affect his looks. And America would
flock after a wounded war hero. But I don't want a
seriously wounded man. It's not part of the plan. So,
Harry's off the list. The best I have now is Hamilton.
He writes dozens of letters, each one more lovey-
dovey than the last, spinning dream-webs about
holding me in his arms and kissing me at dawn. His
best letters have long paragraphs about adventures in

big cities and fancy parties and, yes, being discovered.
He says he could imagine himself playing the hero in
films about the war or entertaining soldiers in a USO
show. I hope he doesn't get killed. That would ruin
everything. There's just so little else to choose from.
Some of the other boys have lost their romantic nature
and only write about battles and how scared they are.
What do they expect me to do about it? I've got more
important things on my mind. This war can't last
forever and I've got to be ready to head for Hollywood
as soon as possible. In fact, I'm planning to take
Harry's money and drive on out there in his car. Then
Hamilton can come there as soon as he gets out of the
war.

    14 -- Hamilton was hurt, not enough to kill
my dreams. Thank goodness. But he insists on
recovering before we set out. He writes that coming
close to death has shown him what's really important
in life. I write back yes-my-darling-whatever-you-
say letters. I have to let him think he's in charge.
For a little while longer, I'll have to wait. But Myrtle
Reed is finally going to get her reward. He wants to
get married. He's coming home soon. Soon. Soon.
Soon.

From the diary of Myrtle Reed Graham, the bride:
    1 -- The wedding was straight out of a movie.
Hamilton was handsome and blurry-eyed with love.
I was breathtaking, of course, and when I sang to
him and danced our first dance, the guests were
spellbound. I could see their faces as we spun around
the floor. Some of them were actually standing
with their mouths open. I wanted my father to do a
dance routine with me, but he pretended he couldn't
remember the steps and that his back was aching

and that his shoes were too new. But the truth was
he'd been replaced as my partner and he knew it.
He couldn't stand to dance with me for the last time
in public where he would dissolve into pitiful tears,
regretting the fact that he had failed to carry me off
to Hollywood himself. Well, it was his loss. I was
elegant and charming and witty and sparkling as I
entertained the guests with my act. Imagine years
from now when they can tell their friends that Myrtle
Graham sang and danced for them before she was a
star.

     2 -- I am dying of niceness. Post-war jubilation
has left America relaxed and yawning. The months
since my wedding have passed in sweet boredom. I
could scream down the walls of this lovely honeymoon
cottage. Hamilton dotes on me. He caters to my every
desire, touching me and bringing me little presents. I
don't want silly pansy earrings and hankies with lace
edges. How can he be so naïve and small-town? He
has become a picket-fence husband, always wanting to
improve the yard with shrubs and trellises. The house
is pleasant enough for any normal woman. Henry and
Ruth are the perfect best friend couple and Hamilton
is a tamed pet. But I am not just any normal woman.
I have a destiny, a fate beyond compare. We would
have been in Hollywood by now if I hadn't gotten
pregnant so fast. I accepted the fact that we'd have to
wait until Hamilton was completely over the war and
his injuries, but that was only supposed to be a few
months, a year at the most. Who would have thought
I'd be pregnant less than a month after the wedding?
But that didn't have to be the end of everything. We
could have still been there, all three of us. When I
miscarried, it was sad enough, but I got over it. I
was ready to move on, but Hamilton was devastated.

Overnight he became controlling and demanding,
impatient and over-protective. Everyone watched
me like I was going to do something irrational, like I
was fragile and depressed over losing a baby. If they
only knew. I was depressed over losing valuable time,
over losing years when I could have it all. Now all
Hamilton talks about is having another baby.

3 -- The doctor has given me medicine to calm
me down. My parents are both gone and they're
telling me to be calm. I think my father drove the
car into the tree on purpose. I think he was sick of
life. He had every reason to be. And my mother.
She was born sick of life. I'm just plain sick to death
of life. They tell me I lost control at the funeral. I
don't remember a thing about it, but now everyone
is tiptoeing around me like I'm crazy or dying or
dangerous. I'd like to be a threat, a force, a fatal
mistake. Oh, God, get me out of this life. Let me be
Myrtle Reed Graham, the way I was supposed to be.

4 -- Well, Hamilton finally got what he wanted.
I'm pregnant again. Ruth smothers me with attention,
tells me how lucky I am to be having a baby. She
can't have one of her own. Well, I'd like to give her
my repulsive stomach and that disgusting morning
sickness. I'd even like to give her the baby. And
Hamilton. He is the most exasperating man in the
world. I should have married Henry instead. I could
have been in control of him. Without Hamilton's
looks, he never would have been a star, but he would
have been so much easier to contain. Maybe I'll lose
this baby, too. If that happens, I will leave Hamilton
and go to Hollywood on my own. I can't wait much
longer.

5 -- At first I didn't want to be a mother. At
first I thought my life was finished with the birth of

that squalling, red-faced baby, but then my precious little Gerald started kicking his tiny feet in rhythm and I knew my destiny was wrapped up in the diapers of an incredibly handsome baby. My purpose is to train this child to perform for the multitudes that will adore him and lift him up on the shoulders of stardom. Gerald Graham, the child star with talents well beyond his years. Gerald Graham, who will be more famous than Shirley Temple. Gerald Graham, who will sing and dance with his mother, the beautiful Myrtle Graham, forming the perfect Hollywood partnership of innocence and sophistication. My time will come.

Drafts of letters written by Myrtle Reed Graham:

Dear Harry,

My darling, how I miss you. I pray every moment that you are safe and will come home to me. Our little nest egg is growing. Each month I take some of the money you send to buy sets of sunny yellow dishtowels or matching coffee cups or the loveliest embroidered pillowcases. I'm going to make just the sweetest home for us filled with laughing and kissing. And, of course, my darling, we'll have the joy of singing and dancing. I can't believe I've found a man who shares my dream of life in Hollywood. I've always had a hidden hope, but never thought it would really come true since I am just a small-town girl. Who would have ever believed that this war would bring me a wonderful man with the talent and the courage to try for stardom? I must tell you this, even though it sounds silly. Last weekend I went out to the lake where we met. It's so important to keep our boys cheerful. I tried to have a good time so that

they would be entertained, but I missed you so much
I couldn't keep dancing. I had to get away for a few
minutes so I went out to the dock. It was a starlit
night and as I was watching the twinkling reflections
on the water, a shape began to form. It was you in
your uniform, looking so brave and strong. Suddenly
you were in evening clothes and you were dancing
across the water. You held out your hand and a vision
of myself stepped down from the night sky. We
danced beautifully. I could hear music and clapping
and a voice saying, "The world is yours." Do you
think I am crazy? Crazy in love with you, that's what
I am. You are my life, Harry. I know, with you as my
partner, I can have all my dreams come true. Kisses
and hugs. Be safe. I love you. Myrtle.

Dear Hamilton,
        You were here and gone so quickly, yet I feel
so much love for you that I am overwhelmed with joy
and anticipation for our future. Imagine, in the midst
of a war so terrible, meeting a man so wonderful
who shares your dreams and hopes. It's incredible
and, I know, we have a destiny together. I love you,
Hamilton. Please be safe and come home to me so
we can start our life together. The road to Hollywood
may be long and hard, but our love will make it a trip
to paradise. When I think of us in the years to come,
I see Champagne in crystal glasses and love on a bed
of mink. You and your handsome face court me in my
dreams at night and dance me into your arms. Oh,
Hamilton, I am the envy of all the girls. We'll have
our own little bungalow with real orange trees in our
own backyard and every morning I'll squeeze you and
then I'll squeeze fresh juice for our breakfast. I love
you. Myrtle.

Dear Mrs. Graham,

     By now, I'm sure Hamilton has told you all about me. Your son is a wonderful man. So wonderful, in fact, that he has neglected his own dreams because he wants so much to please you by staying in Tennessee. What he really wants is to try his hand at show business. This may come as a surprise to you, since he has probably never revealed his desire. But his handsome face cannot be denied. He will be every woman's dreamboat. When a man goes to war, he often thinks his hopes will die on a battlefield somewhere, but I'm going to do my best to make Hamilton's dreams come true. I'm just a small-town girl myself, but I'm willing to give the Hollywood life a try if that's what Hamilton wants. When this awful war is over, I know Hamilton will want the two women in his life to meet and love each other. Until then, please know that your son's love is safe with me. Warmly, Myrtle Reed.

Dear Hamilton,

     Please forgive me, darling. Of course, I thought you would have already told your mother all about us. It wasn't my intention to upset anyone. I love you much too much to do that. You're so far from me. If you were here, I could show you how sorry I am. I would shower you with kisses and tickle the back of your neck and oh, so many other things I would do to you. Perhaps your mother doesn't want to share you with another woman just yet. Maybe she still thinks of you as a little boy. But Hamilton, you are a man, and I love you that way. Tell her we love each other. Tell her we have dreams. Stand up for the woman you love. You're my hero. I love you. Myrtle.

Dear Mr. Claven:

 The death of my parents was, indeed, a shock.
It may be true that I was not in full control when
I made the arrangements for the services, but let
me inform you, my dear Mr. Claven, that I do not
appreciate your going behind my back to confirm
my plans. My husband is not the person to make
decisions concerning my parents. I am, and do
not forget that. My wish to sing was my affair and
something I know my father, at least, would have
wanted. It was not inappropriate, as you led my
husband to feel, and I am highly insulted. I know
the funeral audience was most impressed. Your
decision not to inform the organist of my plans was
inexcusable. Fortunately, for you, I am accustomed to
singing without accompaniment. When I face death
in the future, I would greatly appreciate it if you would
mind your own business and let me grieve in my own
unique way. Yours truly, Myrtle Graham.

McKenna Talent Agency
New York, New York

To Whom It May Concern:

 Congratulations. I am pleased to inform you
that you have been selected to receive the once-in-a-
lifetime opportunity to represent the biggest talent
of the future. Gerald Graham is not only handsome
and talented, but also charming and magnetic. He
sings, dances, and acts. He commands the stage even
though he is only a boy. Enclosed are photographs
of him in various costumes. You will notice how he
jumps off the page at you. Do not miss this chance.
Act now to secure your future. Act now and you may
also be able to sign Myrtle Graham, the talented

mother of Gerald and a veteran performer, as well.
Don't let this pass you by.

Gerald's Eulogy:
Notes: How I knew I was supposed to lead Gerald's
destiny
-- voice in a dream, vision of mother and child,
mysterious writing on wall, angels, dream of dancing
shoes, voice from sleeping baby
-- Why Gerald died -- evil forces, terrible disaster,
higher purpose in heaven
-- Big ending - something with memorial shoes, poem,
song, memorial dance, read letter he supposedly left,
another vision

Ladies and Gentlemen and Friends of the theater:
         From the first time I saw Gerald, I knew he
was destined for greatness and I knew it was my
purpose in life to give up my own dreams of stage and
screen in order to prepare him for his future. How
did I know? I could simply say, a mother knows, but
the truth lies much deeper. This is something I have
never spoken of to anyone except Gerald, but the time
has come now to tell all. In the hospital a few hours
after the birth of my beautiful son, the nurses left me
alone with him. I was gazing at the downy hair of
my sweet sleeping boy when he opened his eyes and
looked at me, clearly and with adult intelligence. His
little hand lifted from the blanket and he pointed
toward the window. I looked where he indicated,
out the window at the soft, rainy morning and there,
before my very eyes, was a vision. My mouth dropped
open and I quickly looked again at Gerald who smiled
and pointed yet again. The vision was a glowing
woman with long hair and graceful hands. She lifted

the hem of her flowing gown and on her feet were tap
shoes. At once the shoes were off her feet and in her
hands and she held them in front of her as a tiny angel
boy skipped down from the clouds and took them
from her hands. At once the shoes were on the tiny
angel boy's feet and he began to glisten as if tingles
of glitter were alive in his pores. Suddenly the skies
cleared and the sun filled the hospital room with a
sparkling rainbow of light that arced down on Gerald's
head. And I knew, for Gerald and me, it was more
than just a mother/child bonding. It was a bonding of
performers that reached farther than any mere family
tie can. For you see, I had not only gone through the
agony and travail to give him life, but also had passed
my talent on to him. I began very early in Gerald's
life to train him and teach him and provide the skills
he would need to achieve his dream. I remember he
would beg me to dance for him. "Light up the room,
Mommy," he would say. Sometimes I would indulge
him, but more often I would refuse. It was Gerald's
turn to shine and I didn't want to discourage him by
doing steps his tiny feet could not yet comprehend.
Yes, we had a special relationship, Gerald and I. He
would giggle and promise that someday he would
marry me and we would go away to Hollywood. Of
course, all little boys idolize their mommies but with
Gerald, it was different. I think he realized what I
had given up for him. As Gerald grew, I knew I could
not keep him to myself, I must send him forth so
he could be to others what I had been to him. Thus
he became the light you all saw in the dance studio
and on the stage as your hero and your teacher. He
influenced so many, and others far from here had
recognized his talent. Even at the time of his death,
I was negotiating with agencies worldwide to bring

his gifts to the masses. But many of you did not know other forces were at work in Gerald's life, forces that were tempting him to stray from his purpose and from me. He confided this to me and I believe he somehow knew that the only way to combat these forces was to leave this place. Gerald is gone from us to a safe haven where his talent will always be pure. Is he an angel? I think not. I believe he is now the brightest star in the heavens performing nightly in God's Show of Shows. And now I'd like to read a letter I found in Gerald's room shortly after his death. It was in an envelope stuffed inside the right toe of his favorite tap shoes, addressed to "Mother."

My dearest Mother, Lately I feel that our dreams are not to be. I am filled with a sadness, not so much for me, but for you. You, who have given me all the support and love. You, who gave up your own career to give me mine. You, my wonderful mother, deserved much more than the preparation. You deserved the satisfaction of making it big. I cannot stand to disappoint you. Please forgive me. I feel I will not carry out our destiny. Call it a premonition, if you will, but I feel an ending is near, an ending that will happen so I can remain as I am now, your pure and golden son. I love you with all my heart, more than anyone or anything in the world. You understood I was different. You understood that I was special. Make them understand, please. Your loving son, Gerald.

Letters from "Harry Malone" (Joe Graham) to Myrtle Graham:
Dear Liar,

You thought I was dead, didn't you? Well, I am alive and ready to ruin you and break your heart

the way you broke mine. I gave you money and my
car, not to mention my love. And what did you do?
You spent it all and used my car to drive yourself to
fuck with other men, like the lying bitch that you are.
I've been watching you all these years, waiting for the
perfect time to expose you. Well, you deceitful hag,
I've waited long enough. All my love forever, Guess
Who?

Dear Myrtle the Wicked,
        I'll bet you're happy to hear from me again after
all these years. I'll bet you've been worrying yourself
to death wondering what happened to your poor
sweet, stupid Harry who loved you and believed you
and wanted to give you the world. I'll bet you cried
yourself to sleep every night when my letters stopped
coming and you knew your dreams of a perfect life
were over. Well, you can stop worrying now. Harry
Malone is back and he's going to change your life just
like you changed his. See you soon, sweetheart. All
my hate forever, Harry.

Dear Myrtle,
        Do you ever have the feeling you're being
followed? Close your blinds, Myrtle. Lock your doors.
How's that unsuspecting husband of yours? I might
have to write him a little letter and introduce myself.
We'd have a lot to talk about, wouldn't you say? Rest
easy, Myrtle, it's not money I want. It's not even my
old car back. It's revenge I dream about now. The
truth will set me free. Harry.

Dear Myrtle,
        Have you figured out a way to trace these
letters? Wonder where I am and when I'm coming

to see you? Like the end of the world, it'll be when you least expect it. Ahh, Myrtle, I can't wait to see your blood red hair again. Blood. Now there's an interesting word, don't you think? Harry.

Dear Myrtle,
        Bum, bum, bum. Here I come.

Dear Myrtle the Fool,
        For the time being, I'm not coming to haunt you, at least not in person. Of course, now that you know I'm around and watching, will you ever really be safe again?
        I don't think so. But since I'm not going to get the chance to see you myself and have my little chat with your unsuspecting hubby, I want to get a few secrets out in the open. Remember all those nights during the war when you thought all the soldiers were carrying a torch for the popular Miss Reed? Well, old girl, they weren't. They were laughing at you and your ugly hair and huge arms and legs. You were like an old barn cow to them. Something to milk for a bucket of fun. They joked about that fruit-filled brick you called a cake. Guys danced with you, sure, but it wasn't because you were adored like you thought. They had bets on you and losers had to hold you close. A dance with you made going to the battlefield a relief. So how's it feel hearing the truth? Don't forget me, Harry.

Notes found on a yellow legal pad:
        Arsenic, hanging, carbon monoxide, sleeping pills, drowning, gunshot, slashing wrists, burning,

driving car into overpass, gas oven, jumping off
building, exposure, suffocation -- too plain, too plain,
too plain

Need something different, attention getter,
scene-stealer, showstopper. Newspapers. Media
coverage. I'm no ordinary woman. I am bigger than
life. I am bigger than death.

Painful vs. painless? Pain for them, definitely,
pain for them. A will? A note? A mysterious
disappearance?

Covering up the truth? Blaming them all.
Leaving a legacy of guilt. Letting me down. Stripping
my dreams like dirty linen from the beds. The
ruination of my life. Men. My mother was right.

Myrtle Graham's Leavings:
A recipe box for Ruth. Inside? Nothing but
blank cards and a note.

Dear Ruth,
I made this list for you because you were
constantly hounding me about my cooking, begging
me to tell you the secret ingredients in my specialties.
The truth was so simple that I was laughing to myself
the whole time. It was all a matter of adding one
extra spice or unexpected little surprise, of leaving
out something you thought you couldn't live without.
And lots of substitutions. Life is full of substitutions.
Nobody knows that better than I do. In cooking, you
can get away with it. I'm tired, Ruth, tired of making
do. A stove doesn't applaud when you sing. You can't
dance with a dishwasher.

In my chicken salad, I chop up a Granny Smith
apple and use salad dressing instead of mayonnaise.

The famous fruitcake recipe takes applesauce

and honey to moisten the batter.

When you make the applesauce, use two teaspoons of horseradish.

To make the meatloaf lighter, use a cup of water.

Use dill pickles instead of sweet in tuna salad.

Also I add dill pickle juice to my hamburger meat.

Before you flour the chicken for frying, marinate it in apple juice.

To cut the bitterness of the tomatoes in spaghetti sauce, use a little brown sugar.

Cook your grits in buttermilk instead of water.

After you boil chicken, use the broth for cooking your rice or potatoes.

For the squash casserole, mix ground peanuts with sour cream and cream of chicken soup.

Squeeze a lime into your banana pudding.

When you cook a turkey, fill the cavity with jellied cranberry sauce and two peeled oranges.

When you make iced tea, steep the tea bags with a couple of mint leaves.

Put a little orange juice in your sweet potatoes.

Use Parmesan cheese in your deviled eggs and that fancy mustard.

Milk goes in the cole slaw.

A dash of Texas Pete in the pimento cheese.

Never use raisins, no matter what the recipe says. They're dried up excuses for grapes.

Tell Hamilton to give you the old Betty Crocker cookbook that's missing the cover. Inside I've written all the other changes I've made over the years. Don't tell anyone else about my secrets. They are yours now.

Myrtle's letter to Calvin:

Dear Calvin,
        I guess by now you've realized who you really
are. Your mother kept you away from me. If only I
had been able to start you off early, you could have
been well on your way to being a stage and screen
personality by now. Gerald would have been so proud
to watch me work my magic on you. Thank God, it's
not too late. You see, I still have the power to help you
even though I, myself, will be gone. That's part of the
bargain, you see. This may sound crazy, but I have
had a vision. I was in the attic, spending time with
Gerald, looking at his photographs when suddenly
the room began to glisten with a silvery light and the
picture I was holding, the one of him in his white tie
and tails, floated from my hands. And then Gerald
stepped off the page and stood in front of me. He was
positively glowing with excitement, his smile as bright
as a spotlight. His top hat was angled on his head like
a cocky but debonair Fred Astaire. I started to speak,
but he put his finger to his lips, and then pointed to
his throat where I could still see the faint bite marks.
I knew we had to keep silent. He lifted his top hat
from his head. Once again I saw his beautiful hair like
sunspots. He smiled again, raised one eyebrow, and
made a flourishing gesture to the hat. As if he were
a magician he reached in, but instead of a rabbit, he
pulled out a small boy which he placed on the floor
beside him. As we watched, the boy began to grow
and I realized it was you, Calvin. It was you. Gerald
looked at me and I noticed a tear had formed in the
corner of each of his eyes. They began to roll down his
cheeks and when they hit the floor, the tears became
tap shoes. Like in a Disney cartoon, the shoes came

to life and tapped over to you, jumped on your feet, and you danced around the attic. From trunk to trunk, on the walls, even on the ceiling you danced with joy. You were Gerald's destiny. You were mine, too. When you were finished, Gerald applauded. Then he turned to me and held out one hand. The other he held out to you, as if to say, "Only one can meet destiny." I knew then that for you to find your dreams, I must surrender mine. But don't be sad, Calvin, for Gerald allowed me a glimpse into his hat where I saw our names in neon lights. We have top billing, you see, in God's Show of Shows. So, my dear, here are your magic shoes. Wear them when I am gone for you are the reason I am going. You must. It's part of the bargain. Do not let me go in vain. All my wondrous love, Myrtle.

Myrtle's letter to Henry:

Dear Henry,

Don't be mad at me. I needed you to help me. Destiny. It was all a matter of destiny. I should have married you. You would have been better to me than Hamilton was. I knew you desired me. I knew you would matter in my life. And you see, you did. You mattered more than anyone else. I'm finally going to be where I belong. Someday you'll see me there. I'll get you front row tickets and backstage passes. Maybe a private show just for you as a reward. Don't fret, Henry. No one needs to know a thing. Secrets are safe with me. We washed away the past, Henry. It's like I'm being born again. Don't you see, it's like a womb—warm and wet and dark and safe. I'm sparkling now. I'm new. But I know what you're feeling. Remember the part in *The Wizard of Oz*

when Dorothy was leaving for home and she said
good-bye to the Scarecrow. She said she'd miss him
most. Well, Henry, I think you'll miss me most. I'll
miss you, too, more than I'll miss Hamilton. Secretly
yours, Myrtle.

Rough drafts of suicide note:
　　I wish I had those red poppies from *The
Wizard of Oz*, the ones that made Dorothy fall asleep.
Only this time the good witch wouldn't make snow fall
to wake me up. There was nothing at the end of the
yellow brick road, anyway, except a man. A man like
Hamilton who had no power or magic. Tragic excuse
for a wizard.

　　Good-bye forever. I'm sorry my life didn't turn
out the way I wanted. It was not my fault. A snake
came and Eden was taken away from me. No garden
for my life.

　　Gerald has appeared to me and shown me how
to leave you all, how to cleanse myself. I don't want
any homegrown roses on my casket. Give me orchids
imported from Hawaii. I want rare ones with exotic
greenery and heady fragrances. God, don't let me die
ordinary. Living that way was punishment enough.

ABOUT MUDDY FORD PRESS

Muddy Ford Press is a family-owned, boutique publishing company located in the South Carolina Midlands. Muddy Ford Press is dedicated to providing a publishing home to the best of the Southeast's growing community of poets, artists, and authors. For more information please visit us at MuddyFordPress.com, or contact us at Muddy Ford Press, 1009 Muddy Ford Road, Chapin, SC 29036

CPSIA information can be obtained at www.ICGtesting.com
Printed in the USA
LVOW10s0618110216

474590LV00016B/104/P